ENRY TURNED HIS HAT IN HIS HANDS BUT WENT ON looking at Diana in a way that made her want to crawl into his arms and stay there forever. She was surprised at herself, and a little angry, for still having feelings like that. "I don't love her, Di."

She closed her eyes and rumpled her brow. "You certainly have all New York fooled," she said, rather unconvincingly.

"I don't even go to bed with her."

She opened her eyes then, the thick lashes fluttering back from her rich brown irises. "Never?" she whispered.

Henry shook his head and watched her. "How could I, when you're the one I want?"

ALSO BY ANNA GODBERSEN

THE LUXE

RUMORS

SPLENDOR

Envy

A *Luxe* NOVEL

ANNA GODBERSEN

HARPER

An Imprint of HarperCollinsPublishers

Produced by Alloy Entertainment
151 West 26th Street, New York, NY 10001

ON THE COVER: Dress by St. Pucchi

Library of Congress Cataloging-in-Publication Data

Godbersen, Anna.
Envy : a Luxe novel / Anna Godbersen.— 1st ed.
p.   cm.
Summary: In Manhattan, in 1900, the Holland sisters and other socialites fight each
other, face off over men, and rail against the strict rules of society.
ISBN 978-0-06-134574-6
[1. Sisters—Fiction. 2. Conduct of life—Fiction. 3. Social classes—Fiction.
4. Wealth—Fiction. 5. Love—Fiction. 6. New York (N.Y.)—History—1898–1951—
Fiction.]
PZ7.G53887 En 2009   2009275632
[Fic]—dc22   CIP
                                                                      AC

Design by Andrea C. Uva

10 11 12 13   CG/RRDH   10 9 8 7 6 5 4 3 2
❖
First paperback edition, 2009

For Edna and Marge

Prologue

OR A CERTAIN KIND OF NEW YORK GIRL, EVERY-thing must be always in its place. She keeps her jewels in her jewelry box and her laces in her lace drawer. If she walks, she wears her walking costume; if she goes to the theater, she wears her theater bonnet. In the afternoon, when she visits that friend she especially wants to see, she will know at what precise hour to find her alone and most receptive to confessions. And afterward, when she makes the obligatory stop at the home of the friend she has no real desire to call upon, she will of course arrive at a moment when that lady is known to be out. Such a girl would not be seen on the street without a hat or in mixed company without gloves. So it might have come as a surprise to any little sparrow, fluttering around in the clear air on the first springlike day of 1900, to see that none of these ladies were quite where they were supposed to be.

It was the beginning of March, and though snow had clung to the sidewalk as recently as yesterday, the evening held the far-off promise of a warm season to come. As our little bird settled on the Italianate stone ledge of a certain Fifth Avenue matron, his tiny heart began to flutter beneath his white-feathered chest. For that lady—recently married into one of New York's great families—was unhooking her corset in the company of a man who looked nothing like her husband. Her cheeks were flushed from the champagne she had drunk at dinner, and because she was unused to removing her clothing without the help of her maid, she found herself repeatedly subsiding into giggles and fits of hilarity. Eventually her companion crossed toward her and began to slowly undo the ribbons himself.

But by then the little bird was off, his mottled wings spreading to catch the night breeze as he coasted south high above the avenue. He soared past the brightly lit doorways of millionaires and over the heads of their coachmen on the curb in their perpetual pose of waiting. When his talons next set down, it was on the iron rail outside the leaded panes of one of those new, stylish apartment houses for the wealthy. The light from the street reflected in the glass, but the figures within were clear enough.

The girl was known for her family's reputation and for her family's address and for one very grand engagement. The apartment house was farther north on the little island of Manhattan than her people had ever lived before; the man calling her away from her place by the fire was not at all like

the one whose ring she'd once worn. But the sparrow's dark eyes were already roving, and before anything more could be glimpsed, the bird had swooped down and away.

From there he looped southeast, his round tufted head twisting at the pictures framed by the windows of polite people. There was the heiress whose new wealth did nothing to prevent her from unrolling her stockings in the company of a man whom no one had ever heard of. There was the favored son of upper-class New York, who not long ago surprised everyone by ending his bachelorhood, gazing at the city's receding reflection in the Hudson River. There was his wife, whose spring wardrobe had not yet arrived from Paris and was still dressed in heavy winter velvet, without a dance partner in a very good room.

Who could blame our little bird, then, for alighting eventually on the sill of one of those old-fashioned families to whom decorum still meant something. But when he chose the sill of No. 17 Gramercy Park, well, that was still no guarantee of staid lives within. And yet, on this particular evening, Diana Holland might well have been the only girl of her set who was in fact where she was supposed to be. For there she sat in her own room, alone, her shiny and unruly curls brushed and falling down around her neck. The rosy skin of her cheeks had been carefully scrubbed, and she looked into the elaborately carved and dark-stained vanity mirror where she had so often prepared for gay evenings out.

There was nothing gay about her appearance now. Her usually dewy, deep brown eyes had cried themselves dry and her small round mouth was twisted in despair. She blinked and blinked at her reflection, but she could not bring herself to like what she saw. She no longer approved of the girl who stared back at her, and she knew that despite the many tragedies her short life had hurled at her, she'd never been so low as this. She ached with what she had done, and the longer she sat alone, the worse the hurt became. Then she relaxed her shoulders and raised her small, defined chin. She blinked again, and resolution settled on her features.

Her gaze did not waver from the mirror as her hand felt across the table for a pair of gold-plated scissors. Once her fingers curled around the handle there was not even a second of hesitation. She brought them to her curls and began to cut. There was such volume to her hair that she needed several breathless minutes to shear it all off. It was only after it was done, when shiny brown heaps were amassed at her feet, that she pushed back her chair and broke away from her own reflection. All that was left were the dark brown roots wisping over her ears and at the nape of her neck.

Later, when the first pale touches of morning were only a promise at the edges of the sky, our sparrow, still resting

on the eaves of the Holland home, watched as its youngest inhabitant exited by the front door. Her old coat was drawn tight to shield her from the cold, and her hat was pulled over her ears. It was too late, or too early, for any human being to note the absolute determination in her stride, but the little sparrow's black eyes followed her as she disappeared into the brand-new day.

One

MR. LELAND BOUCHARD

REQUESTS THE PLEASURE OF YOUR COMPANY

AT A BALL TO BE GIVEN IN HONOR OF

THE MEMBERS OF

THE NEW YORK AUTOMOBILIST CLUB

ON THURSDAY EVENING

FEBRUARY 8, 1900, AT NINE O'CLOCK

18 EAST 63RD STREET

"SURELY A GIRL AS LOVELY AS YOU, A GIRL WHO PER-
sonifies loveliness itself, should not be hidden away
on a night like this, on a night when everyone wants to see a
fine figure and starry eyes, and where yours are the starriest
of all."

Diana Holland looked up innocently from the comb-
crested silk sofa in the library and met the eyes of her friend,
who leaned against the polished mahogany doorframe, having
characteristically used twice as many words as were strictly
necessary. His name was Davis Barnard, and though he wrote
his gossip column under a pseudonym, he was the only famous
writer Diana knew.

Diana glanced to her left, where the eyelashes of her
chaperone, Aunt Edith, were just touching down on that lady's
high cheekbones. In Edith's face Diana could see the future of
her own features, for the small, rounded mouth, the subtle nose,
and the dark eyes perfectly spaced under a generous forehead
were very like hers, albeit with the thinning and etching of age.

Edith exhaled a sleepy, contented breath, and then Diana looked back at Barnard. Over his black tuxedo–covered shoulder were the trilling sounds and electric lights of the Bouchard ball.

"You flatter me too much," she said as she stood, adding a knowing wink for emphasis. She was terribly knowing these days.

The long black chiffon skirt of her gown trailed behind her as she approached the entrance, and she batted her fan open to modestly cover her face. She always did this when Barnard escorted her, because they discussed everyone in detail, and so it was prudent to obscure the view of her mouth from any chance lip-readers. Her hair was drawn into a bun in the back, and her curls descended diagonally on either side of her forehead toward her ears. A black leather belt marked the narrowness of her waist, and at the middle point of her princess neckline was a flower made of ivory lace petals. The gown was new, and she had paid for it herself. She glanced back once, to be sure that no one had noticed her slipping away from her chaperone, and allowed herself to be drawn across the creamy marble floor of the second-story mezzanine.

"Quite a showing," Barnard remarked as they crossed onto the richly gleaming parquet floor of Leland Bouchard's music room. It had been constructed with acoustics in mind, although the music room was rarely used for its titular purpose. Music rooms were for people who held musicales, and Leland

Bouchard, who had built the house for himself at twenty, from money that he had earned off his own investments, was known for never sitting still. The walls were paneled with murals, and a gigantic Kentia palm festooned with tiny lights scraped the twenty-five-foot ceiling.

Her vision swept the rectangular room with its high, vaulted ceiling and met the gaze of Isaac Phillips Buck, who quickly looked away, as though he had been watching her. He was large in every way one might imagine, and the soft fleshiness of his face made his age impossible to determine. He was Penelope Hayes's lackey, Diana knew that much, but she couldn't imagine why he would have any interest in her. Next, Diana's gaze fell on her sister's old friend Agnes Jones, who was resting on the arm of a well-kempt gentleman. She tried to make her eyes widen in a cordial manner, though she still had trouble appearing to like people she did not, which Barnard had admonished as an unfortunate characteristic in both a lady of society and a peddler of secrets.

"Everyone is here," Barnard went on as they watched Teddy Cutting cross the room with Gemma Newbold, who wore a diamond tiara nestled in her reddish curls and was well known to be Mrs. Cutting's choice for her only son. There was a time when everyone had thought Teddy would marry Elizabeth Holland, but that was before she became rather publicly engaged to his best friend, and then very privately married to her true love. Like their mother, she had been widowed; both those ladies were home together tonight. That was among the reasons her younger sister tried to be seen in her place as much as possible, though it was hardly cause for Buck to spy on her.

"Nobody doesn't love Leland," she replied, shaking off the feeling of Buck's swinelike eyes on her.

"It would be difficult not to." Barnard paused to accept a glass of champagne from a passing waiter. "Although I must confess to getting a mystery headache whenever I am in his company too long. He talks too fast, and he is always excited about everything. Me, I am never excited about anything between the hour when I wake up and five o'clock."

Diana smiled subtly at this, for she knew what five o'clock signified to her friend; of course, she had also known him to take whiskey in his coffee at decidedly earlier hours.

"That is a very gaudy gown on Eleanor Wetmore," Diana observed, fixing her sight on the array of custom-made dresses and painted faces before them.

Barnard paused and looked. "Indeed."

"I would imagine she is on quite the search for a husband, now that her younger sister is engaged to Reginald Newbold. That will sting for her, to be twenty-six and a maid instead of a matron of honor at the wedding. I suppose she needs the attention any way she can get it."

"That would make a nice item." Barnard finished his champagne and left the glass on the magnificent carved wood mantel, which had been transported from a grand Florentine house, as Barnard himself had reported in his "Gamesome Gallant" column.

"Why don't you write it?"

This casual offer flooded Diana with nervous anticipation; she smiled behind her fan. "All right," she said after a moment, so as to not seem too eager.

"Don't try to hide your smiles from me, Miss Diana Holland." Barnard turned slightly away from her as he spoke, and motioned to a waiter for another drink. "I hope, for my own sake, that the day you realize that you were made for better things is later rather than sooner."

They had reached the huge, classically proportioned windows that faced northward onto the street, and Diana dropped her friend's arm for a moment to gaze down at the fallen snow reflecting the warm light from above. Behind them the voice of Leland Bouchard could be heard going into raptures about his recent purchase of a horseless carriage, an Exley, which was displayed in the first-floor vestibule so that guests could, upon their arrival, stare at its shiny modernity with covetous curiosity.

Their host was tall, with a uniquely broad forehead and wheat-colored hair that always seemed a little overgrown. "It can cover twenty-four miles in an hour, without undue racing effort," he was saying to Mr. Gore.

"He is an investor in the Exley Motor Carriage Company," Barnard remarked, sotto voce, to his protégé.

Though Diana should have listened for more information, she found her attention already wandering to the street below. The lace flower on her gown rose and fell with her breath, and a delicate sensation settled across her chest. The crowd behind her, which was full of stories that the protagonists would rather not have told, and also of small deceptions certain to amuse the reading public, dimmed for her. Just a moment ago she had felt the cleverest player in a game that obsessed the whole room, but she was overcome now by the strong impulse to hide herself and the brassy sound of her famous laugh.

Down below, Henry Schoonmaker had stepped out of his coach and was lighting a cigarette as he paused by the iron gate that encircled Leland Bouchard's mansion. He was the man who had drawn out Diana's affections last season, and then pounded on them. There was much history between them, but as Diana watched him, posing there with the elbow of his smoking arm rested on his wrist, in a wide, pensive stance, she reminded herself that she felt no emotion for him. And when Henry's wife, Penelope—of the so newly grand Hayes family—arrived at her husband's side, with her fierce

blue eyes cast directly in front of her, Diana reminded herself that Henry had chosen to marry mere weeks after taking Diana's virginity.

"I'd like to know what goes on in their bedroom." Barnard smirked.

"The Schoonmakers are the envy of every young couple in the city," Diana answered mechanically, as though repeating some lesson learned by rote.

Barnard took two champagne glasses from a passing tray and handed one to Diana. She closed her eyes and took a long sip that did nothing to settle her insurgent nerves. In a moment, Henry Schoonmaker would be coming through the door.

He must not see her.

Even as Diana tried to fill her sister's role, acting the part of the good Holland daughter in the wider world, she had scrupulously avoided letting Henry catch even a glimpse of her. In the same manner, she had been careful to burn his letters—which had arrived daily since his New Year's Eve wedding to Penelope—unopened, and to smooth away any feelings the sight of his face might have lit up in her. She had thought once, not long ago, that they were destined to share a storybook romance. But she was an entirely different kind of girl now—she had had her heart broken and all of her naïveté worn off. Nothing Henry said could change her back to the way she had been then, and certainly not if it came in so cold-blooded a form as a letter.

"Are you all right?" Barnard asked, twisting the pale gold flute in his large hand.

"Only a little tired." Diana smiled weakly as she handed him back her nearly full glass. "I ought to be going, but I promise I will learn everything there is to know about Eleanor Wetmore's matrimonial ambitions by Sunday at the very latest."

Her voice rose courageously on that final word. She extended her hand for her friend to kiss, and then she moved carefully through the crowd, always keeping the central palm between her and the entryway. But she must have hesitated too long, for just as she ventured forward, the Henry Schoonmakers appeared and filled the doorframe. Diana let out a little gasp and drew backward, so that the great green leaves covered her figure. She could still see enough, though. For Penelope was wearing a slash of red that might have brought to mind the butcher, were it not made of quite so precious a material.

The new Mrs. Schoonmaker made a friendly gesture across the room at the older Mrs. Schoonmaker, Henry's step-mother, who was only twenty-six and wearing a rather daring dress herself. Then Adelaide Wetmore overtook Henry and his wife, and distracted them long enough for Diana to make

her move. She pulled back her skirt and hurried through the throng toward the library, where she would rouse her aunt and collect their wraps. It was cold outside, and they were more than forty blocks from their own, somewhat out-of-fashion address. A chill, which Diana would have liked to believe was numbness, was settling around her chest. Still, it took everything she had not to turn and look back as she left the party behind.

Two

Society is always particularly receptive to new blood in the winter. It has ever been thus; it is so now; and Mrs. Carolina Broad is only the latest to benefit from this fact of nature. Her climb has been precipitous, for in November nobody had ever heard of her, and by the end of December, her name was in all the papers as one of Mrs. Penelope Schoonmaker's bridesmaids. We hear she lives in the New Netherland hotel, under the chaste wing of Mr. Carey Lewis Longhorn, and she is without question or doubt one to watch. . . .

—FROM THE "GAMESOME GALLANT" COLUMN IN THE *NEW YORK IMPERIAL*, THURSDAY, FEBRUARY 8, 1900

THE GIDDY PIANO MUSIC FROM THE MAIN FLOOR
of Sherry's Restaurant, on Fifth Avenue and
Forty-fifth Street, could be heard even in the ladies' lounge,
and perhaps might even be said to have infected the women
there. For they were clambering forward, in that rosy-hued
space, toward the mirror, which was etched with metallic
curlicues and shrouded in white netting from above, as though
by celestial clouds. It was large, but not large enough for all
those pink-cheeked beauties in their silks and laces, as they
leaned in to blacken their lashes and perfume their décolle-
tages. They had supped on English pheasant and hothouse
asparagus, and they had grown drowsy until the coffee arrived.
Now they were eager for the next chapter of their evenings,
and perhaps none of them so much so as Carolina Broad, who
stood in the center pinching her freckled cheeks to bring some
warm color there, in a dress of pale but unmistakable gold.

The dress was the gift of Carey Lewis Longhorn, the
man often referred to in the papers as the elder statesman of

New York bachelors. It brought out the length and slimness of her middle, while disguising her big, bony shoulders with bursts of gold-edged lace, and her almost unladylike clavicles with five choker-length strands of gleaming pearls. Her dark hair was festooned with strands of smaller pearls, and her lichen-colored eyes were set under recently shaped brows. The pride of her face, her bee-stung lips, were painted glossy red. Any of the women surrounding her would have been shocked to hear that she'd once been a maid in service to the kind of girl she now purported to be, or that she had until recently been known by the plain-sounding name Lina Broud.

This was an inconvenient fact of which Longhorn was perfectly aware, and that his young friend did her best to forget. It was easy to forget now, as she swept her skirt, its lacy underskirts foaming upward like a cresting wave, back from the vanity table and moved toward the central dining room. She walked very well, in a manner almost indistinguishable from the way she had walked only a few months ago, and it was at this ladylike gait that she came through the series of small, dimly lit antechambers and stepped into the margins of Sherry's main dining room. Her figure was shadowed by a second-floor balcony, but she had an excellent view of the vast room, with its columns and posts, its white tablecloths and elaborate flower arrangements, its hustling waiters and pampered debutantes.

Longhorn sat at a prominent table in the middle of the room where the dappled light of the central chandelier shone brightest. When he had dined by himself he had preferred the corners, but once Carolina began accompanying him she had insisted that it was her time to be seen, and he had acquiesced with an easy laugh. He was wearing his customary red velvet smoking jacket and an old-fashioned collar that turned down at its high, white corners and was fastened below the chin with a conspicuous button. His hair had gone gray, though he still had much of it, and despite the wear of a drinking life, which was evidenced in a swollen nose, you could see the good features that had made him so desired as a young man. At his shoulder stood his man, Robert—a constantly hovering, bearded presence—with their capes. Carolina felt a surge of airy anticipation when she realized this, for she knew what those capes signified. It was time to go.

It was not that she did not appreciate the fine china or the champagne cocktails or the elaborate service of her patron's favorite restaurant. She had enjoyed her many courses (perhaps with a little too much relish, she had realized when she caught Robert looking at her from his post), and being observed by all the other diners, who had lately grown as curious about her as she once was about them. But her whole evening thus far had been building to its second act, in which Longhorn took her to a party at the home of Leland Bouchard, whose name now held a place in her thoughts once reserved for that of Will Keller.

Will had been her first love, but she had known him when she was a child, and it seemed a very childish attachment now. Anyway, Will was dead, and while that was a starkly horrible fact, one had to move on, and when one did one discovered ever more new and wonderful things. For had there ever been a name with a nicer ring than "Leland Bouchard"? It sounded like it was made of money and charm, which it almost surely was. She had met him at a ball around Christmas, and he had asked her to dance again and again. His hands on her waist and wrist had been neither polite nor lecherous. He had gripped her earnestly as they talked of many things. She had never felt so lovely or light before or after that evening, and she often filled her mind with memories of it when she rested her head on her pillow at night. For though she had done her utmost to be near him again, she had not managed to see him. Or rather, she had *seen* him—once, from Longhorn's carriage, as he hurried along the street, her heart rattling at the thought that he might turn at just the right moment, and a second time from behind at a ball where she had been too pathetic to go up to him—but he had not seen her. Tonight he was the host, and she was looking her very best; it would be impossible for him not to ask her to dance. Her friend Penelope had promised to introduce them again if he did not—and then he would lead

her into a waltz that would draw her across the floor and into his heart forever.

It was with this winsome fantasy that she stepped forward into Sherry's main room, ready for an evening that she was convinced would come to herald so many new beginnings. She would have crossed straight to Longhorn, and gone on to the front entrance without any need for discussion, but she was stalled by the whisper of fingers on her back. She half turned, with an indifferent semi-smile on her face; when she recognized the person who had touched her, all her pleasant thoughts faded.

"Miss Broad!"

The voice was jocular, but when she returned its owner's greeting, she found she could not match his tone.

"Oh." Her gaze shifted over the full tables to Longhorn, who had not yet noticed her there in the shadows. "Hello, Tristan."

Tristan Wrigley was tall, with wispy light hair and hazel eyes the color of a sunset reflected in muddy waters. Although their acquaintance was still new, he had already hurt and helped her in many ways. He was a department store salesman and a con artist, and he was the first and only man who had ever kissed her. She had been avoiding him, but if this rankled him he did not show it. He was smiling, and a bosomy woman, who wore a garish amount of rouge and foot-high feathers in her hair, was hanging off his arm and grinning entirely too much for the setting.

"This is Mrs. Portia Tilt," he went on, fixing a steady and intense gaze on Carolina. "She and her husband have just moved from out west. Carolina is from out west, too. She is the heir to a copper-smelting fortune, you know, and she—"

"I'm sure your friend doesn't require my entire autobiography," Carolina interrupted coldly. In a moment, she had surmised the whole situation. Mrs. Tilt, having more money than class, had believed Tristan's implication that he might assist her with getting into society, and he, thus assured of her gullibility, had pressed on for money and trinkets and free meals of all kinds. Mrs. Tilt would learn in time—though she did not look particularly swift at the moment—that one does not get into society by walking arm in arm with a Lord & Taylor salesman around one of the best restaurants in Manhattan; Carolina was not such a fool, and she did not intend to make the same mistake. "Goodbye," she concluded, with a bright smile but without explanation.

"Goodbye," Mrs. Tilt answered gaily, too thick-witted to realize she had been cut, and then pushed forward. Tristan— still attached to her by the crook of his arm—was pulled along, but he had time to look back and fix Carolina with such a concentrated look that she felt it down into her toes. It was lucky that Mrs. Tilt began guffawing loudly after that, and all eyes turned in the direction she was heading, which allowed Carolina to return to her seat without anybody taking notice.

"Ah, there you are, my dear." Longhorn smiled at her appreciatively, the way one smiles at a favorite grandchild who has eaten all of the candy one has given her and shortly thereafter requested more. Then she felt the weight of her wrap on her shoulders and allowed herself to be escorted through the many rooms to the front entrance.

Out in the deep purple night it was still, and the lamplight fell in yellowy pools. It was cold, too cold to move, and the coachmen who loitered at the curb were bent, immobile, over their cups of hot cider. The horses were covered in thick blankets, and the breath streaming from their nostrils was visible in the frigid air. Carolina had regained herself after her encounter with Tristan, and she turned to Longhorn now with a look of gratitude. Longhorn knew what she was, but he didn't know about her shameful involvement with the salesman, or that it had been Tristan's idea for her to get close to the old bachelor for both their gain. He thought of her as more guileless than all that, and had given her no opportunity to correct the impression. It was a kindness that she felt acutely at that moment.

Since Tristan's initial suggestion, she had grown truly fond of the older man. She enjoyed his saltiness and carefully observed the confidence and indifference to others' opinion with which he approached the wider world. And he liked what he termed her "candidness"—in truth, this was nothing more than a lack of knowledge and a dumb willingness to admit that she had much to learn. But they made a good pair, and their time together was always of a high quality.

"What a lovely evening this is turning out to be," she said sweetly, tucking her bottom lip under her teeth. Her heavy cape was lined with white fur, which framed her face, and embroidered with gold threads along its full sweeping length.

Longhorn smiled at her, and a twinkle—or maybe the light from the restaurant behind them—passed in his eye. Then Robert reappeared, leading the horses that pulled the coach along behind him. He opened the door to the coach and helped Carolina up. He paused to spread a wool blanket over her lap, and then stepped down to the street. He and Longhorn exchanged a few words, and then Longhorn came inside and took the seat beside her, the small door closing with a click behind him.

"It *has* been a lovely evening." The horses jerked into motion, and Carolina felt her body drawn forward as Longhorn's words evaporated into the air. There was something about his tone that she disliked. "Lovely. But I am afraid I had a bit too much of that heavy sauce, and that I have been staying out too late too often with you, my dear. You won't mind just this once if we go home early? We can have a glass of Madeira in my suite. . . ."

Carolina's heart puttered and began to sink. Suddenly Leland Bouchard's house on East Sixty-third—she had passed the address several times, claiming that she wanted to admire the architecture on that block—seemed the only place in the whole city that contained life. Her friend Penelope Schoonmaker was there, no doubt being admired by all the young men, even as she had eyes only for her dashing husband, the bubbles rising in the champagne, the witty phrases too frequent for the laughter ever to cease for very long.

Carolina felt desperate, and wanted to grasp at any possibility, but she couldn't muster the will to say anything contrary. The coachman had already been given his instructions, and he was pulling them inexorably to the same hotel where, it suddenly seemed to her, they would spend all their nights in an uninterrupted cycle of Madeira and monotony. Her bottom lip trembled with regret, but her companion, whose eyes had already drifted shut, was too fatigued to mark it.

Three

A young woman, newly wed, may find herself in the delightful position of wanting to do nothing without the company of her darling husband. She may indeed discover that she spends all her waking hours with her fellow to the exclusion of every other friend or family member. This is understandable, but wholly unacceptable, to society.

—MRS. HAMILTON W. BREEDFELT, *COLLECTED COLUMNS ON RAISING YOUNG LADIES OF CHARACTER*, 1899

MRS. HENRY SCHOONMAKER, NÉE PENELOPE Hayes, had come far in her eighteen years. As she swept past Leland Bouchard's vestibule, where a gleaming black motorcar was displayed, she couldn't help but muse how she, like the horseless carriage, was a waxy emblem of the future. Ever since she was a little girl she had told herself that she wouldn't meet the other side of twenty without a deeply gaudy wedding band on her finger, and here she had beat her own goal by two years and in the process joined one of New York's most well-regarded families. There were those who still remembered how her maiden name had been hastily salvaged from the odious surname Hazmat several decades ago, but neither appeared on her card these days. Now, moving up the glistening curve of marble stairs toward the sound of a party already in full swing, she could not help but anticipate the joy of entering a room on the arm of her very handsome husband.

It was one of the great pleasures of her life, for Henry

was tall and lean and possessed of a chieftain's cheekbones and a rakish mien that made all eyes turn to him. As a debutante, Penelope had grown accustomed to being looked at, but the envious intensity of the stares she encountered upon entering the second-floor music room, which was full of old money and good connections on that Thursday evening, was superior even to what she was used to. She wore a haughty smile, her plush lips twisted up to the right no more than was necessary, and a dress of cardinal-colored silk that a thousand elegant darts brought in close to her lean frame. Her dark hair was collected in an elaborate bun, and a line of short bangs divided her high, proud forehead.

Penelope cast an appraising gaze at the paneled murals, done by one of the leading talents of Europe, and the polished mantel that had been transported in pieces from Florence. She knew this and much more about Leland Bouchard's home because she wanted Henry to build a town house for them and had collected newspaper clippings on this one and others like it. He had not yet given her any indication that he would do so, but, like everything Penelope wanted, it was only a matter of time and perhaps a little of her own rough brand of persuasion before it was hers.

Above the gentle din of decorous voices and clinking glasses, Penelope heard her name being pronounced with all its most recent and glorious trappings. "Mrs. Henry

Schoonmaker!" went the beautiful sound, and Penelope turned. As she did, the fishtail of her skirt swept across the Versailles parquet. She immediately noted the approach of Adelaide Wetmore, who wore a dress of pewter faille. Her eyes were moist with self-regard, for her engagement to Reginald Newbold had only just been announced, and she was looking pleasantly weak with all the congratulations. She might have been pretty, Penelope reflected charitably, if not for her disproportionate mouth, and the way it garishly showcased her broad teeth.

"Why, Adelaide." Penelope extended her gloved hand so that the diamond bracelet she wore fell down her wrist and caught the light. "Congratulations."

"Thank you," the other girl gushed. She took Penelope's hand and made a dipping motion, almost as though she were going to curtsy. "We were all so inspired by your wedding," she added with painful sycophancy. "What a celebration of love it was."

Penelope communicated her gratitude with a few bats of her black eyelashes, and deduced from the way Adelaide was looking at the couple whose love she claimed to be inspired by that Henry's gaze had wandered, and that he was exerting exactly no energy in trying to seem interested in the matrimonial doings of their peers. Penelope smiled her goodbye, and then she and her husband—who she was now realizing smelled of musk but even more strongly of cognac—pushed farther into the room. That was when Henry stumbled almost imperceptibly, catching himself on her arm, and Penelope felt her self-assurance flag a little over the sudden fear that someone might notice Henry's drunkenness and begin to draw their own conclusions.

As she moved through the crowd, under the high polish of the vaulted ceiling, she tried to secure her grip on Henry. It wasn't easy—but then, of course, it never had been. She gave knowing little nods of her head in the direction of some of the younger Mrs. Vanderbilts, assembled near the vast central palm in the middle of the room, and didn't dare look in the direction of the man she was almost forcibly pulling along with her. She had believed him to be hers, time and again, but still she could not stay the feeling that he might at any moment slip through her fingers.

It had begun between them the previous summer, when her best friend, Elizabeth Holland, had been abroad, and she and Henry had started meeting amorously in the shadowy corners of their family homes. But then Elizabeth had returned in the fall and, with precious little reason, become Henry's fiancée. Of course, that had been according to the wishes of their parents, and Penelope had rescued both of them from an unhappy marriage by helping Elizabeth fake her death. As she felt Henry list just slightly, she considered how poorly her efforts had been repaid, for not long after Elizabeth's "death," Henry had taken up with her little sister, Diana. That turn of events had not been entirely bad, since the fact of the younger Holland's whoring about was the piece of information that Penelope had used to persuade Henry to marry her. All she had ever wanted was to be Mrs. Schoonmaker, and none of them wanted a messy scene.

Penelope possessed the mettle of a society lady ten years older, and there was forcefulness evident in her smallest movements. But even as Mrs. Schoonmaker, Penelope was unpleasantly surprised to discover that her ability to control Mr. Schoonmaker fell somewhat short. They glided amongst the guests, and when a waiter appeared carrying champagne flutes it was all she could do to keep Henry from lunging for one.

"Don't you feel drunk enough already?" she admonished. Her smile never wavered, and she brought her upper lip back just enough to reveal the perfect whiteness of her teeth.

"I've had a lot," he replied slowly, without particular venom, although the drink might possibly have been impairing his inflection. "But not enough to make me want to spend the evening with you, my dear."

Penelope briefly shut the lids of her large eyes and stifled any feelings his comment might have aroused. Then she batted her mascara-darkened lashes and let her lake blue irises roll right and left. No one had heard, she determined with a small release of her shoulders, except perhaps the waiter, who wouldn't have dreamed of looking her in the eye. When she spoke again, it was with effortless ease and a glass of champagne in her hand:

"When you put it that way, I suppose I should have one too."

Thus fortified, the most envied couple in top-drawer Manhattan moved onward through the throng. The members of the Automobilist Club were making grand pronouncements about upcoming races, and the ladies who wanted to be near them were smiling patient smiles and assuming the poses of eager listeners.

"Ah, the Schoonmakers!"

Penelope twisted the length of her white neck so that the full blaze of her smile could be fully appreciated by her host. "Mr. Bouchard," she purred, as he bent his long torso and placed his lips on her gray, full-length glove. The warmth in her voice was studied and convincing; it was a tone she reserved for men like Leland, who was heir to the Bouchard banking fortune and besides that universally liked. He was that rare high-born New Yorker who somehow or other had managed to make more friends than enemies, and was a particular friend of her brother, Grayson. As younger men they had lived in adjoining rooms at St. Paul's. Penelope, ever watchful, noted Grayson's presence by the window, where he was ensconced in conversation with her mother-in-law, the senior Mrs. Schoonmaker, whose dress of opalescent chiffon tiers did little to detract attention from her.

"I hope you're both enjoying yourself," Leland went on earnestly as he clasped Henry's hand. His light blue eyes were open wide beneath his broad forehead, as though their enjoyment really was a crucial issue for him, and for all Penelope knew, it was. "Did you see the motorcar downstairs?"

"Could not have mishedut," Henry answered enthusiastically, slurring the last two words.

Penelope elbowed him while maintaining her steady, bright gaze. "Such a beautiful object, Leland."

"Thank you." Leland's eyes drifted and his chest rose, and for a moment he was someplace else. "Speaking of beauties," he went on, his attention returning to Penelope, and this time with an added touch of sympathy, "how is your dear friend Elizabeth? It was terrible what happened, and not seeing her out has made us all worry."

Until that moment Penelope had maintained a strong, smiling posture, and had stayed uncowed by Henry's misbehavior or any askance glances from whichever young ladies in the room flattered themselves by imagining that they were the rival of the former Miss Hayes. But now her mouth constricted and she heard herself swallow hard. Leland went on looking at her with that same concerned expression. Henry's weight on her arm bobbed a moment and then grew heavier. She only hoped that her face did not betray the insecurity this inquiry brought on, for of course Elizabeth was her dear friend by reputation only. Penelope had barely seen her since her unexpected return from what was supposed to have been a long exile in a western state—for truly, what was there to say?

"She is very well." Penelope began to regain her composure, and even as she spoke reminded herself that she really would have to make a show of seeing Elizabeth, one that the papers took note of, and soon. "But it is still early for her to be going out. After her trauma. You understand, of course."

"Of course." Leland bowed his head, appearing almost embarrassed for having asked after a girl who had gone unaccounted for for over two months, and who might indeed have suffered any number of grave injustices. But before he could further anyone's discomfort, he succumbed to the calls of his fellow driving enthusiasts, and excused himself. "Please do enjoy," he said as he slipped into the crowd.

Penelope did not look after her host as he left. She stared straight ahead and reminded herself what a lucky thing it was that he was not a gossip and that he wouldn't be searching for signs that Mrs. Henry Schoonmaker's marriage or friendships were not what they seemed. For a moment she reflected on how to avoid such a mistake again, and then she turned toward Henry.

His dark eyes were focused in the direction of the huge windows and the night scene they held, and they looked less glassy than before. There was something almost like clarity in his face when he turned toward his wife, and when he spoke, it was deliberately.

"Promise me," he said, meeting her gaze, "that if someone brings up the Hollands again you'll take me home."

The new dressing room on the second floor of the Schoonmaker mansion, which had until recently held Henry's collection of unread first editions, was dark. Once she had been undressed, Penelope sent her maid away, instructing the girl to shut off all but one of the lights before she left. Penelope stood, looking into her full-length triptych mirror with the polished cherrywood frame, and let her head rest back on her neck. It was only in September that her family had moved into its Fifth Avenue mansion, an event that was widely understood in the press as a declaration of the Hayeses' presence in society, and now half a year later she was living at an even better address, with an older family, on a more established section of the avenue.

She let her head sway back and forth, and as she appraised her reflection she thought—as she had thought before—how perfect she and Henry looked together. For they were both tall, both dark-haired. They had the same long limbs and the same haughty posture. There were times when she wondered if they didn't look *like* each other, if God in his infinite wisdom had not created them out of the same impeccable stuff so that they could recognize each other when they met. She was not wearing any of her lingerie, which was very fine and which had been handmade in France. She was wearing stockings and a black shirtwaist and nothing else. From the next room she could hear Henry's rising, whistling breath, and hoped that he was not snoring, that he had not fallen asleep.

She did not wear lingerie, because lingerie had already failed. What she wore now had a special significance for her—for both of them. She had answered the door wearing the same thing last June, the first time she invited Henry to the Waldorf-Astoria, where she and her family had lived while their house was being constructed. He hadn't left until the following morning, by which time she had already imagined herself as his bride.

She put out the last light, and stepped past the aubergine damask–covered screen and into her bedroom. It had been Henry's room originally, but she had banished the black leather club chairs and hunting trophies to the basement when she moved in. The broad, simple tables, which he had vaguely protested were from Great Britain and possessed historical significance, had been given to the servants. The room was now all white and gold and rococo, and the edges of every piece of furniture curved voluptuously. A waterfall of white and gold brocade descended from the high canopy at the head of the bed, and under it, on the ivory bedspread, lay Henry, with his hat and shoes still on. His hat tipped slightly over his eyes, and his legs were crossed at the ankles.

"Henry." Penelope kept her voice soft and rested a hand on her hip. He took a breath and stirred just enough to shift the hat on his head. In a moment it tumbled, softly, onto the plush white carpet.

"Henry," she said again. "Henry!"

He sat up then, his eyes a little wild with surprise. His dark hair had been neatly pomaded to the right earlier in the evening, but it was now sticking up in various places. He pulled at his white tie, which came undone in his hand. For a moment he looked at her, and she felt the old tingling warmth.

She crossed to him, her high-heeled slippers sinking into the carpet, and sat down on the edge of the bed. She reached up and took hold of his tie, then gently pulled it off. It fell soundlessly to the floor beside his hat, as she let her fingers glide from the point of his chin down his neck and to the first button of his shirt. She had succeeded in undoing one when he pushed away from the plush bed, and rose unsteadily to his feet.

"Henry?"

"Good night," he answered, pausing only to pick up his hat and tie as he walked into the adjoining room, where he sometimes took his tea, and to the black leather sofa with the piles of kilim pillows in its corners.

Penelope threw herself back against the bed and exhaled hotly, feeling—in her shoulders and all over—an aching for something just the slightest bit beyond her reach. Her disappointment was monstrous and her pulse quick, and she could not stop the fearful thoughts about what might come to pass if the news got out that this was how every night of her short married life had ended.

Four

We are all eager to catch glimpses of Elizabeth Holland, so lately returned to the realm of the living, but it is like trying to see some especially rare royal. Though her younger sister was seen out at the Leland Bouchard ball last night, the elder Miss Holland remained behind closed doors. Does her mother fear future kidnapping attempts? Have the young lady's delicate sensibilities been so flattened by the violence she was witness to in the Grand Central Station? Or is there some great secret that the public is being shielded from? We remain curious as ever.

—FROM *CITÉ CHATTER*, FRIDAY, FEBRUARY 9, 1900

$\mathcal{A}$ FIRE HUMMED IN THE DRAWING ROOM OF THE town house at No. 17 Gramercy Park South, which had provided shelter to three generations of the Holland family. It was easy to hear the snapping of kindling in the flames, because the occupants of that room were uncommonly quiet. They had settled into three of the several somewhat-the-worse-for-wear bergère chairs—which were arranged across the room at seemingly random distances from the hearth—after breakfast. Mrs. Holland sat closest to the warmth in her black crepe dress with the high neck and narrow-buttoned wrists; her elder child, Elizabeth, sat not far off. A book was open in the girl's lap, but she did not read. Snowden Trapp Cairns, who had been a business associate of the late Mr. Edward Holland and who had so often lately made himself their savior, lounged to her right. A portrait of Elizabeth's father peered down at them from above the fireplace, with an expression perhaps more skeptical than sage.

"It looks strange that you weren't in attendance at

Mr. Bouchard's last night." Mrs. Holland did not look up when she spoke, and the lines around her mouth grew taut. She had been reading the morning papers with her usual fierce attention. Diana had been at the ball—she'd returned after Elizabeth had gone to bed and had not as yet emerged from her room. Their aunt Edith, who had chaperoned, hadn't yet made an appearance in the parlor that morning, either. "It would have been a lovely evening, and you might have danced some. Anyway, your sister cannot represent this family alone."

Elizabeth's gaze rose slowly from the flames to her mother, who still held the folded broadsheet in her hand. In contrast to the orange hearth, she looked almost blue in that light of early day. Elizabeth opened her mouth, although not to speak. She knew that she had done the older lady much harm, for Mrs. Holland, who was born Louisa Gansevoort, had been a stern social arbiter before the series of tragedies that had begun to befall their family over a year ago. They had lost their patriarch and then their money, and soon after that Elizabeth had followed her heart—which had not been easy, given her impeccable training as a debutante—and run away with her father's former valet. When she closed her eyes she could almost feel her face against Will's clean, bare skin.

"The Henry Schoonmakers would have been there, and you could have silenced everyone who wonders if you're sour about the match by seeming glad to see them for just a few moments," her mother continued.

Elizabeth put her hands into the lap of her off-white, thick cotton dress with its vertical navy stripes. The dress was narrow at the waist, but ballooned in the torso and the hips and in the arms, enveloping her small frame. She blinked, for these days tears were never far away, and silently wished that she could obey her mother. It would be so simple, and it would make the lady so happy. But Elizabeth had never felt a stronger instinct than the one that insisted she stay in the house, that she never go out, that she never again appear pretty or gay.

It was her fault that Will had died, because he had been shot—suddenly, repeatedly, in a fusillade that caused the most horrendous sound she would ever hear on this earth—by men who thought they were protecting her. They would not have cared to protect her if they had not believed the illusion she had so carefully constructed: that she was a perfect, virginal society girl, possessed of impeccable manners and lavish gowns, and not in the least capable of leaving New York of her own volition, in pursuit of a coachman. She lowered her eyes, chastised but still silent.

"Perhaps it's too soon. After all, the events of New Year's Eve . . ."

Elizabeth turned toward Snowden, whom she was surprised to hear speak in contradiction of Mrs. Holland. Then again, he was the one who had married Will and Elizabeth, a few days before Will's death, in the room across the hall, where the Hollands used to have parties, when they still did such things. Oh, to be a widow at eighteen . . . but Elizabeth could not think that way, for it was self-pitying, and she had other atonements to make.

Mrs. Holland leaned forward and dropped the newspaper into the flames. Only when it shrank to ash did she let her obsidian eyes meet Snowden's.

"Perhaps you are right." Elizabeth's mother spoke in a clipped manner and went on looking into the eyes of her guest. She did not, however, marshal the full coldness that had famously been her response to anyone who caused her displeasure. But then, she could not have, even if she'd wanted to, as Elizabeth well knew, for Snowden had been very generous with them at a time when their inherited wealth had dwindled to nothing, and their bills had begun piling up. "But it is not her readiness that matters most, I am afraid. It is society, and what everyone will say. What they are already beginning to say. Unfortunately, the truth is not on our side, and we must be ever mindful of appearances."

"Elizabeth is very delicate now," Snowden returned without pause. "I'm sorry to say it is quite evident."

The girl in question glanced from her mother to Snowden, and saw that there was kindness in his simple, blocklike features. His eyes, which were set far apart under thick brows, and which were never quite brown or green, widened in her direction. He wore a shirt of sturdy white linen, and a vest of worn brown leather. It was his uniform of sorts. He was right, of course: She'd hardly had an appetite since Will's death, and had trouble keeping down the meals she did eat. She had grown gaunt, and forgot to care for her hair, which nowadays often had the limp look of having gone unwashed.

"And," he went on, "it would be doing none of the family any favors for her state, or the reasons for it, to be publicly speculated on. If you fear people saying that something untoward befell our girl between October and December past, her frailty might only seem to confirm that."

Elizabeth's smile was not what it used to be—in her days as a much-discussed debutante, she had been known for the radiant genuineness with which she had greeted her friends and peers, but that was a facial expression she could scarcely dream of now. Still, she tried to smile a little then. He was making the argument she might have made, if only she felt up to the task. She let her thin eyelids drift shut for a moment, and then she was back in California. Her body was warmed by the sun and close to Will's and she was almost blinded by that light, which was so clear and direct in a way she could never have imagined in New York, where the sun set at five in the winter and the walls were all stained with the residue of oil lamps. When she opened her eyes, she was again in that cluttered dark room, with its embossed olive leather paneling and carved, stained wood ceiling, with its many antique pieces.

Mrs. Holland's small, determined chin twitched in Elizabeth's direction. She drew her long fingers over her forehead and then rested her temple against her fingertips. She thought a moment, and then asked, "What do you suggest, then? That she stay indoors forever, like a prisoner of this house, as though she were some deaf mute who could not understand the world? And then what should I say to my friends, who were once merely happy that she was alive and now wonder suspiciously at our shielding her?" She paused and brought her hand down swiftly to her lap. "Those friends I have left," she added darkly.

Snowden stood and answered in the inverse tone. "I think I know what to do." He moved to the fireplace, the light from the flames catching his preternaturally blond hair, and made swooping gestures with his hands. "We should have a party here, at home, where Elizabeth is most comfortable." He paused thoughtfully. "Not a dance. A luncheon. Quiet, lovely, during the daylight hours. We can invite all the people Elizabeth used to know. The young ladies that she was friends with. Not too many, but enough to spread the word that she is quite all right and will be back in the world once the winter is over and she has begun to feel normal again." He turned to Elizabeth. "For surely, she will be normal by then?"

That remnant of a smile that had just crossed Elizabeth's lips disappeared now. She looked from Snowden to her mother, and saw that his plan was already in motion in that lady's thoughts. There was nothing to say, for Agnes Jones, and the Misses Wetmore, and her Holland and Gansevoort cousins were already as good as invited. They would arrive in the latest creations of their dressmakers, and would all be peering slantwise at Elizabeth to see if their clothing was better than hers. She was queasy with the idea of the pretense— all the greetings and superficial conversation that she would be forced to engage in. She would have to fasten a corset and dress like it mattered.

A log in the fire, burned through the middle, broke and fell then, scattering embers onto the stone hearth. Snowden moved to stamp them out, and Elizabeth put her face into her hands, knowing that she was far more than a few cold months away from normal.

Five

I hear that among the younger generation couples sometimes maintain but one large bedroom for husband and wife. I suppose that this is the hallmark of an intelligent use of space, and after all, the species must be propagated. Still, I prefer the older people's way of doing things: two well-appointed bedrooms, one each for husband and wife, an arrangement that prevents the revelation of so many irksome personal facts. . . ."

—*VAN KAMP'S GUIDE TO HOUSEKEEPING FOR LADIES OF HIGH SOCIETY,* 1899 EDITION

THE HILLS WERE THE INTENSE GREEN COLOR nature reserves for that hour directly following a heavy rain, and the horse beneath Henry Schoonmaker moved so speedily into the damp air that he felt a little dizzy with the pace. Up ahead of him, Diana Holland—her shiny russet curls half undone and whipping against her shoulders—turned her face slightly back to make sure he followed. She was wearing a white gown that reminded him of some Grecian statue in the Metropolitan Museum, and her small body rocked with the galloping of the huge, shiny animal. He turned his gaze down to urge his own horse, already sweaty with exertion, faster, and then, as he brought his face up again to look at her, he felt the rough texture of kilim against his cheek, and remembered the pillows on the couch that he had slept on ever since he had become a married man, and which Penelope's tastemaker, Isaac Phillips Buck, had picked up on some cruise through the Dardanelles.

"Henry!"

For a moment, Henry's addled brain couldn't distinguish what was dream and what was reality, although he held out a poignant hope that the scene with the verdant hills, the racing horses, and the youngest Holland was the one that would soon come into sharper focus. He dragged his face down, away from the harsh voice of his father, and felt again the scratchiness of the pillow against his smooth, golden skin. The feel of those imported Turkish fibers was undeniably more acute than the moist countryside air, which was in any event fading quickly, and there was nothing he could do to stop it.

"*Henry.*"

Henry now twisted the entirety of his long body so that he was sitting up, and then committed the first mistake of that morning: He opened his eyes, an act that caused him great pain when the flooding morning light met his weary retinas.

"Oh," he said feebly.

"Yes, it hurts, I know," his father replied, sitting on the couch next to his son. William Sackhouse Schoonmaker was a man of considerable size, broad-shouldered and full in every way, but whether his body or the sarcasm of his tone weighed more heavily on those soft black leather cushions was open for debate. He wore a suit of dark brown that shone almost purple where the light caught it, and his hair was a deep and artificial black. His face was a study in blunt features and popped blood vessels, but you could see under all that the bone structure that he had bequeathed his son. He had the appearance, now as ever, of being a very rich man. "But what are you doing here?"

"Here?" Henry's tone was dull, he knew, but he lacked the energy to change it. Unlike his father he was still lithe, his features still strong and clean as though they had been carved from marble, but his insides were feeling decidedly crumbly. The room they occupied was adjacent to his bedroom, in the second-floor wing that had always been largely his own. When he was a child his governess had slept here, and when he had dropped out of Harvard last spring it had been converted into a study of sorts for him—he had claimed, halfheartedly, that he might resume his studies at Columbia, where his friend Teddy Cutting had then been a senior. The floor was highly varnished parquet, and on the ceiling was a mural depicting a happy luncheon on the grass in big, loose brushstrokes. His gaze lingered there for a moment, and he was overtaken by a very childish thought: that he could jump in there and amble away.

His father, intuiting the gist of his fantasy, cut in. "Stop thinking like a little boy, Henry," he said.

"All right." Henry, who still could not manage any tone beyond a passive acquiescence, closed his eyes after he spoke. His tongue felt like some swollen fish dying on a rock. Then came the recollection of the drinks that had filled the previous evening and made it blurry and tolerable. Before all that—or

at least before the peak of his intoxication—there had been
Diana, to whom he had tried to be near over and again since
his wedding, without the slightest success. It had only been a
glimpse of her, for as soon as he had entered the music room
at Leland Bouchard's, she had exited. She'd looked as healthy
and rosy as any sixteen-year-old, but with that sharp pride of a
woman who has been scorned and then drawn herself up, ever
more glorious, from the humiliation.

"Now, what are you doing here?"

Henry's hands went to his chest. His memory of how
he had arrived on this couch this particular morning was
incomplete, and he had gotten in the habit on mornings like
these (there had been many) of patting himself down to make
sure he was all in one piece. He seemed to be. He also seemed
to be wearing a rumpled white dress shirt of Italian linen—the
same one, as far as he could determine, that he had worn the
night before—and black dress pants. His feet were covered
in black socks, and his shoes were lying next to his white silk
waistcoat on the floor. His tie was nowhere to be seen.

"Sleeping?"

"Evidently."

Henry stood. "It was a long night," he replied,
sounding—with exactly no effort—like he could sleep for
another hundred years. He bent to pick up his waistcoat, and
regretted it instantly. The swift movement had caused a kind

of stabbing agony around his forehead. He brought himself up quickly, and drew on what energy he had to remain upright.

The elder Schoonmaker stood, cleared his throat, and softened his tone. "Henry . . ." He looked at his son, and for a moment his thoughts seemed to have gone to some place in the distant past. They stood awkwardly there, in that paneled and ornamented room, shifting in their places. "There's been a promising development in my quest for the mayoralty."

Henry, who a moment before had hoped he might escape his father's wrath, now felt a twitch of dread. W. S. Schoonmaker was a ruthless businessman, and he had inherited and made several fortunes already, but he'd recently decided that he wanted his earthly name to ascend a new level of fame and glory, and it was for this reason that he longed to enter the fray of politics. He believed he should be mayor, which caused him to fear and rail against his son's profligacy as never before and to curtail his son's sprees whenever possible. His new ambition made him fond of threatening disinheritance, and it had transformed him into a formidable pusher of Henry Schoonmaker, the married man.

"Oh?" There were very few things that Henry liked discussing less than his father's political ambitions.

"Yes. The Family Progress Party needs a candidate for their mayoral ticket, and it seems we believe in many of the same things."

"What kind of things?" Henry asked ironically. He did not have the courage, or the mental strength, to point out the obvious absurdity of this prospect. For many of the people who voted for the Family Progress Party also had the misfortune of living in tenements that were owned by the Schoonmakers' holding company, where they surely had requested services like heat and hot water and been turned down flat.

"Well, in science and innovation," his father replied impatiently. "In the progress of society, and in humankind's mission to improve the world as they found it. And of course, on the fundamental joy of family as the raison d'être of all men."

Henry smothered his laugh with his fist and turned toward the windows. He had not disguised his opinion about his father's words well enough, however—he could tell by the way the old man loomed behind him.

"I suppose you doubt my dedication to family." His father's tone had changed quite suddenly and was now full of ire. "Well, you know nothing."

"I do know . . ." Henry began, but faltered. He wasn't even sure what it was he had wanted to say.

"Shut up, Henry. It doesn't matter, anyway, what you think of me or what I think of you. It matters what the people of this great city see in both of us. Do they see a family of louche, careless individuals, or purposeful businessmen with wives and children to nurture?"

"I have no children," Henry said. This seemed to him, in the moment, like a true stroke of luck. His physical discomfort was coming in waves now, and for a moment the tide seemed to ebb as he thought of that one crucial way in which he was still free.

"No." His father laughed cruelly. "And you're not going to get them by sleeping on the couch. I've queried the staff, and they say you wake up here every morning. Can it be that you haven't—?"

"No." Henry glanced at his father, and saw a horrid concoction of amusement, rage, and disbelief on his face. The two men stared at each other for a long moment, whole monologues going unsaid across their features.

"Well," the elder Schoonmaker went on, more peacefully than his tone of a few seconds before might have implied, "you'll have to stop behaving like silly children. I want a grandchild by the election. That'll be November of 1901, Henry, so you have plenty of time. A boy would be nice. A big healthy boy, to hold aloft over the crowds. Try for that."

"Dad, I really don't think—"

"Am I interrupting?" The two Schoonmaker men turned sidewise, to the door that adjoined the bedroom and the study. Penelope was standing there, fully dressed in a fluted skirt of blue and white tartan and a shirt of cream chiffon with a high, whalebone collar. Her dark hair rose, silken and shiny, from her smooth forehead. The counterfeit concern on her face melted into an ingratiating smile, and then she tipped her head. "Good morning, Mr. Schoonmaker."

"Good morning, Penelope."

"I *am* sorry to interrupt," she went on like the sweet girl she most certainly was not. "But I've just received an invitation to the Hollands', this Sunday, for luncheon. We must go, for dear old Elizabeth's sake, and show her that there isn't any discomfort between us. She will see, of course, that we were the right match all along, and that we love her no less for having nearly taken my place. . . ."

A terse "no" was ready on Henry's tongue, as it always was when he conversed with his wife, and he wasn't sure whether he was more disgusted with the way his father and Penelope were now smiling at each other, or by the idea of appearing at the Hollands' house as a married man. He had explained his actions with every conceivable combination of words, but he had yet to receive any kind of indication that Diana had even read his letters. But he went on writing to her because he didn't know what else to do, which was the same motivation that led him to hang his head now. "Teddy and I have planned a trip to Palm Beach, to get away from this damned cold and do some fishing. We are leaving Tuesday, and I have precious little time for social events before then—"

"I didn't know you were going to Palm Beach," came Penelope's crisp reply.

"It was a sudden impulse," he replied lamely. Henry knew that Penelope was giving him an accusing look, but he couldn't bear to meet her eyes. "Which is why there is still so much to be done . . ." he mumbled at his lap.

"In that case," Penelope went on with a firm hand to the hip, "I will arrange for your luggage and travel things, and I will book passage for myself so that I can see to everything for you in Palm Beach."

Henry wasn't sure what kind of expression his face assumed just then, but Penelope returned one of triumphant satisfaction.

"I will bring a friend along for company," she concluded, almost to herself.

"Good," his father put in, sealing all of it.

"All right." Henry tried to smile a little at both of them. He could tell that his father wanted to go on needling him about making a family of healthy Schoonmaker babies—an idea so bizarre and wrong to Henry that he couldn't begin to mentally approach it in his current state. He knew the old man would again, but not now. Not with Penelope there, all prettily made up like any guileless, cosseted girl of their class. Propriety was good for something after all, Henry reflected with bitter humor, as he brushed past his wife and went into the bedroom to get a few hours' proper sleep.

Six

Carolina—

Luncheon at the Hollands'

this afternoon? Wouldn't it be fun

if you showed up and reminded

Elizabeth how far beyond her

you've risen? I will come by

in the carriage at noon.

—Mrs. Henry Schoonmaker

"OH, DEAR OLD SEVENTEEN," CAROLINA BROAD SIGHED, her voice dusted by an entirely disingenuous nostalgia, as Penelope Schoonmaker's covered phaeton came to a stop on the south side of Gramercy Park.

When Penelope's note had arrived that morning, asking her if she didn't want to come along to a Sunday luncheon at the Hollands', her initial reaction had been a kind of panic. She had first suffered the recollection of those plain black linen dresses that she used to have to wear—not even the more dignified white-collared uniforms that the maids in the Hayeses' house wore—and of the rough treatment the skin of her hands had been dealt during her service there. But then she had looked into her closet at all the dresses and jewelry, all the shoes and gloves and smart little jackets that she had acquired as the special friend of Mr. Longhorn. And she had thought on the Hollands' poverty—which they had managed to keep secret for so long, but which had inevitably become somewhat known—and she had reassured herself

that now was her time, and that the Holland women should be made to see it.

"I wonder why they want you here," she wondered aloud, realizing only after she had spoken that this question might sound cruel.

Penelope, if she had found it so, did not appear wounded. "Oh, they need me much more than I need them," she answered blithely as she checked her face in her carved ivory compact mirror. Beyond her profile, framed in the carriage window, were the trees of the park, which had become bare and leafless since Carolina had last seen them. "Surely old Mrs. Holland knows by now that I am privy to Elizabeth's dirty little secret, and anyway, nobody in society likes a jilted former fiancée. It is *not* a coveted role. I'm mostly looking forward to how they react to seeing *you* here."

Carolina rested her hand on the brass-edged door of the phaeton and blinked at the house where she'd once laid her head. It seemed rather narrow to her now, and almost dour with its plain brownstone façade. The iron grille of the enclosed porch looked tacked on as an afterthought, and the windows in straight lines up and down stared obtusely at the street. The life she'd lived there felt remote to her, like an awful story she had been told once, or a nightmare she had been jolted from suddenly. She thought briefly of Will—who had been such a good, beautiful boy—and how he had made the mistake of loving high and mighty Elizabeth Holland. It was a mistake he had died for. That was a sad direction, though, and Carolina turned her thoughts back around as Penelope's driver opened the little door and helped her down to the curb.

She took a big, greedy breath of air and looked toward Penelope, who always knew just what to do. They linked arms—a thing Penelope only did with her in public. She had to. It was their agreement to appear to be friends; that was what Penelope had traded her for the secret about Diana Holland having done unladylike things with Henry, in her own bedroom, late one December night, after his engagement with Elizabeth had ended but before his engagement with Penelope had yet begun. Then they walked up the old stone steps, Carolina's long, gray, fur-trimmed skirt swishing against Penelope's black accordion-pleated one.

The door swung back, and a young woman with neatly brushed-back copper hair welcomed them. The planes of her face were broad and fair, rather like Carolina's, except that Carolina's were darkened by a smattering of freckles even in the cold middle of February. The girl's welcoming smile faded, and she paused dumbly in the dark and narrow foyer.

"Mrs. Henry Schoonmaker and Miss Carolina Broad." Penelope indicated how she would like to be announced as she removed a hat festooned with small black birds. "Mr.

Schoonmaker is preparing for a trip and will not be able to join us. Miss Broad came in his place. She is a particular friend of mine."

Carolina, too, removed her hat, which was a rakish, top hat–style thing, and handed it to the maid with a wink. The maid was well known to her. She was in fact her sister, Claire Broud, who loved to hear stories of beautiful people and their doings but was too good and shy to join them herself. Not so the younger Broud—now Broad, since a typo in a society column had announced her presence in elite New York and forever re-christened her. The sisters saw each other whenever possible—although it was often difficult for Carolina, what with all her new friends—and still understood each other enough that Claire was able, with a few bats of her lashes, to let her younger sibling know that she would try her best to act normal.

As Carolina stepped inside, she couldn't help but think how meager and scuffed the rooms here were. The stairs at the end of the foyer moved straight up to the second floor without any grand, looping pretenses, and the pictures that decorated the wall on the way up were really not as fine as the ones the Hollands had had to sell last fall for ready cash. Her gaze drifted to her left, into the lesser parlor, which had not been in much use when she was last in the house, but was now populated with round tables covered in white damask and crowned with silver loving cups filled with red berry–dotted branches. There was a time when she would have steamed those cloths and arranged those cups, she was thinking, when her reflections were interrupted by a fearsome and familiar voice. Both Broud sisters froze.

"Penelope," said Mrs. Holland as she entered the foyer from the back of the house. She was wearing all black, and her dark, white-streaked hair was arranged without the covering of a widow's cap, as it had been for most of the previous year. The hostess approached the younger women and paused. If she smiled, it was only a flicker at the corner of her mouth. She drew out the interlude long enough that even Penelope seemed a little befuddled, and then she bestowed a simple, "Congratulations," on her daughter's onetime friend. "And you are?" she asked, turning her cusped chin at the girl in gray and fur.

For a moment, all of Carolina's nerves reverberated. Then she met Mrs. Holland's eyes, dark as a pool in a forest, and realized that there was not even the slightest cloud of recognition. They were eyes so blank and imperious that Carolina wondered how she had ever had the courage to meet them before, and a second later she realized that she never had. Her former employer hadn't ever so much as looked her in the face, even as she issued thousands of orders, and she did so now with such artful indifference that Carolina wondered—briefly,

but nonetheless—if she had really risen from her place in the Holland house at all.

"This is Miss Carolina Broad." Penelope seemed not to have noticed or cared that a confrontation with the hostess had not materialized, and was already looking into the lesser parlor, to see who else was there. Then she added a rather cursory explanation: "She is new to the city, but already beloved."

"It is such a pleasure to be among your guests," Carolina managed to say through her disappointment. It was only after the opportunity had passed that she realized how much she'd wanted to be recognized, that she had in fact been nursing the desire for Mrs. Holland to recognize her nascent grandeur and quaver at how far she had come.

Claire, who must have been petrified with fear during this exchange, gave her sister a warning glance and retreated toward the closet underneath the stairs laden with the two new guests' many cold-weather trappings. Penelope had now moved, along with Mrs. Holland, into the mahogany-framed entryway, where people whose every waking hour was occupied by one delightful leisure activity after another filled the room.

"You see, we have restored some of our old paintings, and done away with those pieces that really weren't the style anymore . . ." Mrs. Holland was saying.

Behind her in the foyer, where the draft was most

chilling, Carolina paused awkwardly. She was aware of every hair on the back of her neck, as she often was when she suffered from the condition of not knowing quite where she was supposed to be or quite how she was supposed to stand. Her sister had disappeared, and was no doubt wishing that she had been born an only child so that she could at least depend on steady employment. Already Carolina's connection to this event had stepped into the adjacent room, leaving her behind with a suffocating need for attention and approval. She took a step forward, but faltered. Suddenly, her surroundings had stopped seeming quite so small and shabby.

"Lina."

The name was like some ill-fitting old garment that scratches the skin even as one tries to hand it down. The sound was humble and plain. It was her own name, Carolina knew, or at least the one that she had been most often called in her seventeen years. But it gave her no pleasure to hear it out loud. Instead it brought heat up into her wide cheeks, the same heat that the speaker's very presence used to cause. She turned her eyes—now intensely green against her reddening skin—and saw Elizabeth, alive after all, and not nearly as lovely as she used to be.

"Hello." Though she had not intended one tone over another, the sound of that single word hung in the air with certain satisfaction. The last time she had seen Elizabeth she had spilled hot tea all over her white skirt, an act that had swiftly resulted in her being let go. Her former mistress's face was gaunt now, and that blond hair, which Carolina had once arranged, was stringy and pulled into a tight, unpretty bun. There was nothing to indicate that any of the intervening months had softened Elizabeth to the girl who had once tied her corsets.

"What are you doing here?" Elizabeth asked as she drew close. Her voice and movements lacked energy, but that did not preclude hostility, which was evident all over but especially in her darting brown eyes.

"I might ask you that very question. I thought you *drowned*." Carolina shifted to a cockier stance, for all of a sudden she knew precisely how to stand. Her smart jacket, which was fitted in the waist and puffed elegantly at the shoulders, had quite obviously been made by a skilled dressmaker, and was of extravagantly expensive cloth. She leaned closer to Elizabeth and went on in a low, pointed voice: "Or was that just a story to cover up your intentions regarding a certain boy who used to work in a stable?"

Elizabeth shrank a little at that, and her eyes filmed over as though tears might follow.

"Oh, don't." Carolina curled her upper lip back and held her former mistress's gaze. "I once loved him too, or did you forget that while you were so busy feeling sorry for yourself?"

"He was my *husband.*" Elizabeth's voice wavered over the words, and when she finished speaking, she pressed her lips together firmly, as though she were trying to contain some violence of emotion.

The girl who would have felt jealous or devastated or anything by this news was gone. If Elizabeth wanted to lose control, that was her decision—Carolina was past making such mistakes. She raised her chin slightly and allowed a sense of her own prowess to radiate across her clavicles and down into her fingertips. She arched one thick eyebrow with slow purpose and allowed the standstill to lengthen a few seconds.

"I wouldn't want that one getting out."

Elizabeth closed her eyes. "You wouldn't tell—"

"Probably not." Carolina laughed her most insouciant laugh. "But then, I *am* awfully thirsty and I *was* under the impression that I was attending a luncheon party."

The brown eyes under Elizabeth's fair brows opened again. She looked at Carolina with greater vulnerability than ever before, which was quite remarkable considering the two had known each other almost since birth and had been friends as little girls.

"Of course," she said in a new tone. It was the sound of weakness feigning strength, but it fooled neither party about what had just transpired. Carolina was no longer Elizabeth's subordinate, and she had a piece of gossip on her once again.

"Won't you come in? Perhaps you would like to sit with me, at my table, where I can be sure that you are getting the best of everything?"

Carolina, who could hear the strain in Elizabeth's voice, lifted her arm and waited for the other girl to take it before nodding her assent. "That would be perfectly lovely," she said, her blood pumping triumphantly as they walked into that festive room. It was full of well-heeled guests and brightly shining serving trays laden with rich, aromatic food, which she might once have carried in from the kitchen, but which she would now allow to be presented to her from the left so that she might take whichever portion she pleased.

Seven

I have heard from a special source that a luncheon will be held today at the Hollands' house, and that Penelope Schoonmaker is among the guests. In society there will always be fans of low entertainment who hope for a fight between ladies, and that element has predictably been talking up some feud between Miss Elizabeth Holland and the former Miss Hayes, since both girls were at one time engaged to Mr. Schoonmaker. It seems they will be disappointed, if the ladies are meeting so cordially as all this, at the first social gathering the Hollands have hosted since the death of Mr. Edward Holland, over a year ago. . . .

—FROM THE "GAMESOME GALLANT" COLUMN IN THE
NEW YORK IMPERIAL, SUNDAY, FEBRUARY 11, 1900

*D*IANA HOLLAND CAME DOWN TO HER MOTHER'S luncheon a little late but fully prepared to hear all about Eleanor Wetmore's romantic travails. She had colluded with Claire and had her place card switched so that she was sitting next to Eleanor, the better to glean information from that girl, and also conveniently so that she would not be seated too near Penelope. She wore a dress of thick cotton with a looping red and white pattern on it and a neck that rose just an inch above her clavicles; her head of curls framed her face with their natural architecture. She arrived on the first floor with a thoughtless stride, but found herself shocked still, her plum mouth opening slightly, when she saw the figure on the other side of the front door's glass pane.

By the time conscious thought returned to her she had already crossed to the entry and placed a palm against the glass. It was as though she had been pulled there by some magnetic force. She closed her eyes, because she knew they had taken on the wide, innocent longing of a little girl's. When she opened them again, they shone with a harder quality. Henry, however, had not gone away, and so in a few seconds she twisted the knob.

"What are you doing here?" She kept her voice low and unfriendly, and her body partially obscured by the door.

"I believe I was invited." There was that jocular, entitled tone that had served him so well in his twenty years. He must have known it was a mistake, because he closed his dark eyes and shook his handsome head. She was surprised how handsome that face was to her now, when she looked straight into it at close range. A lot of time had passed since she had been this near him.

"I suppose you are here to meet your wife," she quipped, almost just to distract herself from the line of his jaw. "She's here."

"No . . ." Henry stopped shaking his head. A moment later he let his gaze—so tentative, so full of desire—meet Diana's. "No."

"No *what*?" She relaxed her grip on the door and let it open just a few inches wider. The park was quiet behind them, the naked branches of trees reaching up hungrily toward the white sky. All of the coachmen kept their noses in their newspapers and studiously ignored the two people on the stoop.

"No, I didn't come to see my wife." He paused and pressed his fingers to the place on his forehead just between his brows. "I wasn't going to come at all. But then, the idea of being in the same room as you—I'm sorry. I sound like an ass. I hadn't anticipated that I would actually be able to *talk* to you, like this, so close. You will probably leave any moment now and I won't have said any of what I want to say to you and . . . Oh, God."

Her heart, the damned thing, had begun to race, and she only hoped that the rapid inflation and deflation of her chest wasn't visible beneath her fitted bodice. She knew that she should do what Henry expected her to do and walk away. Then he could ring the bell, and Claire could show him in more formally. But instead she stepped out onto the stoop and let the door close partially behind her. "What did you want to say?"

Henry took off his hat and held it pensively between his hands. "Well, it's like I said in my letters. . . ." His sentences were broken, as though he were having trouble drawing breath. "Didn't you read my letters?"

For a moment, all of Diana's emotions had been under siege, but that was now replaced by a simple, simmering irritation. "No," she said. She began to notice the chill air. "I burned them."

Henry let out a breath and a sound approximately like "Oh." He looked at Diana for a long time, and while she recognized some great emotion in his face, she couldn't be certain if it was sympathy for what he had done to her, or self-pity for what he himself had lost.

"Henry," she said after a while. She was trying to sound tough and impatient, but she knew that vulnerable desire to be wooed was still brimming in her tone. "They'll be wondering where I am."

Henry glanced to his left, where the windows of the parlor were, and took a step closer to make sure that he was out of view. She noticed the apparatus of his throat working beneath the soft skin, which his valet had no doubt shaved an hour or two ago. "If I could just have one more minute of your time, Miss Diana."

She looked behind her, as though a whole crowd of snoops had gathered, but there was no one in the foyer. "All right," she said.

"I don't love Penelope, I never did." For the first time during their interaction, his body was completely still. Not even his eyelids flickered. "There was never a time I really thought I would marry her, and when I did it was all to protect you."

Diana's arms moved involuntarily over her chest. The cold was at her ears now, but she had never seen Henry's face so sincere—she felt a little warm noting that.

"She found out about that night . . . in your room . . . and what occurred between you and me. She told me that if I didn't marry her she would expose you. I tried to explain it all to you. . . ." He trailed off, perhaps realizing that none of that mattered now. "You were all I thought of the whole ceremony, and ever since. Protecting you and your good name."

Diana's good name had never seemed so useless to her. She pressed her fingertips into the rough door, and wondered if he wanted her to thank him. Many things had changed in her over a matter of minutes, but she had not begun to feel grateful.

"My letters were to explain all that to you, and to tell you how sorry I am that this is what has happened." Henry turned his hat in his hands but went on looking at Diana in a way that made her want to crawl into his arms and stay there forever. She was surprised at herself, and a little angry, for still having feelings like that. "I don't love her, Di."

She closed her eyes and rumpled her brow. "You certainly have all New York fooled," she said, rather unconvincingly.

"I don't even go to bed with her."

She opened her eyes then, the thick lashes fluttering back from her rich brown irises. "Never?" she whispered.

Henry shook his head and watched her. "How could I, when you're the one I want?"

It was as though she had been pushed forward, through the breeze, on a child's swing. Her lips parted, and a thousand thoughts clamored for articulation on her tongue. She wondered if maybe Henry would kiss her, quickly enough that nobody would notice, but then the moment broke.

"Diana?" a voice called from the foyer.

Her mind rushed with fear and she swallowed hard before turning to see her sister just beyond the door. "Oh, Liz. I was only . . ." Her eyes flickered between the man in the black frock coat and Elizabeth's tired eyes. "Mr. Schoonmaker is here."

"Well." Elizabeth's pale, heart-shaped face was framed by the cracked door. "We are all waiting for you. Have him come in, and take his coat, for goodness' sake."

She gave Henry a serious look, and then turned away, leaving her sister alone with him once more. A silence followed, and eventually Diana asked, "Are you coming in?"

"No . . ." Henry's dark brows drew up and closer together. "I don't think I could stand it."

She nodded.

"I am leaving Tuesday. Teddy and I are going to do some fishing. Tell them I was called away to get my luggage and plans in order, if they saw me. And if they didn't, don't mention my coming here at all." He paused and put his hat back on his head. "Penelope invited herself along, of course, and now she plans to invite Elizabeth. I think she wants to create the illusion that they are still friends." Henry was babbling now, saying words that implied his departure even while he

stayed put. He went down a few steps, looked at his shiny dress shoes, and then back up at Diana. "Would you come?"

"Where?"

"To Florida."

She looked nervously over her shoulder. "But how would I . . . ?"

Then he grinned at her, and for a moment the bad weather broke. She felt that old giddy lightness, as though she were capable of anything—it was the sensation he used to give her, just by being in her general vicinity. "You are very clever, and I'm sure you will find a way."

He lifted and then lowered the brim of his hat, before turning and walking briskly to his waiting carriage. She brushed the curls away from her face and tried to feel a little calm, but all her cool distance had left her. When she finally returned to her family's gathering, her whole body was at an entirely different temperature.

Eight

A young lady's most natural ally is her sister, although sometimes our own relatives are as inscrutable to us as an antipodean.

—MAEVE DE JONG, *LOVE AND OTHER FOLLIES OF THE GREAT FAMILIES OF OLD NEW YORK*

THE PLATES BEARING HALF-EATEN TIMBALES OF chicken were being removed from the right-hand side of the Holland family's guests, to be replaced—Elizabeth knew very well, for she had overseen the menu—by filet of beef with asparagus. She had also arranged the silver loving cups with brightly colored winter branches, carefully inscribed their guests' names on place cards, and helped Claire with the steaming of the old damask table linens. The money that Snowden had given them—it was their father's share of a claim they had jointly owned in the Klondike, or so he had insisted—had enabled them to hire a new cook for the occasion. Elizabeth had worn the dress of her mother's choosing, an iridescent navy with tiny buttons drawing the fabric close to emphasize the thinness of her neck and wrists, but not her torso or arms, and she had managed to meet their guests with something like the welcoming mien expected of one of the old Dutch families' eldest daughters.

But she had made a fatal mistake. It was the kind of

mistake that the girl she used to be—the one people thought of when they uttered those names, "Elizabeth" and "Holland," sequentially—never would have made. She had let an ugly emotion (anger, tinged with unquenchable sadness) rise in her in public. She had revealed too much to an ungrateful girl who hated her, and who in any event already knew enough to hang her. Elizabeth smiled weakly in Lina's direction, hoping that Lina was not as unreasonable and vengeful as she sometimes seemed, and asked if she was enjoying the food.

"Why, yes."

Lina smiled with shameless pleasure at the girl she had served since childhood. A small amount of grease was smudged against her lip, which she had not bothered to blot with her napkin, and it glinted in the afternoon light. Across the room, their guests were chatting in polite tones and enjoying Holland hospitality without being so gauche as to note what a rare commodity it had been of late. The lesser parlor looked very well—it had once been the room where they displayed their dowdier paintings, but all of those had been removed along with the cobwebs that had accumulated on the high picture moldings. It was also the room Elizabeth had been married in.

At the hostess's table, Penelope carried on as though she had been a weekly visitor in the house for all of recent memory. Mrs. Holland occupied the chair across from her daughter, and listened to her guests with studied acceptance. She had apparently forgotten that she had once selected Penelope's husband as the groom for her own child, and—perhaps more strangely—failed to recognize Miss Broad as her former employee.

"What a good thing it is to have a home-cooked meal after so many months eating hotel food," Lina was saying. She paused and turned to Mrs. Holland brazenly. "I live in the New Netherland, you know."

"I did not know." Mrs. Holland took a sip of Apollinaris water and assessed the newcomer. Maybe she did wonder why, in a room of thirty-six highborn people, this girl from out west, possessed of an unstoried fortune, should be sitting at her table, but she did not betray any such thoughts. At least not in an overt way. "I remember when it went up, and how garish we all thought it was. And now lovely girls like you live there! It does show you how precious little we all knew then."

"How odious I found hotel life," Penelope sighed.

Elizabeth looked at her old friend and let her eyelids flick back and forth a few times. They had been exceptionally close during the year and a half that Penelope had lived in the Waldorf, and even after Elizabeth had departed for a finishing season in Paris she had received letters overstuffed with accounts of all the marvelous things to be seen and touched and tasted there. Elizabeth distinctly remembered feeling embarrassed by those guilelessly exuberant descriptions. It was during that period, Elizabeth later realized, that Penelope had fixed her ambitions on Henry Schoonmaker, which was among the reasons that she eventually ran afoul of her friend.

"The service is much better in one's own house, where one can control things," she added.

"Do you never stay in hotels anymore?" Lina asked. Her voice was flat and earnest, and Elizabeth realized that she was asking out of true curiosity and perhaps as a cue to her own future behavior. It made Elizabeth pity her a little, despite the earlier scene, because she was obviously trying so hard to appear fine and rare, and yet she was somehow or other under the wing of Penelope, whose money was still considered rather new.

"Of course, when I travel, but only if I have to," that lady returned. She pressed her voluptuous lips together and gave her new friend a certain look. "For instance, when I am in Newport, my family takes a cottage for the season, and when I am in Paris, I stay in our apartment on the Champs. But I am looking forward to one upcoming stay in a hotel—"

"Mrs. Schoonmaker, are you taking a trip?" Mrs. Holland asked. Her daughter, who knew each of the lady's tones, detected a strained politeness in the question, although the guests at the neighboring tables would have heard only warm curiosity.

"Yes, Henry and I are taking a trip to Palm Beach." A proud and involuntary smile sprang to her lips as she said "Henry and I." "He and Teddy are going to fish, and I've been dying for some warm weather, and of course the Royal Poinciana is said to be a very grand establishment. A good wife always oversees her husband's travel, when she can."

Elizabeth set her water glass down at this, and her eyes darted to Diana, at a nearby table with their aunt Edith and the Misses Wetmore. If she was affected by the sound of Henry's name she didn't show it, for she went on animatedly asking Eleanor Wetmore about which beaux she particularly had her eye on that season. It was Elizabeth's belief that her sister had experienced something very true with Henry, and she also believed that his feelings for her were equally pure. She had seen it in his eyes when she glimpsed him from across a busy street, on the morning when she had thought herself to be leaving New York forever. He had been rumpled and a little devastated to see Diana go away from him. She'd recognized that same look on his face an hour ago, when she'd caught him loitering at the door, and she'd hoped that he finally got to communicate to Diana a little of what those letters she'd so impetuously burned had contained.

"I've never been to Florida," Lina said.

Of course you haven't, Elizabeth thought, a little cruelly, to herself.

Something unspoken passed between the faces of Lina and Penelope, and then Penelope said, "You should come of course, Carolina. I will need someone to keep me company while the men are playing. *You* should come too, Elizabeth." Penelope paused and looked into Elizabeth's eyes, the whites growing around those intense blue irises. It was a look that made Elizabeth grateful for her lack of appetite, for if she had eaten anything she surely would not have been able to keep it down after witnessing such blatant falsity. "We haven't been able to enjoy each other's company like we used to since . . . When was it? October?"

For a moment, Elizabeth was overcome by a wave of hateful feeling, but it washed over her quickly and was gone. She knew that she could forgive Penelope, for all the cruelty she had dealt Elizabeth had resulted in one good thing—it had allowed her to live with Will for some months without all the secrecy and guilt that had shadowed their love in New York. And if Penelope had taken from Diana the thing she most wanted, well, she had only been pursuing what she herself desired with characteristic ruthlessness.

Elizabeth's mouth had gone dry as she stared back at her old friend. Across the room, ladies whose lace collars were clasped by buttons of pearl sat at tables in groups of four and went on exclaiming over antiques and Paris fashions and the hunting on Long Island, but at the table nearest the fireplace

everyone had grown quiet. Their gazes held steady in Elizabeth's direction.

"October," she confirmed after a minute.

"Just think," Penelope went on, undeterred, her delicate elbow coming to rest on the white tablecloth. "We can swim in the ocean and walk by the seashore, and we will be very far away from all the gossip and silliness."

The idea of sunshine and palm trees and parasols and bathing costumes made Elizabeth's stomach turn. Already all the women they knew, and everyone at that table, were professionally frivolous. The idea of traveling a long distance at great expense to do all the same things with better lighting was repugnant to her. But before she could communicate this, her mother cut in:

"How generous of you, Penelope." Elizabeth looked across the table, with its piles of brown bread and its little china butter dish and all the other dainty china pieces that a midday luncheon was an excuse to display. One could detect, in every slight twitch of the older lady's face, a sternness that could not be denied. "Of course Elizabeth would love to go."

Elizabeth's eyes grew round with bewilderment. She couldn't go—all of her insides were in revolt at the very idea. He mother's small obsidian eyes were settled on her daughter, her crow's feet spreading confidently as she waited for Elizabeth to enunciate the appropriate response. Penelope's smile, meanwhile, had transformed to a smirk. Elizabeth turned her fair head just slightly and glanced at her sister for help.

Diana was sitting at the adjacent table, and she propped her left elbow on the wooden back of her chair and leaned over when she realized she was being silently called upon. Her large, soft brown eyes blinked once, and for a moment Elizabeth believed her sister might come to the rescue. Then Diana called, over the voices of the Misses Wetmore, "Florida? That would be such a very good time!"

Elizabeth's gaze darted back to her mother, and she realized that Diana's comment had elicited an uncharacteristic smile in the old lady. "But it's so far away," she mumbled.

"I will go with you, if you fear the distance." Diana's tone was jovial, and in another moment Elizabeth realized what she was about. "I am hardier than you and would see that you were comfortable."

Penelope removed her elbow from the table, as though she were confused, and rearranged the shiny black pleats on her lap. When she had regained her smile she turned to Elizabeth. "How wonderful. It will be a party!"

Elizabeth opened her eyes and looked from her insistent mother to that supremely false face, realizing as she did that her instinct to stay far away from Penelope was based not only on the new Mrs. Schoonmaker's past deeds, but what she was capable of in the future. Penelope's ambitions no longer made any sense to Elizabeth, but it began to dawn on her, as she observed that painfully ingratiating expression, that hiding was a useless and futile way to spend her time, and that it wouldn't keep any of them safe in the least.

"You're sure you have room for Diana too?" Elizabeth noted, in the far corner of her vision, that Diana's breathing had grown a little dramatic and that she was following everything at the table closest to the fire with vigilant eyes. Her face was nakedly hopeful. "It's only that I'm not quite myself again, and I would need the company of my sister to feel at ease on so long a trip."

"Of course!" gushed Penelope. "Although," she went on a little more loudly, so that all the nearby tables might hear, "I think of *you* as a sister and believe we could comfort each other very well. But your sister is my sister"—here she paused to flash her eyes at Diana—"and haven't I always said the more the merrier?"

"It will be very lovely for both my girls," Mrs. Holland said with uncharacteristic deference. "Thank you, Mrs. Schoon-maker."

"What *fun* we'll have," Penelope concluded with terrible emphasis.

As a slightly younger debutante, Elizabeth had been an expert practitioner of small equivocations and white lies— always in the service of propriety and politeness, of course.

She had never liked big lies, as she had not liked anything that might fall in that dreaded category of "too much." But looking at Penelope, at her large, fine, attention-getting features, at the rabidity in her giant eyes, Elizabeth began to see that putting on a false front, on a truly grand scale, was the only way to protect herself and her sister. She thought of Henry and Diana on the stoop, gazing at each other with the confusion and sadness of two puppies who have just stumbled into their first puddle and not yet come to understand what has happened to them, and found that she wanted to lie extravagantly. She brought herself up, allowing air into her delicate lungs, meeting Penelope's gaze.

"*Such* fun," Elizabeth said, and then she smiled, the kind she used to employ when cooing over balls or high-heeled slippers, the kind that suffused her cheeks and throat an affectionate pink. Her old friend beamed back. They regarded each other for several seconds, and then Elizabeth rested her long, slender fingers—not as well maintained as previously, but still elegantly constructed—over Penelope's. "I cannot wait."

Nine

Where did Carolina Broad come from? Who were her parents, really, and how did she establish herself among us so quickly? Is she the creation of Carey Lewis Longhorn, or is there some other author of this latest girl on the make?

—FROM *CITÉ CHATTER*, SUNDAY, FEBRUARY 11, 1900

"*I* THINK THAT WENT OFF VERY WELL," SAID SNOWDEN Cairns, who was standing somewhere behind Diana in the more used of the Hollands' two parlors, as the last of their luncheon guests crossed the sidewalk to their waiting carriages. Diana, who had no particular eye for social events or their success or failure (the grand sweep of an evening could never compare, for her, to its secret, stolen moments), shrugged indifferently. She didn't know if it had gone off well, although she did now know who Eleanor Wetmore had her eye on, and that she was determined to be engaged by the younger Wetmore's June wedding. Diana also knew that she was going to Palm Beach, with her sister, and Penelope, and—most achingly, most confusingly—with Henry, who still loved her.

Through the lace undercurtains, down on the street, Mrs. Schoonmaker and Miss Broad could be seen crossing to the former lady's carriage. Mrs. Schoonmaker went up first, pausing before she did to spread her fingers across her black, accordion-pleated skirt and pull it back from her feet. She had not replaced her gloves after lunch, and so the ceremonial diamonds she wore on her left ring finger glinted in the winter sun. The prospect of seeing Penelope and Henry together made Diana's heart a little sore, but her mind could not keep quiet about all the things he had not gotten to say. She longed to hear the rest of his explanation, and about all the times he had thought about her in the months since they had been together. She did think, a little wistfully, of all the letters she had burned, wondering what sweet confessions they had contained. But she was glad she'd gotten to tell him how dramatically all his words had perished, and anyway she was distracted by the idea of how he would kiss her if they were alone together now.

Carolina went after Penelope, somewhat too quickly. She had not yet learned how to pause and preen like a lady of leisure, although her jaunty, shiny black top hat certainly looked like it might have cost her half a Holland family lady's maid's yearly wages. Diana had taken no small part in the creation of Carolina Broad—she had in fact sold the item that had introduced her to society, although somehow the spelling of her surname had changed in the printing—and though she wasn't sorry that she had done it, she couldn't help but feel a little proprietary regret that her onetime friend had taken up with Penelope. It had been undoubtedly good for her social standing, but it made her rather less likable, especially now that it was dawning on Diana how Penelope might have come by the information that had sealed her marriage to Henry.

Standing in the window, Diana could not help but think how all of Carolina's stature and finery could be traced back to that one little item in the paper. At the time, her only true motivation had been money. But now she knew how satisfying writing could be, how you could create a whole person and event with a small insinuation. Why, she wouldn't be surprised if her item on Eleanor Wetmore transformed that sorry girl's desires into reality, or if she couldn't turn Henry around with a few well-formed sentences. Already she was imagining how happy Barnard was going to be about the trip, and all the stories that she could wire him.

"Yes," Mrs. Holland, warming herself in a chair by the fire, agreed. "I was worried about you at the beginning, Elizabeth, but by the end you seemed like your old self."

Diana's gaze traveled to her sister, who was standing nearer the high windows that faced down on the walk. Her hair, which had returned to its ash blond shade since December—it had still been sun-streaked from her time in California then—was drawn into a low bun, and she was turned so that Diana could see the side of her face at a quarter angle. The halo around her head was lit up and pale, but the dark shadows under her cheekbones were pronounced. She looked tired, and Diana wondered guiltily if she hadn't pushed her too hard.

Envy

"I do worry about the proposed travel plans for Miss Elizabeth, however," Snowden continued. Outside, Penelope's driver urged the horses forward. Elizabeth did not respond immediately, and instead watched as they pulled away from the curb. Diana moved toward her sister and put her arm around her waist, as though that might shore her up to lobby further for their southern journey.

"It's all right, Mr. Cairns." Elizabeth turned her back toward the window and allowed herself to be hugged by her younger sister, who grew ever more aware of her fragility now that they were in each other's arms. "I think it would be good for me to be out in the world a little."

"You don't have to go," Diana forced herself to say, though she knew that the way she was looking at her sister made a quite opposite statement. How she wished she had Elizabeth to herself for a little, so they could discuss what Henry's real intentions were, and also how high and mighty Penelope had acted at lunch, and what a tremendous insult it was that she'd come at all, and did anyone really think she was beautiful with those oversize features anyway?

"But it wouldn't be so very difficult if you came with me." Elizabeth spoke in a soft but determined voice as she pushed one of Diana's stray glossy curls behind her ear. "And we will be with our old friend Henry Schoonmaker, whom we have barely had time to see since his marriage, and perhaps put to rest any lingering discomforts he may have over our former connection. If you go with me," she went on, giving Diana a purposeful look, "then it will be all right."

Diana pressed closer, trying to somehow or other impart a bit of her own strength to her older sister. The fluttering of her heart, and the yearning to see Henry's face up close again, came involuntarily at the sound of his name. She hoped her mother did not notice. Already she was imagining the sight of him on a railway platform, and how his expression would change subtly when he recognized her among the crowd. In this fantasy she was able to read all his feelings for her in a few minutes, and afterward the horrible wondering that kept her up at night and ruined her sleep would cease.

Even when a girl is married, she still never completely leaves her mother and father's home.

—*LADIES' STYLE MONTHLY*, FEBRUARY 1900

PENELOPE SCHOONMAKER HAD NOT YET TAKEN off her burgundy wool coat with the black piping and high, proud collar, and already she was slouched on one of the striped settees in her bedroom in the Hayes mansion at 670 Fifth Avenue. Penelope had hurried straight upstairs because she couldn't stand the idea of seeing her parents, who were so stupid and useless, and who had caused her so much pain by not giving her a more tasteful and established family to begin with. Sometimes she felt like a changeling of the most elegant variety.

Her former bedroom, very much like her current one, was a study in white and gold, except that it was larger and had been built with the idea of housing many, many gowns. She shot bitter looks at the pile of monogram canvas–covered Louis Vuitton trunks, with their little Japonisme initials, which she had bought in the shop on Rue Scribe in Paris long before she was married. They were her official excuse for having returned home that day. The real reason was that Henry's indifference—reluctance, if she were to be honest, which was not among her native characteristics—to her plan of accompanying him to Florida was growing more obvious, and she feared the Schoonmaker servants would begin to talk.

"I don't even want to go anymore," she said to Isaac Phillips Buck, her closest confidante, who had arrived several hours earlier to oversee the packing of the warm-weather clothing that had not yet been moved into her new wardrobe at the Schoonmaker residence. He glanced at her from the bed, where he had been folding laces, his large girth perched against its chenille edge.

"Oh, but you must, for my sake, to tell me what everyone is wearing," said Mrs. William Schoonmaker, her mother-in-law, who had accompanied her that morning. Her tone was dry and her pretty features were framed in white fur. She had lit a cigarette somewhere between the door and the window, and she exhaled before qualifying her statement: "William is such an ass for not letting me go. I don't know how he deludes himself that I actually like attending those silly political functions with him."

Isabelle, who had proved such an ally to Penelope in her campaign to marry Henry, had been moody lately, and not a bit of fun. Penelope ignored the older lady's words, pushing herself up and walking over to the bed with its heaps of decorative pillows and neat piles of accessories. She picked up a vermilion sash and turned away from Buck as she examined it, letting her fingers glide slowly along its length.

"Don't go," Buck said.

"I do have to, of course."

She didn't mask her impatience, for Buck knew that to back out of the trip would be to shatter all appearances. He usually introduced himself by stressing his surname, as though to suggest that he was one of the old Buck clan who lived in country gentility somewhere up the Hudson, but in fact his prestige derived almost entirely from his exquisite taste and from the firmly held belief among a certain kind of New York lady that he was absolutely necessary to have on one's payroll when there was a party to be thrown. This was the reason he had first become known to the Hayeses, and especially to their youngest member, and it meant that he was well aware how very new their reputation was, and how assiduously it was to be maintained.

"The papers all reported how you attended the luncheon with Elizabeth Holland, and that your friendship is as strong as ever." Buck shrugged, as though that was all that might be concerning her.

"It's not Elizabeth I'm worried about." She sat down on the bed, and drew the smooth fabric over her face thoughtfully. "Elizabeth I can handle. But how will it look if my husband goes on a trip without me, after only two months? What will everybody say? I couldn't let him go alone, *you* know that."

"No." Over by the window, Isabelle had lit another cigarette. "You couldn't in a thousand years do that."

"Well, at least you're going to escape this dismal, gray city." Buck's small eyes, which were enveloped in well-moisturized flesh, rolled to the elaborately frescoed ceiling as his tone sank dramatically.

"True." Penelope felt hot all of a sudden, and she jerked the buttons of her coat open one at a time. "It won't be so bad, and I think a little sunshine might bring Henry around, but now of course I've gotten myself outnumbered. I mean, Miss Broad is on my side, I suppose, but she's not as grand as she looks, and if anybody knows *that*, it's Elizabeth. The two Hollands together will surely be always looking for some way to step on my skirt. And Teddy will be there, and everybody knows that he was always infatuated with Liz. . . ."

She removed her coat completely now and, leaving it on the bed, stepped across the thick carpet. Her day dress of mild cerise trailed along behind, and Robber, her Boston terrier, fell from the ottoman where he had been resting and scooted under an armchair when he heard her coming. Penelope was not a girl who cried easily, but she felt capable of tears of rage, thinking of Elizabeth and Diana and their soft little faces giving her accusing glances all the way to Florida.

At the window, she took one of the cigarettes from the gold case that Isabelle had placed on the sill and allowed her mother-in-law to fuss with her bangs briefly as she cooed sympathetically.

"You know what you need." They both turned to see Buck cross and uncross his legs contemplatively.

Penelope lit the cigarette and exhaled. Then she turned back to the view down Fifth Avenue, with its stately parade of carriages, and waited for the rest of Buck's advice. Those people below were looking at the colossus that the Hayeses had constructed with their shiny new money, envying them and hating them all at the same time. It was a stage that her father had built for his wife and daughter, and though Penelope knew all the right lines and wore all the right costumes, still she was never the star. At least that was how it felt to her just then, as she clutched the gold drapery and despised everyone who was not in thrall to her performance and clapping and crying out brava.

"You need an ally."

"An ally?" Penelope knew instantly that he was right, but she wasn't ready to be reassured yet.

"So that you're not so outnumbered."

"I can't possibly invite *more* people." Penelope looked at Isabelle as though for confirmation of this statement—after all, it was her husband who would get the bill for this trip.

Isabelle shrugged. "Of course you can. It's a party." She made a little gesture with her right hand, leaving a cloud of smoke suspended in the air.

"People broaden the guest list all the time," Buck went on. "Anyway, you'll need someone to help you, especially so that *you* don't ever have to worry about appearing to scheme. Miss Broad has all the right clothes, but she hasn't learned to be clever yet."

"That's true." Penelope glanced at the deflated blonde at her side. "I wish you could come, Isabelle. It's so unfair that mean old Schoonmaker says you must stay here."

Isabelle smiled at her sadly. "Thank you for saying so," she replied in a tone that suggested that the younger girl couldn't begin to understand her suffering.

Penelope might have asked herself if Buck didn't want to come along, and whether or not he might have been her choicest ally, when she looked down below and saw her older brother hopping off the driver's seat of a four-in-hand. The horses were gleaming with sweat as though they had just been ridden hard, and Grayson handed over the reins to a servant and began to trot up the Hayeses' grand limestone steps with the clipped assurance of a born aristocrat. Although she liked to think of herself as the brighter, more cunning sibling, she had always known that he was like her—they had the same natural excess of ambition and total deficiency of sentimentality—in a way that could only be explained by shared blood. She had always been a little proud of that fact, and as she watched him disappear into the house below, an idea began to form in her mind.

Then she heard her mother-in-law exhale a romantic little sigh, and looked sidelong at the older lady. Isabelle Schoonmaker's face had taken on a far-off, dreamy quality. It was embarrassing ever to be so obviously weak with infatuation, Penelope believed, especially when one was a Mrs. She would have searched out a way to subtly point this out, but she was distracted by the thought that it was rather impressive of Grayson to have felled such a sophisticated and desirable married lady. It was in fact a very useful skill, and might prove quite fatal when turned on a more naïve girl.

When she spoke to Buck next, Penelope's tone had brightened considerably. "I'll invite Grayson along. He's my brother, so he *has* to love me."

"No, don't take him," Isabelle gasped. Then her gaze darted to Buck and she lost the imploring tone. "It's only that there are so many more ladies than men to dance with at all the balls this season, and it would be a shame to rob us of a gentleman so light on his feet."

"Oh, you'll get along without Grayson." Penelope took a final inhalation of her cigarette and dropped the end of it in a potted plant. As she crossed the room again, to select her wardrobe with renewed focus and vigor, she left a trail of exhaled smoke behind. "And anyway, I already know just how I'll use him."

Departing today for Palm Beach by special railcar are Mr. and Mrs. Henry Schoonmaker and
their guests, Mr. Edward Cutting, Miss Carolina Broad, and the Misses Holland, Elizabeth
and Diana. The latest addition to the party is
Mrs. Schoonmaker's brother, Mr. Grayson
Hayes.

—FROM THE SOCIETY PAGE OF THE *NEW-YORK NEWS OF
THE WORLD GAZETTE*, TUESDAY, FEBRUARY 13, 1900

TUESDAY DAWNED GRAY AND MISERABLE, AND MR. Longhorn coughed all the way to the ferry station where Carolina had been told to meet the rest of the Florida party. They would cross the Hudson, she had been told, and then, in Jersey City, board the deluxe railcar that Henry Schoonmaker's family maintained. As a maid she had overheard plans of this kind being formed, although actual travel had remained stubbornly out of her grasp. It was always her well-behaved and ever-suffering sister who had been taken along to resorts and leisure places, while she remained behind to repair old camisoles and shams at No. 17.

Thoughts of what it would be like to flee the city for an exotic locale, and to be described doing so in the papers, had kept her up most of the night, and by now the anticipation had grown almost unbearable. At times she very nearly shook with excitement. And so it was only when they turned and started their southward journey that she began to detect something imploring in the old man's wheeze.

"My Carolina," he said, once they had finally come to a halt at the designated pier. The color in his face, which had previously been a constant and jovial red, was all washed out now, and he seemed to be catching his breath at every word. "I wonder if you won't consider remaining with me in New York. You know I don't like to keep you from your youthful fun, but I woke up this morning with a terrible feeling in my lungs. I would like your company very much—I find myself wanting it more than usual. . . ."

For Carolina, it was as though a decadent chocolate cake had been placed in front of her and then whisked away before she had taken even one bite. She felt such agitation at the prospect that she might not be able to go to Florida, that another party might flare up and be extinguished without her so much as knowing of its brightness. The very idea rattled her thoughts and caused a distinctly sour taste to grow in the back of her throat.

"But my luggage is all packed . . ." she returned weakly. She could smell the ocean now and hear the trampling of feet on the docks.

A poor excuse for a smile crossed her face, but she could not sustain it after looking another moment into Longhorn's eyes. They were milky and lacking the usual sharp appraisal. For a moment all her nervous desires to be on the train already, to be one of the bright, lovely things leaving the city behind, quieted. She couldn't remember ever being asked to stay any-where with such ardency. Though there had never been even a hint of romance between her and her benefactor, she felt for a moment the warm glow of being needed spread across her chest.

"Your maid will fetch them back."

The words hung in the air as she recalled all the new dresses that her dressmaker, Madame Bristede, had been paid extra to rush so that they would be ready for that morn-ing. Carolina had imagined wearing them to the dances and dinners in Florida, and perhaps on the train, which she had heard was quite elaborately equipped. Her maid, a girl slightly younger and far more competent than she had been in that capacity, had arrived early with the several new trunks in which those dresses were packed, just to see that they were loaded to the ferry with care. She was wearing a black coat and hat—Carolina caught a glimpse of her through the bustle, standing quite formally on the wooden planks. Carolina longed to be already there, amidst all the workers and the travelers, in her far better coat, which was trimmed in blond mink. She would tell the girl—Cathy was her name—that she should hurry up and board with all the other servants, and then they would be off.

"That's true," Carolina acquiesced at last. She put her bee-stung lips together and her dark eyebrows rose delicately at the awful prospect.

"We'll have another evening tonight, and you may invite whomever you like," Longhorn continued. The effort of speech was apparently too much for him, however, because he subsided into a fit of coughing and had to bend away from her to disguise its intensity. Carolina had to admit that she'd enjoyed the little evening he had thrown to wish her a bon voyage the night before. She and Lucy Carr, the divorcée, had played cards and talked of clothes and screamed with laughter over something or other, she couldn't remember what anymore. It had been entertaining, but she didn't want to do it again. She wanted to go someplace new, and she wanted all the readers of all the gossip columns in the city to know what very good company she kept.

"Is he all right?"

Carolina blinked and tried to put away her self-pity. She glanced from Longhorn, who was doubled over and hacking uncontrollably, to Robert, who stood just outside the carriage window, his dark beard and eyes full of concerned skepticism. She was about to tell Robert that no, she didn't think so, they should probably turn around now and go back to the hotel, and could he summon Cathy and give her the new instructions? But then Carolina's gaze drifted, by chance, over Robert's shoulder to the place on the wide pier where Leland Bouchard stood. The yellow tones in his overgrown wheat-colored hair stood out against the horrible gray backdrop—the day was so overcast you could scarcely see the other vessels in the Hudson River—and he was wearing a scarf with black and white stripes that was tucked into his fitted, knee-length coat. He helped his valet bring a single trunk onto the high wooden platform, and when he stood up again, he paused with all the grand self-possession of a Roman statue. Then he turned in her direction.

"Miss Broad!"

She blushed when she realized she had been staring. Her blush deepened when she realized that he remembered her name, and then she could not help herself from leaning forward against the coach's window and reaching past Robert to wave eagerly at him.

"Hello!"

"You're not with the Schoonmaker party too, are you?" he called out.

"Yes," she said. The cold air outside was bracing, and in that moment she saw clearly what it was she had to do. "Oh, yes!"

"I am, as well—Grayson Hayes invited me. I will see you on the ferry, then!" He removed his hat and made a gallant swooshing bow motion, before disappearing back into the crowd. Carolina watched the bodies that swarmed the place where he'd been, obscuring her view of him in moments, and then she turned back to her companion.

The coughing had subsided, and he brought himself back up and gave her a smile with just a trace of apology in it. He opened his mouth to speak—but Carolina didn't want to hear any of the reasons he wished her to remain with him in New York.

"But I have never been off this little island," she gushed hopefully. "I'll be back before you know it. Perhaps you will already be feeling better by then?"

Longhorn's smile faltered. "You're right, my dear, you should not miss any of the fun on my account. Go, but don't forget me when you do, and come back soon."

Carolina was so pleased to have his blessing that she threw herself forward and embraced him. "Thank you. I will. Oh, I will, I will, I will!"

"Bon voyage, my dear."

He clasped her hand for perhaps one moment too long, and then she pulled away and allowed Robert to help her to the street. She tried to tell Longhorn's valet how important it was to get the old gentleman home and out of the cold quickly—she thought she did. But she was hardly paying attention anymore. Already she was moving forward, her skirts drawn back from the filthy street, as she joined the crowd of travelers streaming to the ferry. All she could think of was the fact that Leland was out there, among them. The very idea made her heart race.

Twelve

How I wish I were a fly on the imported French wallpaper of the Schoonmakers' private railcar, the ARIES, for this week it carries not only the young scion of that family but also his current wife and former fiancée, Elizabeth Holland, and her younger sister—the tensions in such a party could not fail to amuse.

—FROM *CITÉ CHATTER*, TUESDAY, FEBRUARY 13, 1900

*H*ENRY KNEW THAT HE WAS NOT HIS BEST PICTURE of himself, and suspected he might still be drunk from the night before, although these were not his only reasons for avoiding human contact during his party's departure from New York. He wasn't sure how his Florida escape plan had been turned into a group event, overseen by the nefariously flashing red smile of his wife, but he knew that he must continue to play along, that he must not shame Penelope too publicly, or there would be terrible consequences. His original motivation for marrying her, to protect Diana from Penelope's scheming, was as important as ever, although over the months, his reasoning had grown hazy in his mind. He'd often found himself blinking furiously in the mirror to make sure this was still him, that this was still his life, even after all the bizarre twists.

He was not a habitual reader of the society columns, but ever since he had become enamored of Diana Holland he had found himself scouring them compulsively for any little mention of her. That was how he could be sure she was there, on the boat, wrapped up against the cold. Overhead, clouds amassed and loomed as the boat made steady progress across the water to New Jersey, where they could board the train. It made the trip much more palatable to know she was nearby, but he was nervous for her, too, and he feared what would happen if Penelope noticed him staring at Diana in the way he knew he could not help.

Upon arriving in New Jersey and boarding the *Aries*, Henry chose a path that was well known to him. Even before the train departed he went to the common bar car, several cars removed from his own, and sent a messenger boy to fetch Teddy. Since he was fairly certain that sobriety was upon him now—the chill from the river passage was still under his skin—he undid his cuffs and removed his jacket and ordered a bourbon. The cheap tasseled curtains were drawn, and a player piano kept a syncopated rhythm in the background. The car was full of soldiers, smoking and shuffling cards, and none of them so much as looked up when the train whistled to announce its exit from Pennsylvania Station and lurched into movement. They would not reach their destination for another day and a half at least.

"You don't waste any time do you?" said Teddy as he emerged through the fogged glass door and pulled up one of the rickety wooden stools. He watched his old friend, who was two years his junior, with steady gray eyes.

Henry did not get up from his drink, but did try to sound like a host. "How did everyone get settled in?"

"Well, I think." Teddy motioned to the bartender.

"I'm sorry our trip was commandeered this way."

"Oh, that's all right. I rather like having ladies along. It was a rough ferry ride, wasn't it? But everybody made it to the station, and they're all settled in their seats now—your wife's brother, Bouchard, Miss Broad, and the Misses Holland. Your wife was at great pains to welcome the Hollands, and Elizabeth seemed to be doing her best to return the enthusiasm."

Both men sipped from their drinks and let the strange sound of the word *wife* float away unexamined. Teddy always seemed vaguely perplexed by what Henry had done, and Henry, not wanting to make himself more of a cad, could not bring himself to divulge the transaction that had resulted in his marriage. They sat in comfortable silence, drinking slowly and trying their best to seem like the other men in the car, which they most certainly were not.

"Schoonmaker, Cutting!"

Teddy looked up first, and Henry's gaze followed after a moment's delay. Coming through the door, cigarette already lit, was the figure of Penelope's brother. Since his wedding, Henry had found himself always unnerved by the sight of Grayson Hayes, even though he had seen him in gambling halls and late-night haunts for years and thought nothing of the familial connection. But now Henry saw that Grayson had his sister's face—the proud nose like a downward-facing arrow, the extreme blue of the eyes, and the pale oval face set off by slick, dark hair. These features gave him the appearance—probably falsely, Henry believed, although it was still impossible to ignore—of being his younger sister's emissary.

"Nice style your family travels in," Grayson went on with an appreciative smirk.

"Thank you," Henry answered.

There was one striking difference between the Hayes siblings' looks, which was that Grayson's eyes were set too close together. It made him seem a little stupid, which he almost certainly was about to be. It was well known amongst the young men of genteel New York that young Hayes was an inveterate, and not a very good, gambler. If Henry had placed a bet on what Grayson would say next, he would have done quite well indeed.

"Are you ready for a game of poker?" Grayson dropped his cigarette to the floor and stubbed it out with his toe. There was a manic light in his eye, and his shoulders were strung with energy. On another day Henry might have hesitated, or

Teddy might have thought better of it, but at that particular moment young Schoonmaker had had enough of the rotten feeling that apparently came with doing the right thing.

"We're in," he said.

"We need two more for a proper game." Grayson motioned, almost as though he were summoning the help, at two soldiers who were idly sipping bottled beers at an adjacent table. They watched for a moment as the man in a wing collar and ascot tie pulled back the chairs from the simple wooden table and sat down. He was all business and his attention was already fiercely on the cards. Then they approached, pulling back their chairs, taking their places. "Welcome, gentlemen," he said as he split the deck and began to deal.

Henry sat, noticing as he did the simple dignity of the men's uniforms. They both wore fitted blue linen drill jackets with a parade of brass buttons down the front, worn but clean trousers, and knee-high gaiters over their well-traveled boots. The man with the frothy handlebar moustache put his campaign hat on the back of his chair and the clean-shaven one mimicked the gesture. It was impossible for Henry to tell how old they were—the clean-shaven one might have been younger than he was, and yet they were both so much more aged.

"Where are you boys headed?" he asked as he peeked at his hand.

"Tampa," said the mustachioed one, as though the place held significance that people of leisure could not possibly understand.

"With the Fifth Infantry, sir, going down to keep the Cubans in line." His companion grinned, looking up from his cards.

"Cuba!" Henry placed a bet. "Doesn't your friend Bouchard have sugar interests down there?"

"Yes," Grayson answered without looking up from the table. "Although he doesn't gamble," he added, as though that disqualified him as a topic of conversation.

"Doing our best to keep the island safe for American interests, sir."

Teddy made a small, appreciative saluting motion.

"Ever kill anybody?" Grayson asked abruptly. Every thought in the man's head was about cards, Henry knew, but still he winced at his brother-in-law's boorish comment. He began to feel uncomfortable, and realized he didn't actually want to hear the answer.

"Perkins saw action during the war against the Spaniards," the clean-shaven one replied, gesturing, genially enough, to his more hirsute friend. "And was wounded in the charge on San Juan Hill."

Henry and Teddy both looked to Perkins, and though his pale eyes betrayed a reticence, he obliged them by saying, "I enlisted after the massacre of the *Maine*. No American could have known of such treachery and failed to act."

Henry could think of three examples at that very table that disproved this notion, but he nodded as though it were gospel truth.

"My brother was on that ship." The clean-shaven one shook his head and considered the card he had just been dealt. "He died in a filthy Havana hospital, and when they shipped his body back my mother couldn't even see him because all his skin had been burned off."

There was a long, grave pause, but then Perkins's face relaxed a little. "Well," he concluded, "that's what makes us all drag ourselves up for reveille when it's still dark. That's what makes being away from home bearable."

The tones in which men speak of life and death were heavy in the air around them. More cards were dealt and more money tossed into the center of the table. Teddy, who was already out of the game, was watching the soldiers intensely, but Henry could hardly look up from his hand. He was aware, in a vaguely embarrassed way, not only of his waistcoat but also the fine linen of his shirt, soft against his well-protected skin, and the elegant cut of his trousers and of the series of railcars ahead of them with their elaborate trappings, some of which he owned, or his family did, anyway. And when he thought of his railcar, it was impossible not to dwell on who sat within it. His head was still full of Diana, and the way her nose turned pink and eyes grew shiny in the cold.

Henry folded, followed shortly by the beardless man. Then the final two players turned over their hands. When Grayson saw that he had lost, he shoved the money at the center of the table toward Perkins in frustration.

"Again!" he cried, almost fiendishly, and began to collect the cards to deal another hand. Henry and Teddy acquiesced, though with less enthusiasm this time. One of them had become quiet and serious, and the other was too absorbed by the idea of a certain young lady's presence somewhere down along the train as it moved ever southward, ever closer to the sun, to care very much how he spent his hours.

Thirteen

G—

I have a special task for you, one

you will enjoy. Come to my seat

as soon as possible, won't you?

—P

*P*ENELOPE RECLINED AGAINST THE EMERALD GREEN seat in her little section of the Schoonmaker railcar, her heavy ivory skirt fishtailing to the polished wood paneling of the floor. They had traveled many miles already and had arrived at that slow hour before dinner. Her guests were enjoying aperitifs in their seats; she could observe them, down the aisle, only partially obscured by the sliding doors that separated each section. Her arms, which were covered to the wrist in billowing rose-colored chiffon, were crossed over her chest, and she kept a dark brow arched as she gazed down the aisle. Miss Broad was in the next section and situated across the aisle, still sporting the camel-colored traveling suit that she had worn when they boarded in the late morning.

She was looking about her, at the hooped and fringed surroundings, at the ferns and cut flowers, as though she had never seen such finery before. It was quite possible she had not. Every time a man walked down the aisle she glanced up expectantly as though it might be Leland Bouchard; her heavy lids drooped down over her sage green irises each time she realized it was not. She had a crush on him—this was perfectly clear to Penelope from the way she always asked if he would be present at events they attended—but she didn't have to be so pathetic about it.

Beyond Miss Broad and on the same side of the aisle were the Misses Holland. They sat together on the seat, the russet tones in Diana's hair brought out by the green velvet upholstery. The older sister's eyes had closed, and she rested her head on the younger's shoulder, which looked to Penelope like an over-the-top and probably insincere display of affection. The brunette sister, meanwhile, read a book. She was lovely—Penelope knew it, even while the knowledge burned her. The girl's curls shone, her eyes were bright, and her features were gorgeously composed. Although Penelope had used the news of her defilement in order to secure her own marriage, her husband's former paramour maintained an aura of purity that Penelope would have liked to slap off her tart face.

Meanwhile, Penelope's impatience grew. She had sent the messenger half an hour ago, and still nothing. She tilted her head back against the full cushions and looked at the beveled mirror above. The lips she saw in the reflection on the ceiling were generous and scarlet, the hair dark in contrast with her incandescent skin. Her hair was done up elaborately, with curls and braids and the little bangs dividing her unblemished forehead. She would not have thought that Henry's affections would have lasted this long, or that Diana would be quite such competition for her. But Penelope had to grudgingly acknowledge how much space the younger Holland still occupied in Henry's heart, for whenever he was remotely near her his whole bearing changed.

It was not that Penelope felt weakened, or even particularly unhappy. She was at that very moment utterly comfortable—it was her policy to always be comfortable unless beauty demanded otherwise—and she was enjoying hosting a bevy of guests in the grand cars that everyone knew were owned by her family-in-law. Henry's indifference was irritating, but it could not detract from the pride she felt at being so publicly known to be his consort, or to be seen as the equal owner of his many treasures. And though she did feel Isabelle's absence a little—that lady always knew how to enjoy fine things—she was exceedingly pleased to be the only Mrs. Schoonmaker onboard.

"And what does my favorite sister want?"

Penelope twisted around to see, at last, the figure of her brother approaching from the rear of the train. He moved quickly to kiss her cheek, and then fell into the velvet-covered seat opposite her. There was a sheen of sweat on his forehead, and his cuffs had come undone. She considered but decided against pointing out that she was his only sister, and that there were no others to play favorites with.

"I have an assignment for you," she answered eventually.

"An assignment?" Grayson's mouth went crooked at the corner and he watched his younger sibling attentively with his matching blue eyes.

"Yes." Penelope paused, and let her gaze wander back down to where Diana was. The girl looked up from her book and let her rich brown eyes stare back at Penelope for a long moment. She and her sister had both dressed for dinner, although Diana's pale blue dress with the deep and lacy décolletage and the puffed sleeves was clearly not a new one. "I don't think you'll object, after you've heard it."

"You're little schemes are always amusing, Penny."

The younger Hayes sibling felt another stab of irritation at the sound of her childhood nickname, especially after she had done him the compliment of waiting for him. "Please don't call me that."

He grinned, and the chandelier light that beamed down from the car's ceiling reflected on his white teeth. Darkness was falling on the country passing by in their windows, and shadows emerged to dramatize the architecture of their faces, neither of which was built for kindly expressions. "My apologies, Mrs. Schoonmaker."

She returned his smile broadly. "Thank you, brother."

"Anything for you, dear sister."

"I am glad to hear that," she went on, lowering her voice confidentially, "because your assignment will require special delicacy."

"And that is because?"

Penelope tilted her head to the left and let all of her long fingers rest against her slender neck. "I would like you to be a little nice—a little affectionate—with the younger Miss Holland."

Grayson paused and looked down the aisle of the train; Penelope extended herself so that she could see what he saw. Diana didn't raise her eyes this time, but adjusted her position so that the fading light from outside cast pretty shadows on her peach chest.

"A little nice?" Grayson asked as he pressed back into his seat.

Penelope's eyes rolled coyly to the mirror above her head. She straightened her bangs and considered her words. "Yes, but not *too* nice. Get her to like you, but then hold back. You understand, don't you? Keep her busy, but see if you can't toss her heart around a little. She's so young, and she could afford to be played a few times yet." She wrinkled her nose and winked at her brother. She wasn't sure if he was going to ask why, and not wanting to dwell on the rationale, she added:

"Just for fun. We have such a long train ride, and one needs to entertain oneself and one's guests during a seaside stay."

Grayson looked at the Hollands one last time, and then turned back to his sister with a vaguely amused expression. He ran his fingers through his slick, dark hair and then shrugged, as though it were all the same to him. "Well, why not? She's pretty enough."

"I told you you'd like it!" Penelope laughed, although Diana Holland's physical qualities were not the least bit funny to her when, in the next moment, her husband entered the car, looked down the aisle at the girl, and immediately assumed the expression of a man struck by Cupid's arrow. If Grayson—whose gaze wavered momentarily between both Schoonmakers—made any connections, he gave no sign of it. Then Mrs. Schoonmaker stood, extended her rose chiffon–covered arms to her husband's shoulders, and blocked his view. A few seconds passed before Henry's black eyes met hers, but there was scarcely any recognition in them at all.

Fourteen

Travel can be time-consuming, dusty, over-heated, and odious, even for the wealthiest tourist. A lady never shows her discomfort, however, which is why she must approach any steamer or railcar prepared to play make-believe.

—*DRESS MAGAZINE*, FEBRUARY 1900

THE TRAIN SHOOK A LITTLE AS IT RUMBLED toward its destination, but Diana moved down its length with determination, heading north while the iron beast went south, pulling the pale blue skirt clear of her long strides as she did. Her chin jutted forward and her left arm swayed. Her hair, which her sister had so neatly arranged for dinner, was now loosening about the ears; in a less distractable mood she might have acknowledged that that moment when her curls took on a life of their own was also often the peak of her loveliness. But just now her emotions had overruled rational thought and she was so overcome by something—though she hardly knew what it was—that she had found she was occasionally mouthing words to herself and had to rein herself in before she began babbling like a fool.

She was on her way to nowhere in particular, although she was in too featherbrained and selfish a mood to be with her sister any longer. Dinner had exhausted Elizabeth, who was now sleeping in their berth. Most of the other travelers were asleep too—the lights were low in the corridors, which were filled with a stern hush. Back in the *Aries*, Penelope and Carolina were playing cards; the men had retreated to their own single-sex, post-dinner world.

She might have gone to bed too, she knew, but her mind was all lit up. Travel always excited her—the strong and unfamiliar smells, the movement, the anxiety of arrival and departure times, the shouting of conductors, the idea of her tired old self changed by ever new surroundings. The train fascinated her too—it was made up of all the rooms and apparatuses of everyday human existence, except rendered slightly smaller, as though it were some kind of display case for mannequins, and then strung together on a very long necklace.

More than anything, though, her thoughts marched relentlessly back to Henry, and how she had been near him again after so many months. He had worn a tuxedo to dinner and given her only fleeting looks. But he had said that he still wanted only her, and that was enough kindling for her imagination. Now every time he touched his wife she saw his scorn; each time he so much as turned his dark eyes in Diana's direction she felt the brush of lips against her throat. There was no sleeping after that. She was like a heroine in a novel that she herself was writing; the character kept protesting that she was too strong for love, and yet the narrator went on describing her desire.

So she had taken off, at a pace that might have been better suited to a jaunt in the park, down the aisles of the train. She had no destination and, in any event, resided more in head than body. Parts of the country that she had never seen and ordinarily would have been curious about were passing in the windows, illuminated by moonlight, but she did not pause to look. Time passed and she continued in the same way. The only thing that stilled her restless walking was the sound of her own name, followed very quickly by the feeling of hands on her arm.

She spun and focused her gaze on the man whose path she had crossed. They were in a narrow passageway—her back was against a paneled wall, and Henry Schoonmaker was standing in front of her, the golden quality of his skin obvious even in the dim light. His eyes were a little puffy, she couldn't help but notice, and they were on her, boring into her, the way a man just coming out of the desert might stare at a glass of water.

"Di, I'm sorry," he whispered wearily.

She glanced up and down the corridor to make sure no one was watching them. He had caught her at a windowless juncture, and there was only the light of a few sconces. "Whatever for?" she replied, her voice straining in an attempt to sound careless and witty.

She inhaled the familiar smell of him, of cigarettes and

musk and all those other undefinable masculine things, and she wondered if he wasn't maybe a little drunk. She wondered how he could drink—she herself felt entirely too light-headed already, just from being in his general vicinity. Then he looked away, just long enough to catch his breath and let his eyes dart right and left before settling on her again.

"Your being here is such a risk. If Penelope told anyone what we have been to each other it would never be the same for you. I fear I've been very selfish. . . ." Diana was distracted by Henry's broad, aristocratic face, with his long, narrow eyes and fine nose and the lips, which she wanted, even now and against all her better judgment, to press her own against; she had lost track of what he was saying. "If that is the case, I am so sorry."

"I'm not," she said.

"Oh, Di," he replied hoarsely.

She was acutely aware of the speed with which the floor she stood on was passing over the earth, rendering landscapes and idle observers blurry, if only she could see them. She herself felt blurry and rushed. One part of her wanted to listen to Henry for hours, but another part—the one that was all tingly—knew that someone might come down the aisle at any moment and see a married man in a dark corner with a vulnerable girl. Then she would never find out how this story ended.

The train rattled on its tracks, the movement of the car unsteadying Henry, so that suddenly he was much closer to Diana. He was still looking at her with those ardent eyes, and for a brief moment she was sure that the same idea was in both their minds.

Diana's lips parted. He was close enough to her now that she could feel his pulse, which was quick. Her breath had grown short, and she knew his had too, because she could feel it against her face. He hesitated for another second, and then a door opened at the end of the car. All the loud, outside noises broke the moment. Diana turned her head toward her shoulder and Henry lowered his chin. They would have to move fast. He let his hand run down her arm and across her fingers, and then he turned and walked toward that opened door, his shoulders squared with the old, inveterate entitlement. A moment later, she heard him intercept the porter.

Diana turned left and hurried in the opposite direction. There was plenty more train to walk, and already she knew that she wouldn't sleep at all that night.

Fifteen

A woman coming out of mourning, especially if it is her husband who has passed, must be ever vigilant of her nerves. I have known not a few ladies who, when they went back into society, with its excess of voices and tendency to overstimulate, saw stars, became dizzy, and had to be taken hastily to bed.

—*VAN KAMP'S GUIDE TO HOUSEKEEPING FOR LADIES OF HIGH SOCIETY,* 1899 EDITION

"OH, LIZ, IT'S SO GOOD TO HAVE YOU ALL TO MYSELF away from the city." Penelope approached at a rapid gait and reached for her old friend's hand. Over her hostess's shoulder, Elizabeth could see the bobbing heads of the other guests, and perhaps she made a doubtful face, because Penelope went on quickly: "Or all to *our*selves, rather, which is the next best."

Elizabeth managed not to appear disgusted by these false sallies and opened the small roundness of her mouth into a generous smile. Yesterday, after the train had finally departed and after so many hellos, and also after being corseted by the train's on-call lady's maid and rouging her once-famous alabaster complexion so that it did not appear quite so deathly, she had felt a little tired. This was to be expected, and anyway, she didn't mind so much, because every time she grew weary, she knew she might find her eyes drifting shut, and then she might be with Will for a time. But this morning she was feeling better than she'd expected, not in the least because of the contented little sighs that Diana had let out in her sleep. She was glad that she had helped her little sister come on this trip, and that knowledge made her feel not so weak.

"What a lovely and gracious hostess you are, Penny," Elizabeth replied as she drew her onetime friend closer to her. She had known Penelope for some time, and was quite aware how little she cared for that diminutive.

They made a pretty picture, which had probably been one of the former Miss Hayes's motivations in befriending her in the first place. Their long necks were both emphasized by high collars—intricate, shimmering lace for Penelope, fine blue cotton for Elizabeth—and their narrow waists were showcased by fitted tailoring. The girls' opposite coloring set each other off. Elizabeth had taken a little extra care with her hair that morning, and it rose in a hazy blond cloud over her forehead. She looked back once and saw her sister give a little exhale of disapproval, and then she focused the full force of her social capabilities—what was left of them—on the dining car's private room, where breakfast was being laid out on silver trays.

"You've lost so much weight since the fall, we'll have to get some food into you quickly," Penelope went on as they swept into the room. Elizabeth noted the subtle sadism of that last bit, but chose to ignore it as they joined the rest of the party, who were gathered in a loose group just beyond the door.

A long table was placed below a gothic ceiling of carved

and engraved walnut with arched windows set high above them to let in the morning light. Penelope passed Elizabeth off to Teddy Cutting, who escorted her to her place at the table. She had been glad when she saw his name in the paper, alongside her own, in the column that reported notable departures from the city, and had felt a kind of relief at his presence in the dining car that morning. Teddy did not play games like the rest of their peers. He pulled her chair back, and she tried not to reveal the dizziness that came upon her as she sat. Penelope's brother, Grayson, who was wearing a coat the color of a dove's wing, took Diana's arm, and Henry took Lina's, and they all moved to the table, the gentlemen pulling back chairs and then seating themselves so that no lady sat beside a member of her own sex.

Elizabeth smiled—faintly, but with the old grace—as Teddy took the napkin resting on her silver plate, shook it open, and laid it across her lap.

"Thank you, Mr. Cutting," she said. "But I'm not an invalid, you know."

Teddy glanced at her, but only for a polite moment of mute, gray-eyed concern. His blond hair wore less pomade than usual, although it did by habit part on the left side of his head and cross to the right. She had not seen him since last September, when he visited her family on Sundays, when people still did such things.

"I know," he replied after a moment. "It's only that you seem so delicate after your . . . trials, and one always wants to protect you." He paused and took a long sip of water. "I find myself always wanting to."

Elizabeth felt her cheeks blushing, as much because of his earnest tone as his familiar words. But Teddy was an old friend and a constant gentleman, and she supposed it was normal for him to have spoken to her with such care, just as she supposed the word *always* had no special connotation. Nobody else seemed to have noticed. He picked up a tray of scones and proffered it to her. The train rattled on through the countryside and Henry, who was sitting at the head of the table on her right, looked absently into his juice as his wife spoke loudly of Newport cottages and favorite architects and other things very few people could afford.

"I find his work utterly self-aggrandizing," came Leland's reply with blazing animation. He expressed everything with his whole body and with total conviction, as Elizabeth remembered him doing when he was more of a boy. It was just one of the characteristics that set him apart from his peers. "Although I appreciate the Islamic influences that he occasionally incorporates. Their architecture is so fascinating to me, all the minarets and mihrabs, all the arches and tiles, all that intricate calligraphy. Did you know that they use the calligraphy in decoration because images are forbidden? Oh, yes . . ."

Elizabeth smiled privately, thinking how frustrated Penelope must be to have engaged herself in a conversation in which she was destined to be the less active participant. Leland, meanwhile, continued unabated, as though delivering a sermon. Beside him sat Lina, wearing a suit of light brown herringbone trimmed in dark brown velvet. Everything she wore looked ill-fitting in the way that brand-new things often do; none of her clothes had yet softened to her body, and they seemed to be occasionally laughing at the less than fluid way she moved in them.

That was uncharitable, Elizabeth admonished herself. For though she had not quite gotten over the discomfort of seeing her former maid socially, losing Will made it difficult to sustain a feeling of hatred for anyone not made of pure evil. And of course what Lina had said at No. 17 was true—she had loved Will too, and so she couldn't be *all* bad. She did look pretty in a way, Elizabeth could see now. With her lichen-colored eyes and her hair done up, she reminded Elizabeth of her childhood nurse, Lina's mother, who was beautiful and kind and always so calm amidst the Hollands' chaos.

Elizabeth broke off a ladylike portion of scone and put it into her mouth, hoping that a bit of solid food would have a steadying effect. She felt Teddy watching her, and tried to smile at him reassuringly. Just then the train went round a bend. She became aware of how fast they were going and had to reach out to steady herself on the table. The curve had destabilized everything else in the dining car too, it seemed. The cups trembled in their saucers, and the serving bowls on their platters. Everyone stopped taking, except Leland, who always moved so restlessly that perhaps he was uncomprehending of the train around him. He gestured wildly and his hand met with a carafe of water, which tipped, trembled, and eventually splashed Lina. Elizabeth's eyes darted to her. For a moment the former maid looked as though she'd dropped a strand of pearls and was watching as they broke apart and rolled away on a hard marble floor.

"Oh!" Penelope cried, snapping her fingers at servants.

"I am *so* sorry," Leland gasped, horrified with himself, as he began to blot Lina's skirt.

"I'll have some more juice," Henry said to no one in particular.

"Oh . . . it's all right." Lina was blushing from all the attention and seemed to have already gotten over any potential devastation about her dress. She was staring at Leland as he furiously tried to soak up the water from her lap. Black and white–uniformed servants descended on them with fresh napkins and a new carafe. Henry received a glass full of juice. Down on the other end of the table, Diana leaned forward and plucked a croissant from a silver tray, several shiny dark curls spilling forward across her chin as she did, then sat back into her chair.

"Miss Diana," Grayson, Penelope's older brother, said. "Can I pass you the butter?"

"No, thank you, this is quite deliciously buttery enough," Diana replied tartly. She was full of some strange energy that morning. Her every movement had purpose and life, and she seemed to find satisfaction in every little thing.

"There's quite a lot of *deliciousness* here, I must say. . . ."

Penelope's brother was positioned at the far end of the table, and though Elizabeth wanted to look at him to make sure he wasn't flirting with her younger sister, a sense of propriety kept her from turning. She disliked his lascivious pronunciation, and it did *sound* like flirting, though perhaps it was just a casual comment, she told herself as she glanced at Henry. But when she glanced over, Henry simply stared into his juice glass. Everyone was acting so . . . strange.

"Miss Elizabeth," Teddy said. His voice was gentle, even as everyone else began to babble. He reached forward and placed his fingers lightly on her wrist. "Are you all right? You don't look well. It was a sharp bend, and I suppose there may be more. . . ."

Teddy's fingertips, resting on her pale skin, communicated such exquisite kindness that for a moment she felt a variety of glowing happiness that she had not experienced in a long time. It lasted only a second and then it was overwhelmed by a terrible turn in her stomach. She realized with dread and self-disgust that she had allowed herself a pleasant sensation—something she surely could never deserve again—and that it had been inspired by another man, a man who had been born lucky and safe and who most certainly was not Will. In an instant she knew that she was going to be sick.

Her head was very cold and her body was very hot. Everyone at the table was caught up in their own loud voices and pressing thoughts. She let her eyelids droop for a moment and prayed that she would make it to the washroom; then she pushed back her chair and rushed from the private dining car.

Sixteen

We have it on good authority that society's latest point of interest, Miss Carolina Broad, is accompanying the Schoonmaker party to Florida, which no doubt impresses all of her new friends. She is reportedly traveling with only a maid and without her usual chaperone, Mr. Carey Lewis Longhorn, which may make some of those new friends chary, although it will certainly make none of us lose interest.

—FROM *CITÉ CHATTER*, WEDNESDAY, FEBRUARY 14, 1900

"Miss Broad, I am so sorry about this morning. I will make it up to you by taking you for a drive in my motorcar when we arrive in Florida. Would you like that? Have you ever been in a motorcar? I assure you, my clumsiness only reveals itself in drawing rooms and at fancily laid dining tables. You can trust me to be your driver. In a motorcar . . ."

Carolina beamed and nodded enthusiastically. It was difficult to catch everything Leland said, because he spoke so fast, and she also sometimes lost track of whether she was supposed to be nodding or shaking her head, since he asked so many questions in passing and she wanted to answer them all in a way that would ensure her spending more time in his company. She felt so giddy and delicate with him and not even very much like herself. She had changed out of the water-soaked dress after breakfast, into a smart suit of navy silk with complicated darts and white ribbon detail, and ever since then he had been showing her around the train. There were little explosions of lace at her wrists and around her throat, and she made demure flourishes with her hands whenever she got a chance to say something because she liked to see how they looked in flight. Leland had already taken her to visit with the train's engineer and hear the brakeman's assessment of the state of the train. (The brakeman was certain they would all reach Palm Beach in one piece.) Now he led Carolina from the observation car onto its deck, which looked back along the tracks that trailed behind them, curving so that they disappeared amongst the bare trees.

The day was cool and crisp, and the afternoon landscape lazily unpopulated under the blue sky. Carolina's dress rippled in the wind as she stepped out behind Leland and felt the air— it was warmer than in New York, but still a little bracing. Like the parlor car behind them, which was outfitted with stuffed sofas and huge maps and velvet drapes, the observation deck was grandly constructed, with a domed and tasseled roof held aloft by gold-plated pillars over a half-circle platform. The railing was made of finely whittled wood with a high shine.

"I love the way the land just falls behind you when you travel on a train. Can you imagine what it must have been like for our great-grandfathers, who hardly knew what a train was and never would have experienced travel with such ease and comfort? What a privilege it is to live now, at just this moment, and to be able to go anywhere. . . ."

Suddenly he paused and looked out at the trees. It was almost a shock to see Leland standing still, and Carolina's breathing became irregular as she gazed at him and saw how truly, unbelievably, preternaturally handsome he was. There was still the rocking of the train, however—he reached out and put a hand on the gold pillar. She blinked, but could not help but continue looking at him. He was so big-boned, and yet so slender, his torso tapering away from his broad shoulders. It made her feel petite to be next to someone of such considerable physical presence. His hair was a little overgrown, and it flapped over his ears. When he turned back she realized she'd been staring again and felt a stab of shame.

"We should be in Florida by tomorrow afternoon," he said, his voice uncharacteristically soft and measured.

Carolina, whose gaze had wandered bashfully to her shoes, now gave herself a little speech. Surely he would not have spent so many hours with her if he did not already find her pretty, she rationalized, and if he had not yet said anything sweet to her, perhaps it was because he didn't want to take advantage, or because he himself was shy in that department, or for a dozen other reasons. For a moment the inevitability of her own seat and the specter of returning to it without sharing a single romantic moment with Leland rose, horribly, in her thoughts. She looked at his wide-set blue eyes and decided it was up to her to show him how she felt.

She passed her parasol into her right hand and took a step toward Leland. She knew that she should be smiling, but the nervousness had already spread through her and she had forgotten how to make even the most basic gestures. All she could think to do at the moment was complete the series of steps that she had imagined for herself: toward Leland, then a little twirl, so that she would land between him and the railing and very close indeed. Then maybe she would remember how to smile. He was watching her intently now, and she moved backward coquettishly, leaning against the rail. She never got to smile, however, because at just that moment the car hit a bump and she lost her footing and her whole weight fell against the wooden bars behind her.

There was a terrible snapping sound. The wind came rushing past her ears, and in an instant she knew she was going to die. The wheels were shrieking on their tracks and the headlines were already reverberating in her mind. SOCIETY NEWCOMER'S GRISLY END SOMEWHERE SOUTH OF MASON-DIXON, they would read, or UNGRATEFUL PARVENU ABANDONS MEAL TICKET, MEETS MAKER ONE DAY LATER. She knew that her body, which had experienced so little in its seventeen years, was going to be crushed and left behind by all the more graceful and lucky people still safely on the train.

Then she opened her eyes and realized her life wasn't over, after all.

Leland had her by one arm, and was holding on to the gold-plated pole by the other. There was a serious steadiness about the way he was looking at her, even though the sky above and land below were falling behind them so frightfully quickly. Her heart beat with such rapidity that she wondered if the thing wasn't going to jump out of her throat, but there was also an eerie calm settling inside her. Leland's face was red from all the blood that had rushed there—she could tell he was engaged in a tremendous effort. Beyond him, the clouds were shot through with gold from the sun. He pulled with all his strength, and then Carolina was righted again. She glanced at the broken rail and had to close her eyes as the full realization of how close she'd been to being torn limb from limb dawned in her consciousness.

"Oh, thank you," she whispered.

"Are you all right?"

She looked at Leland, and saw that he was just as shaken as she was.

"Yes," she said. "Or I will be in a minute or two."

Her fright at what might have been had not yet subsided when she began to see all the bright, shining possibilities of the moment. She was not a deft manipulator of social situations—not yet, anyway—but she knew an opportunity when she saw one. She let her lids flutter shut, let her lips part weakly, and then threw herself forward into his arms.

"Oh, *Leland*, if you hadn't been here . . ." she went on. But she didn't have to say anything more, for already his arms had folded around her, and the full spread of his palms was pressing against her silk-covered back.

Seventeen

The Schoonmaker party is said to arrive at the Royal Poinciana, Palm Beach, Florida, this evening, barring any travel complications. I can assure the most exclusive details of their southern getaway. Many notable people have been wintering at the hotel, including the Frederick Whitneys, the family of Lord Dagmall-Lister, the British ambassador, and the Prince of Bavaria and his retinue. . . .

—FROM THE "GAMESOME GALLANT" COLUMN IN THE *NEW YORK IMPERIAL*, THURSDAY, FEBRUARY 15, 1900

$\mathcal{H}$ ENRY LOVED A GOOD HOTEL, AND WAS KNOWN TO take rooms either for a party or for a few days' rest in several of the New York establishments, even when one of the clubs he and his father belonged to would have done just as well. He found very little pleasure, however, in the Royal Poinciana, a great lemon yellow wood structure with white trimming sitting between Lake Worth and the sea, on the evening of his party's arrival there. He was by then wretchedly sober, and he had been watching the ruthlessness with which Penelope attended to their guests. It was as though she wanted them in a state of controlled awe at all times. Now that he was more clear-eyed, he wondered if there were any limits to her behavior when something she felt was hers was on the line.

"There we are, Mr. Schoonmaker," said the concierge, who had accompanied them personally to their suite. Henry watched the flurry of bellhops and housekeepers before them, still struggling all across the room to place the luggage just so, as he reached into his pockets for tips.

"We are a very large hotel," the concierge went on. "Our hallways cover over four miles, and our grounds are nearly thirty acres. But for you, we want it to feel like home. We want it to feel personal. Please do not hesitate to call on us at any moment, for any little thing. Do not hesitate . . ."

Henry stared off at the fine white net canopy of the gigantic bed—which was made of polished black walnut and stood on a raised and carpeted platform in the far corner of the palatial room—even as the concierge prattled on. The elder Mr. Schoonmaker and Henry Flagler, who owned not only the hotel but most of Palm Beach, had done railroad business together in their youth, and so Henry suspected that the sycophancy would continue apace until the last bellhop had received his reward. He had heard many speeches like this before, in all kinds of hotels, and had often entertained himself by asking impossibly arcane questions about the history of the building or by demanding specific vintages of wines that were impossible to acquire on short notice. None of those antics appealed to him now.

"The bathroom in this suite," the concierge was saying, "is seventeen feet long, and has a sunken bathtub of imported Italian marble. Perhaps Madame would like a bath before dinner? I could have one drawn up—"

"No," Henry interrupted sharply. He paused and let his index finger dart to the inside corner of his eye, where he

scraped after an invisible spec of dust. "No, that is really quite all right."

He could see how abrupt he had been in the faint flitting of the concierge's fair eyelashes. The negative ripple continued across the room, which was now littered with great pieces of patterned luggage, bound in buckles and straps, so that the housekeepers turned their faces to the floor and the young boy with the brass cart moved to exit, until it reached Penelope, who removed her hat and turned to give Henry a cold look. Her dark hair was in a high, rigid form, and the two pieces of her red costume met in an impossibly narrow waist, where she placed her hand.

"My wife loves dirty rumors, you see," Henry heard himself say with stale jollity, "and so she has never been over-fond of bathing."

Penelope turned away, the curve of her back catching a late-afternoon blaze of light, and then spoke in a voice he had never heard before. It intimidated precisely because it was so low and soft. "You may all go now," she said as she handed her hat to her lady's maid without looking at her.

The maid took the hat, which was small and plumed and had been fastened with black velvet, and stepped down from the platform onto the main Spanish-tiled floor. As she walked to the door, she gave Henry what he imagined to be a pleading look. The hotel staff began to shuffle past him toward the door, and as they went he extended his hand to slip them coins. The concierge gave him a crooked smile that confirmed he had been rude to his wife in front of the help, followed by a deferential nod, and then left the room, closing the huge bronze door behind him.

When they were alone he noticed the warm breeze from the French doors that opened onto a terrace, where Penelope stood. Her back straightened and she kept her slender figure facing away from him, but even so he detected in her stance a kind of challenge. There was no doubt that the thoughts in her head were all about how she was going to keep him away from Diana forever, and the idea that anyone would hurt Di made his blood steam.

Henry removed his jacket, and tossed it carelessly onto a satinwood settee. He moved across the floor toward the terrace with a certain restless aggression, undoing his cuffs and then dropping his monogrammed gold cuff links onto the little decorative table by the door. They clattered against its marble top, causing a noise that startled both Schoonmakers.

"Henry?" Penelope had turned to assess the situation, and though she assumed a thoughtful, questioning tone, it carried an undercurrent of decided malice.

"What is it?" They faced each other across the great shining floor, both stiff and wary of each other. All the furniture between them had been polished that day, and it glittered expensively in the fading light. When Henry began to undo the top buttons of the shirt he had worn all morning on the train, his fingers moved with an almost bellicose energy. Penelope's anger was just as clear in the fierce batting of her black lashes.

Eventually she put her hand on her hip, and then she let her whole body relax into what she said next. "You know it's in neither of our interest to make the servants talk."

He exhaled sharply and stepped toward her as though to contradict that notion. But she was right, and he couldn't forget the angelic faith with which Diana had waited to be kissed in the corridor of the train. No matter how much he hated his wife in the moment, he could not be impulsive, for it was not his reputation that was most at risk.

"I'd rather not tell everyone that my husband once deflowered one of the famous Holland girls, but I will if I have to," she went on pointedly. Each word met the air like the whistling thrust of a rapier. "It would be unfortunate if you, in your own stupidity, let this information become known passively, to some maid or other. Don't think I haven't noticed how happy you are to have your former lover along on this trip."

He grimaced, but there was no way for him to return her words. She was frightening when she was like this, and she was also right.

Penelope took another step toward him, and went on, "If I notice, someone else will too, so you had better start playing the good husband before we find ourselves in a situation that makes everyone want to cry."

He nodded, and turned to the view. Diana was somewhere out there, amongst the breezes and the palms, and this knowledge filled him equally with happy anticipation and dread.

Eighteen

Miss Diana—

I sent my valet to check,

and his word is that the water is

exceptional today. Won't you

join me for a jaunt down to

the seashore? I will be waiting

on the veranda for you. . . .

Expectantly,

Grayson Hayes

$\mathcal{L}$IKE THE REST OF THE SCHOONMAKER PARTY, DIANA had gone to bed early and slept soundly through breakfast. She woke to the invigorating sense of a new locale and salty sea air, and decided to take the little trolley to the shore. Her sister was still too fatigued from the journey to accompany her, but when Diana stepped across the sloping sand beach, she found she didn't mind being alone, for her surroundings were perfect company. The turquoise water stretched before her in glaring contrast to the long white strip of sand, while over her shoulder were all the same pure, bold colors, punctuated occasionally by soaring green palm fronds. It was the kind of landscape where fierce creatures lurked amongst the mangroves and a lady of certain persuasions might hunt pumas.

In New York, every inch of land was used up in some human endeavor, and below even the least haloed site were layers of brick and bone that had been buried along with so many forgotten histories. Here it was simpler and wilder, although that had not prevented all the sea-bathers from dragging civilization onto the landscape. They polka-dotted the stretch of beach and had erected all kinds of shelters for themselves, as though they could not quite accept the notion of being so far from the city and all its modern conveniences. Diana smiled a little wryly at this, but then she caught sight of another kind of savage beauty. There, amongst the crowd of bathers, and not far from her at all, was Penelope Schoonmaker, her black straw hat tipped over her flawless face as she reclined, stocking-clad feet pointed toward the breakers.

Standing beside her was Henry. He wore a black tank swimsuit, which covered his strong torso and half his thighs, and was staring out to sea. His chin had that soft, babyish quality it always did after a fresh shave, and his eyes, already long and slender in a way that frustrated easy revelation, were narrowed to slits in the bright white light. They were not looking at each other, or even talking, but they were so clearly two of a kind that she experienced a wilting effect on all her good feelings. Penelope noticed her then, and a slight smile emerged on her large lips.

"Henry, I'm going to need a sunshade," she announced, as though the thought had spontaneously occurred to her.

"Do you want me to rent you an umbrella?" he replied. He turned to hear her answer, and when he did he was wearing the strangest smile—it was not exactly loving, and yet it was a smile nonetheless.

Up until that moment Diana had easily imagined acrimony between the Schoonmakers in every one of their interactions, but her fantasy life sputtered here and she froze, a little stunned, by this composed picture of the couple.

"Thank you," Penelope very nearly whispered. She seemed to be waiting for a kiss, and Diana was at least relieved that she did not have to witness that. He only nodded and then hurried up the dune to the thatched shelter from which the hotel rented parasols and large standing umbrellas and folding chairs to the newly arrived city folk, whose skin had been rendered vulnerable by all those months in stuffy parlors. Those people—the best of New York and Philadelphia and Washington—populated the beach in little groups, the ladies in their black stockings (the better to disguise their naked flesh when their costumes were soaked by the ocean) and suits of dark cotton that covered their womanly forms.

Penelope herself wore stockings—Diana noticed how their blackness accentuated the slim length of her calves—and a getup that had ruffles at the arms and around the legs. Its neckline was square and low. She did not look back at Diana, and instead surveyed the women nearest her on the sand, and those bobbing out in the surf, with a look of placid confidence that seemed to suggest that she believed herself to be the handsomest woman on the beach.

The air was fresh and cool near the water, and Diana inhaled the salt spray and tried not to be unnerved by the image of Penelope and Henry together. She was trying to decide whether she should approach their chairs or quietly disappear, when she heard someone calling out her name from behind. She turned, placing a flattened palm over her brow to shield her eyes, and saw Grayson Hayes approaching.

"Tried to give me the slip this morning, did you?" He grinned at her, but Diana—taken aback by the familial resemblance, which was so striking in the clean, midday light—just stammered. "I would have liked to escort you to the beach, but here we are now."

Until that moment she hadn't thought much of Grayson's attentions, which had begun on the train and only increased upon their arrival. Though she was unabashed about her own charm and appeal, it suddenly seemed too convenient that he would be there, at just that moment, in the exact same kind of black swimsuit that Henry wore, gazing at her appreciatively. The Hayes siblings were up to something, she realized—but then, that didn't mean it couldn't be convenient to her, too. That was how the heroine of a book would play it, and Diana was still writing her own story; the best heroines, she'd always believed, took their fate into their own hands.

"Here we are," she said. She let her lips part in a slow, inviting smile.

Then they both turned round, and saw Henry rushing

back with a boy who could not have been older than eight or nine. Henry carried the base of the umbrella in the crook of his arm and the boy held the red-and-white-striped shade over his shoulder. When they reached Penelope, the boy immediately began assembling them while Henry stood uselessly looking on. Penelope smiled magnanimously at Henry and at the boy, who wore what looked like a stifling outfit of slacks and waistcoat over a white dress shirt.

"Thank you, Henry," Penelope said when it was all done and her almost iridescent paleness was obscured by an arc of shadow. Then she twisted herself toward where Diana and Grayson were standing, and waved. "Why, hello," she said, without even the pretense of surprise. "Look, it's my brother and Miss Holland."

Henry had just finished tipping the boy, but he looked up as though he had been caught drinking from a flask in church.

Diana was suddenly, acutely aware of all the things that were amiss in her appearance. For she was far shorter than Penelope, and her hair was always in a state, and the bathing costume she wore, which was navy with white edging and anchors embroidered on the wide, sailor collar, was not even a little bit smart. She had been so thankful and appreciative when Claire had remade it from her old suit, which had been purchased for her a long time ago, it seemed—certainly before her father died. Her body had changed since then, and she knew that even the remade version looked like the getup of a little girl. Even so, she managed to wave in return.

"What a nice little colony you have here," Diana said flatly as she and Grayson approached. She wasn't sure if she had meant to load her voice with false enthusiasm or subtle irony, but in any event the words came out as dull as the thudding of her heart. She didn't know, either, what Henry intended with that face he was giving her, but she was quite confident that the sparkly scene she had stumbled upon was not the one that he had lured her to Florida with. "A colony of two," she added, and this time the bitterness was perfectly clear.

"Now a colony of four!" Penelope pushed herself up on her long, white whips of arms and beamed a terrible smile in the direction of Diana and her brother. The skin below her ruffled black sleeves was shockingly visible. The narrow femininity of her whole body, Diana noted with a twang of pain, was on display in her embroidered and pin-tucked black swimming costume.

"There are but two chairs and one umbrella." Diana was speaking to Penelope but staring at Henry, whose features were still assembled in a somewhat sheepish but largely unreadable expression.

"Oh, yes. *Henry* rented them for us. *Henry* knows how

quickly I burn and he could not have that." Penelope tossed her head and laughed and then pressed her face into her shoulder girlishly. "Of course, your complexion is much hardier, Di. Surely you don't need as much protection from the elements."

"In fact, I am quite sensitive to all the brutal parts of nature."

Ordinarily, Diana would never have compared herself to the former Miss Hayes, but she was suddenly struck by the conviction that whatever the older girl required she should have as well. She turned to Grayson, whom she was growing truly pleased to have by her side.

"Mr. Hayes, would you be so kind as to rent me a chair and an umbrella? Just like that one, with the red and white stripes."

"Of course, Miss Di," he replied with familiarity that an hour ago would have irked her but which she now found very useful indeed. At that moment, with the gnawing, desperate feeling that the Henry Schoonmakers gave her, she would have accepted even the company of Percival Coddington, a truly awful bachelor whose inherited wealth had made him seem a possible match for both Holland girls at one point or another—at least in their mother's estimation—and whose presence in the hotel was rumored.

A breeze picked up, rearranging the curls around her

heart-shaped face. For a moment she was distracted and felt almost at ease in the warmth and ocean air, with the pillowlike sand underfoot. But then she let her gaze return to the Henry Schoonmakers and noticed that Henry was mouthing something. There was that same broad, golden-hued handsomeness to him as always, the flat cheeks and narrow patrician lips that routinely left her a little dazed. Then her eyebrows drew together quizzically. Penelope, noting the change in her face, snapped her head around so that he was forced to smile blandly at both of them.

As if in response, Penelope drew a hand across her outstretched leg, unclasped her garters, and began to fold her stockings down so that a narrow patch of the skin of her thigh was exposed. That exquisite area of a woman's leg was well liked by Henry—a fact, Diana realized, that she and Penelope were perhaps equally aware of.

"There!" Grayson declared as he returned with the sunbathing furniture. Diana smiled wanly at him—she wasn't sure if she was capable of something more appreciative right then, but the brother of her rival certainly could not have inspired it. She threw herself gracelessly into the chair, but she couldn't keep from glancing once more at that pale, perfectly formed thigh exposed in the chair to her left.

Apparently she was not the only one who noticed, because the next thing she heard was the pointed tone of the beach censor. "Ladies!" he cried, and they all squinted up into the sunlight at a spindly, prematurely aged man with a cap perched high back on his head. Though he might have been referring to both girls, Diana saw clearly that he was looking at Penelope. "Rules is rules!"

"What?" Penelope whispered as though she were a lamb who, in confusion, had strayed too far from her shepherd. Even in the hot sun, however, she could not force a blush.

"All stockings must meet the swimming suit without flesh visible!" the censor went on truculently, as though he were quoting hotel rules from memory.

Penelope shot Henry a dismayed look, and there followed several seconds during which Diana believed he might tell his wife that she looked like the common tramp she was and that his heart lay elsewhere. But he only leaned forward and passed the censor a folded bill.

"That's my wife," he said, and though it sounded nothing at all like his voice, Diana could not help but acknowledge that they were his words and that they had come from his mouth.

"Then tell her to cover up!" the censor muttered before taking Henry's bribe.

Diana could see which way this was going and, not being one to fall behind, bent forward and unhooked her garters so that her stockings rolled down and revealed a bit of her slightly rounder and decidedly pinker thighs. The censor's eyes widened in excitement and horror and he moved as though he were going to issue her a warning too, but Diana flashed a look in Grayson's direction. Before anything more could be said, money had exchanged hands and the censor was on his way down the beach.

"I'm so thirsty all of a sudden." Penelope reclined backward so that her arms folded up like a pillow and she closed her eyes. "Isn't there someone selling lemonade over there, Mr. Schoonmaker?"

"Yes, I think I see—"

Penelope let one of her arms rise and extend so that her hand rested on Henry's forearm, quieting him. "Get me one, would you?"

Diana's full bottom lip fell involuntarily when she saw how quickly the only man she had ever loved, physically or otherwise, followed his wife's command. In the next minute she had gestured to Grayson. "I find I'm very thirsty too."

When the men were gone, Penelope turned an unsettling gaze on her rival and held it for so long that Diana began to recoil into her lounge chair. She found herself longing for home—not just for the hotel, but for New York and all the real novels that she could lose herself in there. It felt like whole hours before the men returned, and then both girls were left to sip their lemonade angrily and stare out at the surf, which was full of dark swimsuits.

"Henry, I'm ready to swim," Penelope said, once she had finished her lemonade. Her voice was light, but the look she gave Diana betrayed a growing wrath.

Everything about her posture indicated that she believed Diana would mimic this move, too, but Diana disappointed her by putting on a nonchalant smile and relaxing back into her chaise. "I think I'm going to warm up a little more."

A silence followed, filled by the sounds of shrieking bathers and rolling surf. Ladies who would not ordinarily have let their faces betray anything more dramatic than faint distaste for those less well-dressed than themselves were now hanging on to the rope that stretched out into the ocean and squealing as the waves crashed over them. Penelope struck a pose, but Diana was at an advantage, for though she felt nervous around Mrs. Schoonmaker, and less well dressed, and less thin, she was now lying on the wicker seat and had surprised her rival by simply staying put.

"Come, Mr. Schoonmaker." Penelope turned impatiently and began striding toward the surf. If Henry looked reluctant in the seconds before he stood to follow her, that was no longer something Diana could see. His motivations were a mystery to her. What had he intended by dragging her all this distance, anyway? She watched as the Henry Schoonmakers approached the water and then began stepping tentatively into the waves.

She pushed herself up on the chair and assumed the tone of a marriage-obsessed debutante. "They seem *so* happy," she trilled.

"What, them?" Grayson, who had been lying in the chaise next to her, sat up suddenly and removed the newspaper, which he had been using to protect his eyes, from his face.

"Don't you think?" Diana drew her knees to her chest coquettishly and wrapped her arms around her legs.

Grayson shrugged. She could see that the question had never occurred to him, and also that whatever he had done the night before had left him very tired. "I suppose," he said, furrowing his brow. "Although I think she fears what the servants think, and you had better believe I wouldn't be along on this trip if she felt confident of his loving her."

"Oh!" Diana found she remembered how to smile again. There were great, bulbous clouds in the sky, but they were moving quickly, and in a few hours, perhaps, there would be only infinite blue.

Nineteen

It is all very well for Miss Elizabeth Holland to be traipsing around again. Or is it? She has suffered many traumas in the last year, and we can only speculate that her presence in Palm Beach this week is an indicator of how desperately her mother wants to make a match. That might also explain the young lady's enduring friendship with Mrs. Henry Schoonmaker, who would seem to have stolen her beau. . . .

—FROM THE SOCIETY PAGE OF THE *NEW-YORK NEWS OF THE WORLD GAZETTE*, FRIDAY, FEBRUARY 16, 1900

$\mathcal{B}$Y FIVE O'CLOCK THE LIGHT HAD BEGUN TO FADE in Palm Beach, although the humid air had lost none of its heat. The guests of the Royal Poinciana had undergone their fourth change of clothes and were gathering in the Coconut Grove for tea and cake topped with coconut shards. It was a quiet hour out on the grounds of the hotel, where two people who had dressed independently but seemingly with the same idea in mind walked under a canopy of trees. High above them palm fronds drooped like the great lazy wings of prehistoric birds, as the sounds of canaries punctuated their silence. There was also the sound of gravel underfoot, although quietly and occasionally, for they were moving at an easy pace.

"I am glad you felt well enough to walk," Teddy Cutting said eventually. Like his companion, he wore simple white linen. His button-down shirt was tucked into slacks, and his only ornaments were the gold cuff links at his wrists. Elizabeth wore a white shirtwaist and skirt, and there was just a hint of gold on her too, in the form of a chain and cross around her neck.

"I am as well," she replied with a hint of gracious embarrassment.

She had not been a very good party guest thus far, and she had hoped to help her sister so much more than she'd been able. The motion sickness she'd felt on the train had stayed with her when they arrived, which surprised her, for proximity to the seashore had always been soothing—indeed the quiet breezes did, at this moment anyway, have a calming effect.

"I'm not much fun!" she exclaimed, trying to laugh a little. "I suppose I haven't been myself for a long time."

"I imagine it must have been a terrible year," Teddy ventured politely, in the way he had been brought up to. He watched Elizabeth with his serious gray eyes, and she knew that he wanted to say more but did not know how. "I am sorry we have not been able to talk as we used to. I have not been a very good friend to you."

"Oh, Teddy!" Elizabeth surprised herself by emitting a very natural, ringing laugh. Somehow it was all she could do when faced with such a straightforward characterization of recent events. "It has been a very hard year. But you've been the perfect gentleman, as always."

Teddy shook his head and looked at the arch of green above them. "That never seems to do anybody very much good, does it?"

They took several steps in which neither of them spoke.

Elizabeth wondered what he could possibly mean by that, and then she asked him as much.

"During your engagement to Henry . . ." he began, but was unable to finish.

There was a delicate anguish in his expression, and as Elizabeth watched him she marveled at how like her former fiancé he was in appearance, and yet how different the effect was. For Teddy was tall as well, and he had the strong, slender features of American nobility. But where there was a perpetually amused carnivorousness about Henry, there was a subtle constancy to Teddy. She remembered now what a good friend he'd been once upon a time, for though he'd flirted with her and commented on her beauty, he had also posed philosophical questions that he had mulled during his coursework at Columbia, and was always curious about her opinions. When her father had died he had taken her for carriage rides in the park and sat patiently by her and never expected her to make any kind of conversation.

"I knew it wasn't a good match," he said finally. "I might have done something."

"What could you have done?" Elizabeth replied lightly. "I accepted his proposal after all, and I knew better than anyone."

Teddy's arms were clasped loosely behind his back and he glanced at her when she spoke. "You never loved him?" he asked with sudden seriousness.

"It's not a secret anymore that my family has fallen on hard times." Elizabeth spoke cautiously, choosing each word before she uttered it. "What I did—what I *would* have done—was all for them."

"Henry is my friend, but I am glad you did not marry him. I had feared for you that it would be a loveless marriage. Not that I am implying there was anything good about your . . . ordeal. But if there was something good . . ." Teddy's voice had grown low and rushed, as though he had unexpectedly sailed into uncharted conversational waters, and was astounded by the new view. When he returned to the usual finespun formality she felt a little sad. "I hope you don't think I am being too personal."

"Oh, no. In fact . . ." Elizabeth found herself struck by the uncharacteristic compulsion to confess everything. And though she knew Teddy had loved her once upon a time and that he had believed the lie in the papers about her "rescue," she felt somehow that he might understand about Will and the great lengths she had gone to be with him. "Last fall, when I was . . . kidnapped . . . Well, that wasn't exactly how it . . ." Elizabeth glanced at Teddy, at his expression composed of nothing but kindness and concern, and stopped herself. She had wanted to be known completely, but the full weight of her deception descended, and her upbringing got the better of her. Now she was formal again, too. "Someday I would like to tell you the whole story, Teddy. But it was partially my fault, you see, because I knew I couldn't be in a loveless marriage, as well." She laughed lightly and, thinking of Will's callused hands and his skin turned brown by the California sun, added: "Even before my ordeal, I knew that Henry wasn't the man for me. He is practically more delicate than I am!"

She had come to a halt on the walk. Teddy took a few more steps, realized she was no longer at his side, and turned to look at her. The leaves overhead cast shadows across both their faces, and out on the water the blaze of evening sun was doubled and elongated by its reflection. His gray eyes grew round and he took a step toward her, as if he was thinking of kissing her. Stranger still, she found herself imagining the soft pressure of his lips against hers, but then her eyes closed and she hoped that Will wasn't watching her from above. She remembered how jealous he used to be and all the tortures she had put him through, and turned her face away demurely.

Then she forced a bright tone and changed the subject: "How *is* Henry?"

Teddy let out a sound that was not quite a laugh or a sigh. "I know she's your friend, but I don't understand it," he said, gauging Elizabeth's expression to see if he had offended before pushing on. "It's like he sold his soul one night when he'd had too much to drink, and now the devil lives in his body. I don't think he's even in love with Penelope! She was after him shamelessly when we all thought you were . . . gone, you know, and he wasn't the least bit interested. I might even say he was disgusted, if it didn't so contradict what happened next."

"I think she might have been the one to sell her soul at a steep price," Elizabeth replied quietly. She was thinking of what Diana had told her, about how Penelope had blackmailed her way to the altar, and felt a little sad realizing that Henry had not confessed this to even his closest friend.

"She wanted to marry him very badly?"

"Oh, yes, before even—" Elizabeth stopped herself and smiled at Teddy. She still felt uncomfortable being a gossip, even if Penelope was the object of the loose talk, and anyway, she knew that down that route lay her own deceit. But she was pleased to hear that, in Teddy's estimation, too, Henry did not love his wife. The idea that her sister and Henry might still prove a great love story lifted her spirits.

They started off walking again, although they drew closer together now. They moved easily by each other's side, their slender, white-clad limbs carrying them forward in neat tandem. They looked at each other, one after the other, but grew bashful and turned away. She glanced up again, the light dappling both their faces. She blinked, and Teddy returned her smile, which was very natural and based on nothing in particular, or maybe everything. For the first time in months

she believed her life could be long and not all clouded over with misery.

"Don't worry, Liz," he said. "I won't make you talk about any of that anymore, or anything that makes you even a little uncomfortable."

Then he took her arm, imbuing her with a lacy sensation of well-being, and they walked on below the soaring palms. Perhaps, she mused, the thick, clean air in Florida had been good for her after all.

Twenty

A SOCIETY BRIDE'S INSECURITIES!
BEAUTIFUL HEIRESS FEARS SHE WON'T
HOLD HER HUSBAND'S ATTENTION,
WORRIES THE SERVANTS WILL NOTICE

A SPECIAL REPORT BY THE "GAMESOME GALLANT"

PALM BEACH, FL—Here in Florida, we have
been the witnesses of some very surprising
developments: Even Mrs. Henry Schoonmaker
suffers from the paranoias that prey on all
married women—namely, that their husbands
may lose interest in them. It seems that she
clings to her brother, Mr. Grayson Hayes, in
case her new husband abandons her on the dance
floor, and is in fact so insecure on this point that
she will not travel without that gentleman. . . .

—FROM THE *NEW YORK IMPERIAL*,
SATURDAY, FEBRUARY 17, 1900

OR PENELOPE, THE SECOND DAY IN PALM BEACH began auspiciously enough. She pushed her black silk sleeping mask up on her forehead and saw that the maid had come already and drawn open the French doors so that a little bit of ocean breeze permeated the rich surroundings of her suite. After dinner the night before she had washed her hair, and it hung now like a dark question mark over her pale shoulder. The champagne-colored sheets were smooth against the skin of her arms—they were much finer than the ones the Schoonmakers used, and she made a mental note to find out where they came from. Most important, her husband was by her side, and though he was still asleep, and snoring quietly into his plump down pillow, it was the most intimate they had been since their marriage. She hesitated to wake him just yet.

She closed her eyes and rolled into the soft space just next to him on the bed, but she was careful not to come too close. She wanted him to stay there, just like that, awhile longer. He was warm, and she could sense the quiet working of his body even though he was wrapped up in bedding. If she moved too quickly she might frighten him, and she knew he might sleep for a good while yet.

"Mrs. Schoonmaker?"

She cracked one eye open and glared at the girl who had come through the door. It was her maid, in her starched black-and-white uniform, and though her mouth was forced upward into something like a smile, the effect was more akin to distress. Penelope unlaced the sleeping mask and tossed it onto the floor, so that the girl had to tiptoe forward and bend over to pick it up. That was when Penelope noticed the newspapers that were folded under the girl's arm and remembered that she had instructed her to bring all of the Schoonmakers' clippings to her room personally every morning. Penelope knew that distance was the true engine of desire, and had hoped that in her absence all New York would again grow jealous of her many, many possessions.

"You can leave them there," Penelope said, pointing to the table that had been erected and laden with juice and coffee and pastries in the middle of the large room. The girl obliged hastily, though perhaps a little too hastily—there was something ominous about the way she scurried from the room.

Penelope propped herself up and shook off the last, lazy vestiges of sleep. She let her eyes linger on Henry's golden back for one second longer, and then swung her feet to the floor. She tied her robe around herself and went over to the tray of breakfast things, where she had a sip of coffee, took a deep breath, and felt happy for the last time that morning. For in the next second she saw the headline, and all of the hateful parts of her personality surged up.

She read a few lines but stopped as soon as she realized the gist of the article. Then she stormed back to the raised platform, and up to the lavish, disheveled bed, and threw the newspaper at Henry's head.

"What the hell?" he cried, coming to life and tossing off the sheets.

Penelope fell onto her knees and grabbed a pillow, which she aimed at Henry for good measure. He caught it in midair, and grabbed his wife by the wrist.

"What in God's name is wrong with you?" he asked, holding her arms against the bed.

"What's wrong with *you*?" she spat back at him, once she had freed herself and taken several deep breaths.

Henry picked up the paper and then he too fell back into the pillows. He read a few lines before putting the paper down on the heaps of bedding that separated his wife from himself. His hands pressed against his hair furtively, trying to get it all back in place. "I didn't have anything to do with that," he said eventually. His inability to meet her eyes did nothing to quell her ire.

"In what sense, Henry?" She brought her robe tight around her body, which still trembled a little in fury. She turned her face into a pillow, her jaw jutting petulantly, but kept him securely in her gaze. "You mean you didn't personally write it? Or you mean you didn't do anything to give anyone the sense that any of it might be true? Because I'm not stupid, and if you expect me to believe the latter, you are mistaken."

"I only meant—"

"You don't mean *anything*!" Penelope shrieked. "Even after you promised to be good, I saw you trying to speak with her yesterday at the beach. The way you look at her, with your pathetic, longing gaze, you idiot bastard!"

She rose to her knees again, and—only half-conscious of her actions, so heated was her blood—began to rip the paper to shreds. The strips of paper fell down around them, the cheap ink smudging the sheets she had moments ago taken such pleasure in. When she was done Henry just stared at her, his eyes as big as they ever got.

"Why should *I* look like the fool? I am the sympathetic one in all this. What I ought to do," she went on, climbing off the bed and walking hotly toward the tray in the center of the room to retrieve her coffee, "is call the paper and tell them *my* version. I'll tell them how I loved my husband, was faithful to him, packed his bags for his every trip. But *he* had eyes only for Diana Holland, whose virginity he took one snowy night—"

"Don't do that." Henry stumbled off the bed and came walking toward her, still wrapped in a sheet.

Penelope turned her back on him and sipped her coffee. "What alternative do I have?"

She knew she had his attention now, and felt no need to turn around and confirm the fact.

"We'll go to the beach again today," Henry finally said.

"What good will that do?"

"It will show everybody that that column was fiction," he went on tentatively. He had taken a few steps toward her; she could sense him at her back. "Maybe it will inspire some piece that contradicts the one you just tore to pieces."

"It deserved to be torn to pieces," Penelope shot back hotly.

There was a pause, after which Henry said, "Yes, it did."

"You'll take me to the beach?"

"If that's what you want."

"And later, you'll sit with me at dinner, and dance all the dances with me?"

Henry was just behind her now, and he put an awkward hand on her shoulder. "Yes."

Penelope kept staring away from her husband, and so he

couldn't see that her winner's smile had returned to her face. "Oh, and Henry?"

"Yes?"

She closed her eyes and enjoyed the placement of his hand for another few moments. She breathed deeply, and her whole torso moved with the breaths. "You'll never make me look like a fool again, will you?"

"No," he said at last. "Never again."

Twenty One

A man is made in the rough-and-tumble of the world; a lady emerges from the flossy back rooms of her own imagination.

—MAEVE DE JONG, *LOVE AND OTHER FOLLIES OF THE GREAT FAMILIES OF OLD NEW YORK*

"WHAT ARE WE DOING?" CAROLINA ASKED WHEN she stopped giggling.

Leland Bouchard's automobile, which he had had shipped at great personal expense from New York, had come to a sudden stop after several rough leaps and dives. They had traversed more than one dirt road that day, and though Carolina had been to Coney Island when she was a child and gone on the roller coaster, she had never taken a ride quite like this one. It scared her a little, but in a way that made her feel happy and filled her with inexplicable hilarity. Leland, who had long ago done away with his jacket and rolled his white shirtsleeves up to the elbows, revealing forearms that were almost ungentlemanly in their strength, gave her a slightly wild smile. The road was overgrown with jungle, all ropey and shadowy, and from somewhere out in the greenery they could hear the cawing of birds.

"Aren't you hungry?"

There was nothing funny in what he said, and yet she found herself giggling a little again as she replied, "Why, yes."

She had not in fact eaten all day, and had several times grown frightened that Leland could hear the faint rumblings of her belly, although mostly her attention had been occupied by other things.

He leaned forward and looked at her intently. "You sure? You're not tired? I'm not boring you?"

Carolina threw back her head and laughed. "Bored? There aren't any dull moments in your world." She hadn't had a lot of practice in flirtatious tones of voice, and did not have to use one here, for what she said was absolutely true. Besides driving up and down the rough roads, they had already seen alligators and giant sea turtles and all manner of strange flora and fauna. She did think, a little regretfully, of the sky blue day dress with the ruffled hem that she'd had her maid lay out for her that morning and planned to wear to lunch. But that was a short-lived concern. It was well past two and lunch had already been served at the hotel, and anyway, she found that the opportunity to show off another dress paled in comparison to another hour or two with Leland. Her only real complaint was that her yellow gingham jacket and matching skirt had grown a little damp from cavorting all day in the heat.

"Good," he said. "I'm starved."

He came around to her side of the car then, and opened the door for her. She let him help her out of her seat and hold her by the hand as they traveled up a pair of boards, which lay over slightly muddy ground, leading the way toward a small shack that was built against the trunk of a great banyan tree. She clutched her wide straw hat with one hand, and Leland's palm with the other, as they moved upward as though along a balance beam. She had taken her gloves off at some point, and was pleasantly surprised to feel Leland's skin against her own for the first time. She didn't worry even a little about the swampy earth below or what would happen to her skirt if she lost her footing.

Once her eyes adjusted to the indoor light she saw that the roots of the tree had grown through some of the windows, and that the unfinished floorboards had been placed to accommodate them. There was a young boy fanning the room with palm fronds, but the place was not a fancy one. The few diners who were left at that late hour wore no jackets and barely looked up to note the arrival of the fine people from New York. A heavy woman who seemed to know Leland ushered them to one of the red-and-white-checked cloth-covered tables, and asked him how long he was staying this time.

"Not long enough," Leland said happily. "This is my friend Carolina," he added.

"Pleased to meet you." When the woman smiled, she exposed a wide gap between her two brown middle teeth. The skin of her face had grown thick and creased from many years in the sun.

"And you," Carolina replied. Mr. Longhorn had once or twice tried to take her to down-and-out places for a different kind of thrill or to hear the music they played there, and she had balked each time. In New York, she hated missing even the smallest opportunity to display her new things and know that they were envied. But with Leland, she didn't mind that no one of special importance was there to see them. In fact, over the course of the day, she had increasingly come to savor being in his presence alone.

"We'll have two shrimp gumbos, please," Leland said.

"Spicy?"

"Yes." He glanced back at Carolina and she realized she had again been staring at him witlessly. She wondered if it wasn't the hunger and its attendant light-headedness that made her behave so gauchely. "What are you looking at? My nose, I know—it's burned. And too large."

She recognized the painful redness only after he'd called attention to it, and realized that he had not, like her, had the protection of a hat. She couldn't stop herself from reaching out and touching the skin of his cheek. The new color looked painful but also brought out the beautiful blue of his eyes.

"It's a perfect nose," she said, meaning it. His nose was broad, but well structured, like the rest of him.

"You are too kind! My mother blames our French ancestry for the monstrosity."

Just then the gap-toothed woman appeared to place bread on their table. Carolina thoughtlessly reached for the basket, breaking off a large piece and putting it in her mouth. She was chewing exuberantly when her large eyes rolled to where Leland sat beside her, and saw that this time he was staring at her. In the next moment she felt the dampness under her armpits and became aware that she'd sweated through her ivory silk shirt. She swallowed hard, and reached for the little jacket, which she had stupidly taken off and draped on the back of her chair.

"What's the matter?" Leland grabbed her by the wrist before she could reach for her jacket.

"Nothing, I—"

"Your face just fell a hundred stories. Something is wrong. You're bored, aren't you? You don't like this place, do you?"

"No! I love it." Carolina began laughing again at the absurdity of what she was going to say next. "It's only that I'm in such a state, and I fear I smell terrible, and I'm stuffing food in my face like a barbarian because I'm so starved—"

"I love a woman with an appetite!" Leland grinned at her, and then put his perfect nose against her shoulder. "And I like the way you smell."

She looked at Leland and he looked back as though there was nothing strange or inappropriate about gazing at each other in a backwoods shack on an out-of-the-way dirt road in Florida. They might have gone on like that for who knows how long, but their food arrived, and the steam that rose off their bowls was so laden with spice that it made her eyes water a little.

Her hesitation must have showed, because the next thing he said was, "Don't you like spicy food?"

She lowered her face to the bowl and inhaled.

The Hollands, like all the old Dutch families, believed in everything in moderation, and disliked strong tastes of any kind. She had often wondered what it would be like to eat food outside of their narrow tastes, but then, of course, she had been taken under wing by an older gentleman whose stomach could not handle anything very strong, and so she'd never been able to find out.

"Not out west? I would have thought on the ranch you'd have eaten all kinds of things that we New Yorkers would be terrified of."

Carolina's eyes rolled to the beamed ceiling. Suddenly the full import of everything she had said over the course of the day began to dawn on her—for until that moment she had bubbled over with tales of her childhood adventures on horseback and sleeping on the range and staring into mine shafts. She had borrowed liberally from the stories Will used to tell her, for he was an obsessive consumer of any book that touched on the western states. She had guessed, rightly, that all of this would entertain a man like Leland, but had somehow failed to consider the possibility that he would remember any of it, or ask her any further questions. She had also forgotten, in the last hour, that a ranch had become a part of her fictitious personal history.

"Out west?" she stalled. The spicy smell had gone to her head now and her nose had begun to run.

"Yes—don't cowboys love hot peppers and Tabasco?"

Carolina drew her wrist under her nostrils to wipe away the moisture there.

"Oh dear, did I say something wrong again?"

Leland brought his napkin up to her eyes and began to dab away the tears, which had continued to emerge there, even against all her willpower. She tried to think quickly, but already an explanation was tumbling from her mouth. "Father loved everything spicy. Even pancakes! It was our family joke. None of the farmhands or any of his employees could match his taste for it. The memory of all that makes me a little sad, is all, and I haven't been able to eat anything but bland food since he passed."

"Oh, my darling. I'm so sorry to have made you think of all that."

She shook her head, and tried to stop the tears, which were quite naturally running down her face now. "It's all right." A brave smiled played on her lips.

"Maybe you would like it now?" Leland's brows slanted downward at the corners in a show of sincere concern. "Maybe it would bring the memory back in a good way."

"Well, I suppose I could try," Carolina answered tentatively.

Leland dipped his spoon in the stew and brought it up to Carolina's mouth. He watched her to make sure it was all right, but then she nodded and he brought the spoonful forward into her mouth. The gumbo was even hotter than she had imagined. It was delicious and lit up her whole mouth. In the next moment, she felt the heat over her entire body. The one bite made her realize how hungry she had been, and when she had swallowed it she asked for more.

Leland then put down his spoon and reached for her hand. He had made similar gestures in the past, but they had all been to steady or protect her, and this time there was no utilitarian excuse. There was a new sweetness to the touch.

"You know, Miss Broad . . ." he began. Then he put his fist to his mouth and coughed embarrassedly. "You aren't like other ladies."

"No?" she whispered. He'd said it like it was a good thing, but the phrase made her nervous even so.

"Not at all." He shook his head and smiled as though he'd stumbled on some stroke of good fortune he could scarcely believe. "I feel so comfortable around you. Maybe it's because you're not from New York and you don't care so much for all those silly, frilly things, but I find that I'm happier around you than I've been in some time."

A few rays of golden light came through the window then, and Carolina's smile broke wide and relieved across her freckled face. "Oh, me too!" she gasped, and took a firmer hold of his hand. "I feel just exactly that way."

THE WESTERN UNION TELEGRAPH COMPANY

TO: *Diana Holland*

ARRIVED AT: *The Royal Poinciana,
Palm Beach, Florida*

4:00 p.m., Saturday, February 17, 1900

*Great news—Your column huge success—
Payment awaits in NY—Keep up the
good work—D.B.*

"AND TO OUR SPECIAL GUESTS, THE HENRY Schoonmakers, who make such a lovely couple!"

The throng—in their tuxedos and laces, their well-oiled hair shining rosily under the many warm-colored electric lights, which were strung across the ceiling of the pergolalike dance floor of the hotel—twittered and clapped, but Diana Holland couldn't listen anymore. Henry had tried to meet her eyes at dinner, but even of that she could not be sure. Today she had seen him on the beach, and at tea, and playing cards in the garden, all the while with Penelope. Diana felt miffed and more than a little stung by Henry's near complete indifference to her since their arrival in Florida, but had tried to keep within his view at all times that day. It was he who had encouraged her to travel all this way, after all, and it was not in her nature to be forgotten so easily.

She had even enlisted Grayson, who was always at her shoulder anyway, in making Henry jealous. She hadn't gone so far as to let Grayson in on the plan, but when he'd flirted with her she had flirted back, and she'd allowed him to feed her bites of cake at tea and had loudly complimented his croquet skills. That had garnered a few furtive glances from Henry, but it had also been many hours ago, and for Diana hours were beginning to feel like years. Now she was alone. Her sister and Teddy had been wrapped up in each other's conversation all night, and even Grayson abandoned her sometime after dessert and before dancing.

Through the thicket of broad, black-clad shoulders, Diana could see the couple that was now the toast of Palm Beach in profile. They were tall and slim and dark-haired, and though Diana could not discern what was in their faces, it seemed the piece she'd planted in the paper had done nothing to stain them. Perhaps they hadn't seen it; perhaps it would forever escape their notice. She felt a little jittery and depleted by it all, disoriented by doubt, and she stuffed her hand into the pocket of her peach silk dress and crumpled Barnard's telegram. Then she lit out across the lawn unnoticed, ruining a pair of high-heeled slippers her family already couldn't afford in the damp grass.

If that morning, holding her column in the *Imperial* in her hands, she had felt the lift of having played a good hand, she was now experiencing the deflation of any gambler after a spree. She started off walking across the lawn, but soon broke into a run. The dress—which she had chosen so carefully to show off her strong, fine clavicles—now flapped against her legs as she dashed through the humid air. She had pushed her sister, who was in a rare, bright mood, to do her hair elaborately, but all that began to fall apart now, too, and the ribbons that had adorned it trailed behind her as she went.

Was she running from Henry? He was a mystery to her, and every time she tried to solve him it caused her a little more pain. But when she tried to give him up he pursued her in her thoughts, stronger each time. This was as good a reason to keep running as any, and if she had been a less impulsive sort of girl, she might have considered that this was not the first time in recent days she had gone on a restless ramble. But already she'd traveled some distance, lost her shoes, felt the sand in between her toes, and reached the water.

The full moon left a trail of silver across the dark, rippling water, which for a moment looked so inviting that she might have believed she could climb up it. Then a wave came on suddenly, crashing against her legs and soaking her dress, bringing spray all the way to her ears. The sea was not particularly cold or rough, but she was so surprised by it that she burst into tears. As it drew away she began to lose her balance, and for a moment she wondered if she wouldn't drown that night. But then she felt familiar arms around her chest, and was pulled back up to the dry sand.

"Oh," she whimpered, drawing her fingers across her

face and trying to uncrumple her features. The tears were still wet on her cheeks, but her whole lower half was drenched by salt water now, too, and anyway she supposed it didn't matter after everything if Henry saw her cry now. He was standing there in his black jacket and white shirt, and he was looking at her with what she would have named concern and sincerity if she didn't know better. "What do you want?"

"To be with you. Just for a minute."

Diana's chest billowed and heaved. The silk skirt, and all the cotton underskirts, clung to her thighs. Henry was finally right there in front of her, on an abandoned beach late at night, but all the confusions of the day were like a chasm between them. The moonlight was bright, and she could see his whole figure perfectly. "A few minutes? You wanted me to come all this way so that we could have a few minutes?"

Henry's jaw shifted and he glanced away. Somehow he had escaped a full soaking, and she resented him for still looking so put together. "That's all it can be. Penelope, she's so frightful, if she found out I was with you now, if she knew I told you why we married, if she knew how badly I want to kiss you—"

He stepped forward and cupped the back of her head with his palm and put his mouth to hers. A moment ago this would have seemed like a very bad idea, but then Diana closed her eyes and returned his kisses again and again as though they might give her some oxygen she had been sorely deprived of. His other hand had found its way to the small of her back, and despite the state of her gown, he pressed his whole body against hers, ruining both of their evening wear.

"Oh," she said, more softly this time, when he drew back.

His lips were still parted, and the moon was reflected like white disks in his eyes.

Her mouth fell open a little wider. She felt the expectation of another kiss, the way one feels the rain just before it begins to fall. But moments passed, their exhalations mingling in the sea air, and none came.

Henry stepped back. "We'll be missed."

"What?" There was anger in her voice, but the disappointment was stronger.

"Your sister, Penelope—they'll be wondering where we are."

Beyond Henry's shoulder the lights of the hotel twinkled and the palms made grand silhouettes against a purple sky. There were some long clouds moving across it—they would overtake the moon and make it blurry soon. "So you'd prefer to have me a few minutes at a time? In back rooms and corridors of trains? That was what you hoped for when you told me to find a way to come to Florida?"

Henry shook his head, but she knew that what she had said was true. She tried to make her body cold.

"You imagined I would become your mistress."

"No—"

"Good night." Diana summoned all the dignity that she could manage in her bedraggled state and began to move back up the beach. Her dress was soaked and her stockings dotted with sand and her heart couldn't possibly withstand any more. She did want to look back, but she felt that to do so would somehow forgive all of Henry's sins against her.

"Diana!" he cried. His voice had been full of anguish, but then it was gone, and for a moment all she heard was the soft lapping of the waves against the shore. "Diana, I need you"—and from the way his voice broke over her name, she believed he did. But she shut her eyes and kept on toward the hotel, over in the distance, where the lights were bright and the music played faintly.

"Diana," he went on in the same desperate voice as he chased her up the beach, "Diana, I'll leave her."

That gave her pause—she stopped and looked. Henry's face had ever been the clean-shaven and well-constructed face of civilization, but he was looking at her now with something more akin to animal urgency.

"You will?" she whispered.

"I can't be without you."

"You can't?" Diana knew she was in grave danger of being a fool again, but hope bloomed in her heart.

Henry took a few strides and then he looked down on her with new conviction. He brushed the curls away from her face, his hand lingering over her eyes, his thumb pressing against her full lower lip.

"Come, you had better get yourself cleaned up," he said as he put his arm around her shoulder.

For a while they walked like that toward the great, lit-up dollhouse across the lawn, until it was too close. Then they separated so that she could return to her room, and he could go back to play his role for just a little longer. She kept the image of his face in her mind even after they'd parted. Like all his promises, it was now burnished with renewed and won-drous value.

Twenty Three

The recently affianced couple, Reginald Newbold and Adelaide Wetmore, were seen last
night at a little musical evening at Mr. Newbold's home on Madison Avenue. His sister,
Gemma, was there as well, who was said to
be expecting a proposal from Teddy Cutting.
Did she look so sad because Mr. Cutting is
away in Florida, and should we take his prolonged absence to mean there will be no June
wedding?

—FROM THE SOCIETY PAGE OF THE *NEW-YORK NEWS OF
THE WORLD GAZETTE*, SATURDAY, FEBRUARY 17, 1900

"ARE YOU ALL RIGHT?"

Elizabeth opened her eyes slowly, and then the ballroom of the Poinciana came back into focus: the bodies swaying across the parquet floor, the white latticework of the ceiling, the string music soft from behind a screen. She realized that she had rested her head on Teddy's shoulder during the dance, but she answered truthfully when she said, "I am."

"You'll let me know if you would like to sit, won't you?" She had never before noticed the worry lines that sometimes emerged on her old friend's forehead. His skin was otherwise so soft and unblemished, and she wondered when and how he'd come by those marks.

Like the other women in the room, Elizabeth wore light, evening-appropriate colors—her ivory dress was embellished with embroidery of pale pink—but in the hours since dinner she had lost track of everyone else. She knew that the kind of people she had always been comfortable amongst populated the room—they were the people her mother wanted her to be seen mingling with, and she was grateful to feel safe and light enough to do so now. Her neck, as gracious and slender as a swan's, was bedecked with her grandmother's jewels, which her mother had carefully packed for the trip, and her pale hair was arranged in piles above her head. The cooler evening breeze came through the open windows, and for a moment she felt quite perfectly at ease.

"Do I look tired?" her small, plump lips parted, and she let her eyes flutter between open and closed.

"No." Teddy smiled from one corner of his mouth, and moved her, in smooth glides, away from the center of the room. "You look lovely."

She smiled faintly and nodded.

"I've so enjoyed getting to spend time with you these last days," he went on.

"I have as well."

"They are such lovely hours, the ones I get to spend with you. They're something I feared I'd never experience again. . . ."

Out of the corner of her eye, Elizabeth noticed Henry coming in from the lawn. He approached Mrs. Schoonmaker, whose hair was arranged in shiny curls with feathers on top of her head, and whose polka-dot chiffon dress gathered in a low V-neck over her chest. Penelope glanced at his feet and then back to his face, and her eyes widened. Elizabeth knew that look well—she had seen her old friend angry, with servant girls and members of her family and—on one especially notable occasion—with Elizabeth herself.

The Schoonmakers were across the room and there was no way to know what words passed between them, but at the end of their brief conversation Henry removed Penelope's hand, which was sheathed in an elbow-length black satin glove, from his shoulder and left the room. For a reason that she couldn't place, the scene filled Elizabeth with foreboding, and she looked to Teddy to ask him what he thought it was all about.

"Elizabeth?" he said before she could question him.

She nodded that he should speak, but he exhaled self-consciously and had to look away. They waltzed in a few circles before he began again.

"I only wanted to tell you that when I proposed to you, so many years ago now, it seems—"

"Less than two, the last time." A whisper of a smile appeared on Elizabeth's face, even though the memory this conjured was a sad one. It had been in Newport, where she had stayed for a whole month and grown dizzy and lovesick over her distance from Will. He had managed to send her letters—she couldn't remember anymore how they'd gotten away with it—which had been full of his fear that she would lose interest in him while she was away. Her eyelashes sank down.

"Yes, that's right, it was not even two years ago. When you were a guest of the Hayeses."

Elizabeth couldn't yet bear to open her eyes, but she knew from his breathless tone how nervous and in earnest Teddy must be.

"Anyway, what I meant to say, what I *want* to say, is that I was sincere then, and my offer still stands." She had never heard his voice so shaky. "I would still—"

"Oh, Teddy," was all Elizabeth could manage. She was afraid that if she didn't stop him she would begin to cry on the dance floor and then there would be no stopping all the feeling, or holding in any of the secrets. But perhaps he misread her sadness for another emotion, because he went on.

"Do you think you could love me? Perhaps marry me? I mean, not now, necessarily, but maybe in time—"

Elizabeth came to a sudden halt on the dance floor. She thought of Will on their wedding day in a brown suit that he had bought for the occasion, and shook her head instinctively. He had still been wearing that suit when she had rushed away from him, and it was that suit that had soaked up his blood on the platform in Grand Central Station.

"Perhaps in time, Teddy," she said, even though the idea of frothy white flowers and trousseaus and groomsmen in a row filled her with revulsion. She met his gray eyes, which were watching her so sweetly and attentively. She'd known, even that summer when she was still so naïve, that if she had never known a man like Will, then Teddy might have given her a very happy life.

"In time," she repeated. Her voice sounded mechanical, but she meant it as a confirmation. In time, there would be nothing so sweet to her as words like those. She tried to smile, but she knew the effect was no good, for all the color had drained from her lips. "You know, if it hadn't been for my experiences last fall and before—" she began, wanting to give him some kind of an explanation. But she stopped herself, realizing this was neither the time nor the place. "Just now I find I am very tired after all. Won't you excuse me?"

Her skirts and jewels, her gloves and laces, the pins that held up her hair and the strings that held in her ribs, all felt very heavy then. She didn't know if she would even be able to carry them across the room. But she could not be out, among the throng, in all that adornment any longer. She wasn't able to look at Teddy as they parted, and so she had no idea whether he had understood her at all.

Twenty Four

Resort dress is always lavish, but my spies in Palm Beach report that Miss Carolina Broad seems to have arrived with an all-new wardrobe, and that she appears always spangled, sparkling, and encrusted with diamonds. I hope that Mr. Carey Lewis Longhorn is at least receiving reports of all his money has made possible.

—FROM THE "GAMESOME GALLANT" COLUMN IN THE
NEW YORK IMPERIAL, SATURDAY, FEBRUARY 17, 1900

$\mathscr{T}$HERE WERE MANY WOMEN IN POSSESSION OF youth and beauty gliding across the dance floor of the Royal Poinciana that Saturday evening, which was covered by an arched white wood ceiling but remained open to the elements via its large, thrown-open windows. Carolina felt she must be the loveliest of them all. Her brown hair was divided into two sections so that it both rose above her forehead in a high pouf and curled down her neck in a ribboned tail. Around her throat rested a double strand of pearls and garnets that brought out the green in her eyes, and her arms were sheathed in flutes of antique lace. She knew that the skin of her broad forehead very nearly glowed under the varicolored lights, and that in the South her smattering of freckles indicated a kind of thoroughbred tawniness. The only element out of place was her partner, Percival Coddington, whose breath was fragrant with the chicken fricassee he had eaten for dinner.

"What a pleasure it is to dance with you," Percival said. Carolina knew what it was to be uncomfortable in this world, and she understood the meaning of the sheen of sweat on his forehead. He was nervous, poor thing, and she did feel a little bad for him. Still, she knew she was wasting whole minutes. of her promising new life, of her late-blooming loveliness, on him. His cavernous nostrils were just at her eye level, and his damp hands were in far too familiar a position as they swayed to the music of Bailey's Orchestra, which played behind a screen painted with underwater creatures. Hundreds of guests were amassed along the edges of the room, and the dance floor was crowded with young couples. There were far brighter, far richer, far better-dressed people in the rosy shadows, blotted out by the army of waiters, and here she was with a moderately moneyed nobody who had not yet learned to breathe with his mouth shut.

In another moment she might have dwelled on the irony that, only a few months ago, the chance to hold the attention of a Percival Coddington would have seemed to her a very lucky turn indeed. But she was entirely different now. She did not have time for such sentimentalities. Her throat began to constrict, for no matter how rudely she twisted her head around, she could not get a glimpse of Leland anywhere.

Of course, her day with him had already been long and close to perfection. But foolishly she had insisted that she be delivered to the hotel in time to bathe, apply her maquillage, have her hair done, and still leave an hour in which to be corseted and to push all the tiny pearl buttons of her suggestively white dress through their holes. He had agreed almost too amicably, and then he had gone off to play golf with Grayson Hayes. She had worried the whole time that he would not return in time to escort her in to dinner, perhaps so much so that she had made his tardiness come true. That was when she had fallen prey to Mr. Coddington, who had insisted on discussing the caste system of the Fijian islanders through the first three courses. She had seen Leland when he came in late, and she now feared that in choosing a few hours with her maid over golfing (which she had never played) she had lost his interest.

"I never did see what people liked about old Carey Longhorn," Mr. Coddington said—cruelly, Carolina observed—before she finally lost her patience.

"I hardly see how you are in any position to—" she began, but was saved from causing a scene by the sight of her afternoon companion over her partner's shoulder. He was grinning, with that mouth that was handsomely too large for his face, and the blue of his eyes was sparkly in the low light. Carolina stopped dancing, and Percival let go of her hand a second later. "Mr. Bouchard."

"Miss Broad." He tipped his head and then turned on his heel. "Mr. Coddington, may I cut in?"

Percival's nostrils flared, and for a moment it appeared

that he was going to be vocally unhappy about it. But then he acquiesced, and Carolina felt her hand taken up again, with much more force this time, as she was moved backward into the crowd.

"I find I must apologize to you again," he offered, though Carolina was barely listening. The gleam on her partner's strong white teeth, the width of his shoulders, the solid size of him, were too overwhelming. "If I had noticed that you were cornered by that tiresome ass—forgive my language—I would have saved you a long time ago."

Suddenly the music was louder, exultant, as though her own inner sensations were being re-created by horns and strings. She would have liked to go on staring at Leland, but she reminded herself how Elizabeth never seemed to need anything from her suitors, or even to be particularly interested in them. She turned so that he could appreciate her profile and looked out at the crowd and felt very satisfied to be right where she was.

For there was Lady Dagmall-Lister, dancing with her young male companion, and there was the famous architect Webster Youngham dancing cheek to cheek with one of the junior Mrs. Astors. They were all dressed in their finest, as though life really were some magical stage play in which every moment ought to be illuminated with its own bright spotlight. Earlier, everyone had murmured over Mrs. Henry Schoonmaker, dancing with her adoring husband, his dark eyes full of mystery but his hands on his wife. She couldn't see them now, but she noted Diana Holland, who was wearing a different dress than the one she had dined in earlier; Grayson Hayes was nowhere to be seen either.

Carolina was a little disappointed that Elizabeth had already gone to bed, leaving Teddy Cutting without a partner, for it meant that she would not be forced any longer to witness her former maid's entry into the rare world of which she had once been the undisputed princess. For a moment, Carolina wondered uncharitably if her onetime mistress had found another member of the staff to have midnight assignations with. But it didn't matter, really. There were plenty of witnesses to Carolina's total acceptance into the fold, and some of them might even cable their contacts in the newspaper business about it tomorrow. They were all her friends, or something nearly as good—they had to be nice to her, they had to have her on their little trips now. She was possessed of her own intrinsic social value, and none of their petty jealousies or little games could take that from her.

"Miss Carolina Broad?"

When the diminutive man in the bow tie said her name, Leland came to a stop. She realized that she was no longer dancing with the man who that afternoon had given her reason to anticipate a possible proposal, and then she felt herself,

however irrationally, beginning to hate this messenger, who was waiting patiently off to the side, and whatever it was he had to say to her.

"Yes?"

"You have a telegram."

"Well, give it to my maid, then," she replied brusquely, as if she were in the habit of receiving late-night telegrams, before moving back toward Leland. He waited for her beside the white latticework on the far side of the dance floor, which protected the guests from the view of the inner workings of the kitchen. There was a real grapevine climbing up it—Carolina had surreptitiously checked earlier in the evening.

"I did." The man paused, and there was something terrible in the way he hesitated over his next words. "She said that you should be summoned at once. She said you would want to respond immediately. Our correspondence room, where you may want to avail yourself of our telegraph, is on the first floor, just past the—"

A thousand harsh words for this man brimmed in her throat, but somehow none rose off her tongue. Carolina knew that the disappointment of being taken away from the center of things was humiliatingly obvious in her face, although when she looked at Leland she did attempt a brave smile. "I'm sure it's nothing," she managed.

"I hope so." Leland's features were so full of kindness

that she could not look at them. "Do you want me to accompany you?" he offered.

Whatever the news, some instinct told her that Leland must not hear it. She shook her head and turned to the man with the bow tie, who led her away from the dance floor, where everyone worth knowing and everything worth seeing would continue to go on without her. As she stepped back into the main lobby of the hotel, she looked at the elaborate pattern of the carpet and felt the horrible tightness of her high-heeled slippers with the little gold crests on the toe.

The correspondence room was all polished oak and gadgetry edged in gold. It was well, almost harshly, lit, and Carolina felt ungainly again beside the fastidious little man. He handed her the telegram, and for a moment she wished that she could hand it back and make it untrue. She wished she could return to the ballroom and go on dancing with Leland forever. But there was nothing that could undo the finality of what she read:

THE WESTERN UNION TELEGRAPH COMPANY

TO: *Carolina Broad*

ARRIVED AT: 25 *The Royal Poinciana,*
Palm Beach, Florida
2:00 a.m., Sunday, February 18, 1900

Carey Lewis Longhorn dead this evening after a short illness. His final request was your presence at his funeral—You must return to New York posthaste—I have purchased tickets for you and maid on the train 12 p.m. tomorrow—Upon arrival, discontinue her services.

Yours, Morris James, Esq.
Chief Executor of the Longhorn Estate

Carolina closed her eyes and folded the telegram. A long, cold shudder passed through her body. The events of the day, in all its illuminated perfection, seemed very far away now, but she couldn't help but realize what awfulness had passed while she was thinking highly of herself and dashing around in horseless carriages. Her memory was overwhelmed by the image of him, on the docks that day, and how very much he had wanted her to stay.

Then, just as quickly, her sadness gave way to another emotion. It seemed impossible that Longhorn could have expired so quickly, and for a moment she was angry that no one warned her of the possibility. But there was no one to blame, and no matter how her heart yearned for it, nothing Leland could do to save her from this. She tried to look as high and mighty as before, and told the man in the bow tie that she would need tea in her room, as there would be much packing to do.

Twenty Five

Men talk themselves into all kinds of trouble at the card table—that is the true reason that real ladies do not go to such places, ever.

—MRS. L. A. M. BRECKINRIDGE, *THE LAWS OF BEING IN WELL-MANNERED CIRCLES*

HE MUSIC OF THE ORCHESTRA COULD STILL BE heard in the little casino that was adjacent to the ballroom, and though the decorations were all of cheery, sporting green and white, the dark-suited men who crowded the tables gave it quite a different effect. They all had at least one thing in common, which was that they had had enough of dancing. Though for Henry, who bent to slap away some of the sand that still clung to his trousers, dancing was the least of the reasons he wanted to escape.

"Brother!"

Henry's eyebrows lifted, and the rest of him followed shortly thereafter. Grayson Hayes was sitting at a card table, and at some point in the last two hours his bow tie had come undone and his jacket had disappeared. There had been several hours that afternoon when Henry had hated nothing in the world as he hated Grayson, for he'd been flirting with Diana endlessly—*Henry's* Diana—and she had at times seemed to return his attentions. But he liked the man a little better as he was now—far from any women, his heart racing over a game instead of a fine figure.

Henry signaled to a passing waiter for a drink, and then pulled up a chair.

"Could you lend me twenty?" Grayson asked.

Henry couldn't help the droll smile that played at the edges of his mouth. He waited a moment before nodding to the dealer. "Charge it to my room," he said, and then fresh chips were produced. There was some fatigue beginning to show under Grayson's eyes, but the attentive hunch of his shoulders suggested he was many hours from bedtime yet. Henry crossed his legs and lit a cigarette.

"Where's Penny?" Grayson asked presently.

"I don't know." Henry had left her on the dance floor, but he was too consumed with the image of Diana half-drenched, her clavicles exposed in the moonlight, the silk sleeves of her dress clinging to the arms that had once hung around his neck so joyously. Henry's characteristic pose was one of stylish indifference, and he doubtless still looked like that now as he exhaled contemplatively. But he was, in truth, full of fire.

"She's smiling and explaining away your absence now, but she'll have your head later," Grayson said. "Oh, boy, drink up. I wouldn't want to be you tomorrow."

Henry's drink had arrived, and—knowing this last bit to be true—he took a healthy sip. "Who cares?" he muttered.

To his surprise, Grayson chuckled. "And she used to be such a *sweet* girl."

"Oh, I only meant—"

"Don't worry, Schoonmaker. And don't think I don't know she sometimes likes to pull the strings like some puppet master from hell." The hand ended, but Grayson's eyes had lost none of their animal quality. "Could you lend me another twenty?"

Henry waved his cigarette at the dealer in confirmation and finished his drink. He tried to discern the waiter, out there amongst all the other men in black and white, in order to request another drink. But the waiter had already seen him and was on his way, and after Henry had taken a sip of the fresh Scotch he felt loose enough to prod a bit.

"You seem awfully fond of Diana Holland."

Grayson was distracted by his hand, and Henry experienced a terrible moment when his words hung in the air without hope of a response. Eventually his brother-in-law looked over, revealing a sparkle in his eye. "She embodies all varieties of feminine beauty," he said, taking a cigarette from the box that Henry had left on the edge of the table and placing it for a moment between his broad front teeth. "She is perfection in a woman."

Henry's mind's eye filled, briefly, with the chaos that would ensue if he struck his brother-in-law across the jaw.

But then Grayson continued: "Her mother must have been strenuous in raising her, though. *There's* a door no man can crack. She's quite young, quite naïve, more protected even than her sister. I can't get so much as a kiss on the cheek out of her."

Henry's shoulders relaxed, and in celebration of this news he drained the contents of his sturdy glass. He circled his finger in the general direction of the waiter, indicating that he wanted drinks for his friend and himself as well. He knew that he should abandon the conversation there and then, but Diana was everywhere in his thoughts and on his tongue. "She *is* lovely . . ." he continued, almost to himself.

"Ah!" Grayson looked up at the ceiling fans and smiled to himself. "That pink skin. Those dreamy lashes."

Henry closed his eyes, and imagined the sweet, petulant woundedness with which she had stared at him on the beach. He felt a little proud that she could love him. "And she moves so gorgeously."

"I tell you, Schoonmaker, she doesn't know what she has. That's the heart of it. She's like some wild creature who hasn't a clue the worth of its coat." Grayson paused to up his bet and then assumed a philosophical tone. "Whoever wins her in the end will be a lucky man indeed."

More drinks arrived, and the colors in the room grew both brighter and less distinct for Henry. Grayson became engrossed in cards again, and asked to borrow more money, but the last thing he'd said about Diana had lodged itself in Henry's head and begun to put down roots. He lit another cigarette and thought on it, and also on his promise to her, and how he would keep it.

The arrangement of the furniture in the best suite in the Royal Poinciana had never seemed so treacherous. It was all blurry, low-lying forms, although the moonlight did glaze the tiled floor. Henry's eye followed the glittering reflection to the French doors, which were thrown open onto the terrace. The silvery trail ended in a fluted skirt of white chiffon dotted with black that was cinched at the waist and then spread over the bust and up to the shoulders dramatically, where the fabric was gathered with black ribbons. His wife was still wearing her long black gloves, although they had slipped somewhat at the elbows, and she had put all the weight of her long body against the voluptuous carved wood balustrade.

The sky was turning from purple to navy, and beyond Penelope the tops of the palms were just visible, like the unkempt heads of giants. The moon above her had grown hazy under the clouds, but still it glinted in her hair and on her bracelets. He hated her then, not just for having cost him so much, not just for all the hypocrisy and vanity and stupid greed she embodied, but because he had returned to her, even now, when all his being wanted to be elsewhere. He looked at her back—for she showed no signs of turning toward him— and imagined all the ways he might tell her he would leave. But his tongue was as useless as some mud-bound carriage.

Out on the terrace, Penelope remained still, except that she bent her ear toward her shoulder—it seemed to him that no gesture had ever contained such malicious self-possession. His mouth did open once or twice, but his anger had grown and sat in the way of words.

Now his feet were carrying him across the floor, his conscious mind trailing a few beats behind his heavy, drunken footsteps. He had seen how easy it would be. Without any words he could sidestep all the messy legal entanglements, all the cutting judgments of society. His wife was leaning carelessly there, four stories above the gravel walk, and if she leaned too far—trying to catch a glimpse of Lady Dagmall-Lister's bejeweled coiffure, say, or the flight of a parrot from one low branch to another—then she might stumble, lose balance, and fall to her death. Her neck would snap in painless seconds, and then she would have no way of preventing her husband from finally being with the girl he truly loved. The girl who was somewhere in those hundreds of rooms, believing his promise . . .

Henry had traveled across the room with forceful speed, removing his jacket as he did and dropping it on the tiles, but something stopped him at the threshold of the terrace. The warm outside air met him like a thick, damp curtain, and Penelope twisted to look at him. Her bottom lip quivered and the corners of her eyes turned down in sorrow. She watched him, and he watched her, and then he knew that the danger had passed. She had seen the idea in him, and now he recognized the full horror of it reflected in her eyes.

Henry gripped the doorframe, unsteady and panting a little, shocked by what he had discovered himself to be nearly capable of. The rich fabric of her dress was contorted around her long body, and even in the darkness she had the appearance of a woman who had seen too much.

Time passed, and then she said, "I don't blame you for wanting to kill me."

Her head swayed away, as heavy on her long neck as overripe fruit. A few of the short dark hairs on the back of her neck floated down, away from her coiffure and toward the clasp of the diamond and onyx necklace that she had had to buy for herself as a wedding present. Below them women in evening wear and festooned hairpieces were teetering through the Coconut Grove, a little worse for drinking, laughing just slightly too loud in response to the sweet lies of suitors who were growing generous with the waxing of the moon. Her shoulders slumped, and she gave him an imploring look, as though she would rather he'd just go ahead and do it.

"Penelope"—his voice broke over the name—"I could never—"

"Oh, Henry," she sighed. "No one would blame you."

A few moments ago he would have agreed, but he'd climbed some great summit and descended into an unfamiliar valley since then. "It would be . . . I'm sorry."

But she did not seem to hear him. She put her hand farther back on the balustrade, and leaned on it as though she were trying to better hear the faint music of the orchestra. Her position looked precarious, and he worried briefly that she might push herself over. He decided that he was close enough to stop her, but then he took a woozy step toward her and felt the floor wobble under his feet, and in the end nothing dramatic happened. She stood and gazed at Henry with those same aged eyes, and then she took a shaky breath and tried to smile bravely, once or twice, without ever quite succeeding.

"Well then," she said quietly. She moved back into the suite with woeful grace, leaving Henry alone on the terrace. He closed his eyes and allowed the relief of having not acted on that awful impulse to soften in him. His blood was still agitated about it, but he knew suddenly that he was very drunk, and that his already unreliable memory would soon subsume the incident into the realm of the forgotten.

He followed Penelope, although his pace was slower and less sure this time, all sorts of pathetic explanations sputtering in his head. Her hip rested on the edge of the bed, and her back was to him and bent forward in a poignant arch. He shuffled closer and sat down beside her, and when she still gave no acknowledgment of his presence, he put an awkward hand on her back. That was when he realized she was crying, for her body was just slightly racked by silent tears. He found he wanted nothing so much at that moment as to look into her face.

"Don't cry," he said. He had always felt unnerved when anyone cried, and since he was a child had been known to promise anything just to make somebody stop. But then she twisted around to face him and he saw the wetness already catching against her lower lashes.

There was something unbearable to him about seeing Penelope brought low, and to stop her from any more self-abnegations he put his mouth—so fragrant with drink—against hers. Neither moved for a long moment, and then she took his lower lip, very gently, between her teeth. He felt dizzy and charged with emotion. Then he pulled her against him, just as he had the summer they had spent together. His hands fluttered along her face and shoulders and down her back, where they began to undo her corset.

He had watched several corsets being removed over the

years, but had never done the work himself. All the hooks and ribbons presented a complicated puzzle, but despite his drunkenness—or perhaps because of it—he proceeded with great, plodding care. When, finally, the layers fell down around her waist she gave him a mysterious smile. Was it shyness, or gratitude, or some quality he had never seen before? The room was full of stars and Henry wondered for a moment if it hadn't come unmoored from the hotel and gone spinning off into the night. Then he told himself to smile back at her—he did so, a little sloppily, as he batted a leaf of hair back from his face— and moved to push her down into the sheets.

MANY OF OUR GUESTS LIKE TO DANCE
QUITE LATE, AND FOR YOUR CONVENIENCE
WE NOW HAVE OUR COBBLER SET UP
ALL NIGHT LONG. HE IS STATIONED IN THE
LOBBY, JUST BEYOND THE NEWSSTAND,
AND ALL LADIES ARE ENCOURAGED TO DROP
THEIR SLIPPERS THERE BEFORE THEY GO TO BED.

—THE MANAGEMENT,
ROYAL POINCIANA, PALM BEACH

THE WAVES WERE STILL BREAKING AGAINST THE shore, and over on the other side of Lake Worth, in West Palm Beach—the town that Henry Flagler had built for the help—everything had gone dark. But light still poured from the dance floor of the Royal Poinciana onto its manicured lawns. The hotel's guests were eating second suppers or howling in laughter or dancing far closer than they would have dreamed of doing in New York or Philadelphia or Washington, with partners they might not have considered in their regular lives. The music grew faster and some of the husbands snuck off to play cards at the adjacent casino. Then their wives started strutting with the waiters, and more bottles of wine were ordered. The first lavender fingerprints of dawn were visible on the horizon when Diana Holland looked around to make sure that the man who owned her heart was nowhere in sight.

"Did Mrs. Schoonmaker leave?" she asked the waiter with the pretty face and ample lips with whom she had danced the last few dances. She was in too good a mood not to dance, for she had seen her and Henry's whole life laid out in front of her, and it was going to be so lovely and intricate and fine.

"Does it matter?" The waiter grabbed her hand and twirled her back around so that she was facing him.

She laughed aridly and let her smile fade. But perhaps this recalibration of her attitude toward him was too subtle, because he cocked an eyebrow and went on looking at her as though she were a goddess come down from heaven on a cloud for his own personal delectation.

"I think she left a little while ago, by herself, with a sour expression on her face . . ." the boy said, catching his breath. Then he winked shamelessly.

Diana saw his intentions in a flash, and moved just aside of his approaching kiss. Then she yawned theatrically and let go of his hand.

"I'm so tired all of a sudden," she lied. Many of the other dancers were now retreating to the shadows of the room, and only a few wild-eyed guests were still flailing their limbs for all to see. It was a little improper, a small voice within her cautioned, to be up so late without a chaperone, and though she was proud of these touches of rebellion in herself, she wondered if caution might be the right path at this particular moment. But she was wearing a new dress, her skin was fresh and her heart full, and even now she didn't want to go to bed.

"Don't go." As he gazed at her, she couldn't help but acknowledge that it *had* been fun—and she was grateful that he had celebrated with her for a few hours. But her smiles were all for someone else, so she offered him a wan look and then slipped away.

She imagined that he stood there alone for several minutes wondering what he had done wrong. Of course the thing he had done wrong wasn't something he could possibly have helped, for it was the simple fact of him not being Henry. She felt strangely full of energy, thinking of how she had danced and of all the things she had seen. Once the morning was more advanced she would have to cable Barnard, and tell him how Lady Dagmall-Lister had spent the evening with a man half her age whom nobody had ever heard of, but who nonetheless knew all the dance steps, and how Henry Schoonmaker had abandoned his wife promptly after dinner.

And he had, Diana thought to herself as she walked across the wide planks of the hotel's porch, which was empty at that hour, and onto the vast lawn that was just touched with dew. She had abandoned a second pair of shoes on the dance floor, so this time she felt the wetness of the grass against the soles of her feet. Somewhere in that great structure, Henry was probably plotting how to annul his marriage, and perhaps he had already taken a small separate room, and maybe chance would draw her to it in the hours to come. . . .

Meanwhile, the light was growing brighter in the sky, and soon she would have to bathe and dress herself for another day of carefully coordinated leisure. The air was thick and still, even at that hour, and it smelled like nowhere she had ever been. With every footstep she felt that her whole life would be different now. All the details of the landscape were surreal and new to her; it was as though she had crossed over into some new stage of existence. For a long time she wandered underneath the palms, alone, and only when the sun was cresting the horizon and gold played along the waves did she turn back.

By that hour a new shift of hotel workers was making their way from the dormitories, which were hidden from the main building by a forest of banyan trees. They wore starched white shirts and black trousers and skirts and they looked away from Diana deferentially even though she wanted to smile at them. There was something wrong to her about seeing so many black people serving so few whites, and though she knew it wasn't slavery anymore, it seemed nearly as bad. And this was a grand hotel. She had heard that at some of the other places the guests took rides in little carriages that were pedaled by a servant, although the guests sat in front so that they could enjoy an unobstructed view. The idea revolted her.

Diana had been so lost in these thoughts that she had failed to notice where she was going, and found herself back at the vast lemon yellow building, with its little turrets and

ANNA GODBERSEN

gingerbread trimmings, with all its thrown-open shutters and terraces. It was a beautiful structure, she couldn't help but notice. Then she turned her chin and refocused her gaze. High above her a man naked from the waist up emerged on his terrace and looked out across the grounds. Diana blinked twice—his chest was almost golden and his hair was dark as black velvet, but he was on the fourth floor and so it took her several moments to realize that it was Henry.

My Henry, she thought as she moved forward, her footsteps crushing the grass. There was something starry and far away in his gaze and she couldn't help but imagine that he was thinking of her. She felt her lungs balloon with air and then she raised her arm to wave at him, forgetting for a moment all the room cleaners and busboys and bellhops and chefs streaming toward work behind her. Then her arm fell, and shortly thereafter all her hopeful emotions were extinguished.

For there, at Henry's side, was Penelope. Diana closed her eyes and told herself not to cry. When she opened them, Penelope was still there. She had come up behind Henry and draped her arms over his shoulders in a very familiar manner. She was wearing a robe and her silky brown hair fell all around her shoulders. It had been many years since Diana had seen Penelope without her hair in some immaculate arrangement, and the effect of disarray on her in this location, at just that moment, was both beautiful and terrible. The two people on

230

that terrace were far more sophisticated and far more know-ing than she would ever be, but one thing she was grown-up enough to see in them at that moment, despite all of Henry's protestations, was that they were a very intimate married couple indeed. Across the grounds of the Royal Poinciana everything was tranquil, but Diana Holland had been all torn to shreds.

There should have been no crying for a stupidity so grand and so prolonged. Diana had known what Henry was from the beginning, and it was only a wonder that she had believed what he said about his marriage to Penelope being loveless, or that things might have been different with her than they were with all his other paramours. Of course he had just been tell-ing her stories on the beach, of course he only wanted her as his mistress. Though if she had been a good girl and gone to bed, she would never have been the wiser. As it was, she now knew herself to be a fool of the first order.

Diana tripped forward idiotically in her long skirt—the employees of the Poinciana no doubt staring perplexedly at this young girl running around in an evening dress at dawn—hoping to find some very private place to hide herself before she began to truly break down.

Marriage is a mystery that one would be wise not to solve too hastily.

—MAEVE DE JONG, *LOVE AND OTHER FOLLIES OF THE GREAT FAMILIES OF OLD NEW YORK*

$\mathcal{T}$HE LIGHT OF EARLY MORNING WAS COMING IN through the French doors of what every guest and bellhop knew to be the best suite in the Royal Poinciana, where Penelope leaned back into the small mountain of champagne-colored pillows and felt entirely new. She stretched her long arms over her head and crossed her narrow ankles. Who knew that the way to Henry's heart was through his murderous instinct? She did, now, and was planning on manipulating his guilt as much as possible. He hadn't scared her, not for very long anyway, and afterward she knew she had him. She didn't care anymore whether or not the other guests witnessed them together. Let the Hollands and Miss Broad and all the other fine people at the hotel speculate on the conspicuous absence of the Henry Schoonmakers instead—that would be much more satisfying.

"Henry?" she called.

There was no answer, only the breeze pressing the Irish lace curtains against the glass panes of the open door. She stood and wrapped herself in the robe, pulling the last pins out of her hair from the night before and throwing them on the polished walnut nightstand. She sighed happily and proceeded across the vast room. Her movements were light and filled with a new contentedness, for in one evening, months of scheming and climbing, of unreturned affection, had at last been validated. They were now truly man and wife.

"Henry," she said again as she stepped onto the terrace. His back was to her, and for a moment she gazed at him in silhouette, his broad shoulders against the tableau of palm trees, the carefully trimmed lawns, the ocean glittering with the light of the rising sun. It was early, she thought—there was still so much left of this wondrous day. Then she moved forward and let one arm and then the other rest on Henry's shoulders. "What ever are we going to do today?"

There was nothing sudden about what he did next. He took her wrists in his hand, first one and then the other, and plucked her arms away from his skin—but ever so slowly, ever so gently. In another moment he'd turned and his expression told her that he was five hundred miles away.

"It was a mistake," he said as he dropped her wrists.

Penelope tried to regain the vulnerability that she had used to such great effect the night before. The glow she had felt moments ago was beginning to fade, but not quickly enough to look truly stricken and needy. "You mean—"

"All of it." He set his thin lips together, as though putting a stern end to whatever compassion lingered inside.

"But Henry—"

"Last night, the wedding."

"—just think how much *fun* we had last night. Just stay with me now, and we'll have more fun!"

Henry shook his head sadly. "You know very well why I married you, since it was all your idea and your brute force. You can't be surprised now if I want nothing to do with you." His gaze dropped away from her, and she realized that at the very least it was with great difficulty that Henry uttered these words. "I need to think." He rolled his eyes toward the pink sky. "I am very sorry, but I can't stay with you now."

When he turned away and moved back toward the room, Penelope felt all the rage and fear rise within her like a towering wave that might drown them all. Henry paused once and looked back. His black eyes darted up and down at her for a moment and then he spoke with pained emphasis. "I *am* sorry."

Somehow all this careful, distanced kindness was worse than any slap. Penelope's hand fluttered to her chest pathetically, but already he had turned and was walking across the Spanish tiles at a fast clip. A moment later she followed, her pride inflamed but her head still relatively cool. If she could garner some time, some information, perhaps the worst wouldn't come to pass. "What are you going to do?"

"I am going to go to Teddy's room and I will dress there. Then we're going fishing, which was the original purpose of this trip." Henry was picking up his clothes from the night before. He pulled the sleeves of the rumpled shirt over his arms and then stepped into his shoes. It was perfectly obvious to Penelope that he was avoiding meeting her eyes, and she wondered what he was afraid of seeing in them. "And then, when we get back to New York, I am going to find a way to leave you. I'm not sure how yet, but I can't stay in this absurd joke of a marriage any longer."

"What about your little Di?" Penelope moved toward him, her voice reaching a frightening pitch. She knew it sounded like shrieking, but she couldn't help herself, not when everything she'd ever strived for was slipping through her fingers.

"What about her?" Now he did meet her eyes, and she saw that his were fatigued, and a little sad, and washed out by some new maturity that one way or another made his gaze that much more piercing.

"If you love her so much, I wonder that you aren't worried about what will happen when everyone knows she played the whore with you." She was hurling her words now, her mouth constricting unattractively around every sentence. "It would be my pleasure to tell them, Henry."

Henry's black tuxedo jacket fell from his hands, but his

eyes remained level in her direction. "I doubt that," he said. His voice was tentative at first, but when he spoke again it had gained strength and momentum and an angry edge. "I doubt that when you begin to experience the humiliation of being turned out of the Schoonmaker mansion, you will want to add to it by letting everyone know that your husband never loved you, and was already thinking of someone else before you were even married."

Henry paused to draw his clenched fist across his mouth—for he had spit, just a little, when he spoke. Penelope's eyes were the least cool blue they had ever been. What he'd said was true. She had flinched, and she knew that he had seen it.

"You wouldn't want to test me, Henry."

There was no answer, only a moment that felt to her like it might go on forever. But it did end, at last, when he bent and picked up his jacket—successfully, this time. He gave her one final hard look, and then he turned and began to move away from her. She took one halting step forward, but he was already headed for the door.

Then he was gone, leaving her alone in her sumptuous robe, her hair all undone, the careful architecture of her plan for them flattened. She wanted to smash things up, but was uncharacteristically restrained by the realization that none of the objects in that large and lavish room belonged to her.

Before her angry impulses got the better of her, she admonished herself that she was born to win and that one did not win by throwing temper tantrums—at least not outside of one's own home, which could result in vicious, spurious rumors. But oh, how she wanted to destroy things, when so much had been destroyed for her.

Twenty Eight

And what of the famous friendship between Miss Elizabeth Holland and the woman who married her former fiancé, the former Miss Penelope Hayes? The two have repaired to Palm Beach together, but of course none of us can see what they do there. . . .

—FROM *CITÉ CHATTER*, SUNDAY, FEBRUARY 18, 1900

THE GIRL IN THE MIRROR LOOKED PALE AND PUFFY, but Elizabeth tried to take a few deep breaths and regain some of the good feelings that she had experienced yesterday. She would have liked to find Teddy and go to breakfast with him, but after his almost-proposal of the night before, she knew she had better stay away. The warm air should still have been doing her good, as should the change of scenery. But there was a rough current inside of her and a sour streak of bile down her throat, and though she wanted very badly to feel contained and in control before leaving the bathroom of her hotel room, another part of her believed she deserved to feel terrible, and anyway she was on the verge of heaving all over again. She wavered there in the white-tiled room; she pinned back a few loose blond wisps and closed her eyes. When she opened them again there was only the same sad, heart-shaped face and a whole day of sun worship that she hardly had the energy for.

She stepped down into the main space of the little room, and was immediately aware of a hostile presence there.

Penelope looked up from the scroll-edged settee, with its pol-ished dark wood and white cushion, and gave her old friend a hard look. A moment later her red lips sprang into a smile. She looked oversized, too large for the room, which the Schoon-makers had reserved for them and paid for and which was far, far smaller than their own suite. That much was obvious from Penelope's lengthy and loving descriptions of the rooms that she and Henry occupied; she belonged there now, Elizabeth thought, not in the narrow second-floor quarters where the Holland sisters slept.

"Good morning, dear Liz," Penelope said brightly.

Elizabeth's gaze shifted to Diana, who had returned from the party after she herself had fallen asleep, and who was now safely ensconced under a pile of white bed linens on one of the two twin beds with the yellow silk upholstered head-boards. She had tossed restlessly in the sheets throughout the night, but had not yet given any sign of waking. The mosquito netting was only partially down and her lavender dress, which had been lying on the floor an hour ago, was now hanging in the closet. Elizabeth had put it there after vomiting for the first time that morning; afterward she had carefully made up her own bed.

"Good morning." She closed her eyes in an attempt to weather the storm of nausea that was coming over her. "How did you sleep?"

"Oh, well enough. What are you doing today? Would you like to go horseback riding with me?" After these staccato statements, Penelope rolled her eyes and let out a sigh that might have pierced steel. "I'm bored of this place already," she added hatefully.

"Bored already?" Elizabeth was biding her time, repeating what Penelope said in the hope that it would distract her friend long enough that she could form a coherent and polite rejection.

"Everyone is so simpleminded down here, and there is so little to do. It's like being an animal in a zoo, with enforced feeding hours and the constant indignity of display. They're all looking at me—*us*—all the time. We should never have left New York. But as long as we're here, we could get some exercise."

"I don't know—"

"Oh, come *on*, Liz. You're my oldest friend." Penelope leaned forward, sinking her elbows into the voluminous burgundy skirt she wore. "My *best* friend. Entertain me, *please*."

Elizabeth regarded Penelope, who was very neatly done up in white chiffon sleeves, her lap covered in silk the color of crushed rose petals, with a black sash marking the narrow isthmus of her waist. Her hair was layered above her forehead, shiny and dark, like a crown. What trouble did that immaculate veneer obscure, Elizabeth wondered, before she nodded her acquiescence. She was too weak to be contrary with her hostess.

"Oh, goody!" Penelope exclaimed as she stood and clapped her hands. "But you're not going to wear that, are you?"

"No, I—" Elizabeth had to put her hand against the wall to support herself. Her slender form was racked again. She placed her other hand on the plain white cotton bodice of her dress and closed her eyes. She was about to tell Penelope that she needed just a few minutes, but then she realized that she wasn't going to make it that long. She spun and hurried to the bathroom on weak legs. Her knees hit the floor and she gripped the wall as she heaved. The contents of her stomach were few, and what came up came quickly.

"Are you all right?"

Elizabeth turned to see Penelope's narrow figure in the doorframe.

"My God," Penelope added unhelpfully.

Elizabeth drew her hand across her mouth and tried to look dignified. "Yes, I will be in a minute. I just . . . took the traveling poorly, is all. There was the motion sickness and now . . ."

She trailed off, remaining for the moment in a heap on the floor. She would have stood with greater pride and readiness if she thought she could have managed it, but her legs were useless beneath her. Then her old friend extended a hand to help her up. It was an unlikely gesture, and Elizabeth didn't know what else to do but accept it.

When she was on her feet again, Penelope stepped away and crossed her arms over her chest. She studied the other girl without animosity or coldness, but with a notable lack of compassion. "I don't think that's motion sickness that you've got," she said eventually.

"What ever do you mean?" Elizabeth—finally, thankfully—was able to summon the old smile. She was feeling a little steady now, and she parted her lips to show Penelope just a little bit of teeth. They were standing very close to each other on those small, hexagonal tiles, and she knew that Mrs. Schoonmaker was taking in every detail of her appearance.

"Well," Penelope answered airily, "you can call it whatever you like. But if you want my opinion—and you really ought to—I'd say you're expecting."

A soft wind blew in through the little window, tickling the nape of Elizabeth's neck. Fear began to grip her like vines, starting at her toes and climbing up through her whole body. "That isn't possible," she whispered hoarsely.

One of Penelope's neatly shaped eyebrows elevated itself. She held Elizabeth's gaze and then shrugged, before turning away and leaving the bathroom. "Maybe horseback riding isn't the best idea just now. Let's play croquet instead, shall we?"

Back in the bedroom, Diana began to stir under the

blankets, and when she'd successfully pushed the curls off of her sleepy face she looked aghast at the visitor in their room. Elizabeth was by then possessed by the idea that she show Penelope how very normal everything was, how very wrong she had been about the illness, and so she smiled reassuringly at her younger sister. "Mrs. Schoonmaker and I are going to play croquet," she said, as though this were the most normal thing in the world. Then she took a glass of water from the tray by the door, and gulped.

Already the door was open, and she could hear the sounds of breakfast being delivered out in the hall. "Oh," Diana said before rolling back under the covers. If Elizabeth had not felt so wretched herself, she might have noticed how deathly her little sister's appearance was. "Please be careful."

"Of course." Elizabeth smiled a lofty smile and thought to herself, *That's precisely what I'm doing.* She could feel her control again, retuning to her with every passing second, giving her just a little extra height and glow. She was going to need every ounce of it to keep Penelope from growing sure of what she already seemed to believe.

The two girls stepped onto the croquet field, affecting their old closeness and confidence, and they spoke with great exactitude over many small and petty things. The blonde smiled, and the brunette smiled back, and they held their hats elegantly when the breeze picked up and tilted the landscape away from the sea, rearranging their skirts. Elizabeth made sure to play a good game, but not to win, and when they were through she insisted on a rematch with a certain ladylike gusto. All the while she held her shoulders high and casually, though she could not stop herself from once or twice resting her hand on her belly and wondering what she carried there.

Twenty Nine

DIED, Longhorn, Carey Lewis, Saturday evening after a short illness. The last of a great family and a notable man about town. He left no survivors, but a great fortune. Services will be held today at his residence in the New Netherland Hotel. In lieu of flowers, donations may be made to the Society for Young Girls Orphaned by Fire.

—FROM THE OBITUARY PAGE OF THE *NEW YORK IMPERIAL*, WEDNESDAY, FEBRUARY 21, 1900

HE VIEW FROM THE NEW NETHERLAND WAS stark and entirely lacking in reassurance. Carolina remembered spending many evenings looking out at that huge swath of park, with its wealth of trees, imagining that it was the backyard of her benefactor, and therefore very nearly hers. When she'd closed her eyes, she had believed that if she fell back into it, it would catch her gently, the way a feather-bed might. The truth of the matter was as unadorned as all those bare branches down there, as simple as the ice gray sky. None of it belonged to her, and whether or not it had ever belonged to Mr. Longhorn didn't matter now. He was gone and he couldn't help her anymore. With that in mind, she turned from the window.

"Miss . . . Broad." The second syllable was pronounced with great skepticism, the way an anarchist might have used the phrase "Newport cottage" when referring to those sixty-four-room mansions that faced the Rhode Island shoreline. Carolina blinked furiously. Mr. James wore thick muttonchops and large black lapels and was shaped like a pear. He had a manner that might have unnerved generals; it certainly unnerved her.

"Yes?"

"A word about the jewels."

Over his massive shoulder, she could see the last mourners taking leave. Robert stood—sadly, but also warily—by the table of cold cuts and pickles, which had lain out for several hours now and just barely been picked at. There had been few visitors, most of them women who had once upon a time hoped for the crown of Mrs. Longhorn, and this only increased Carolina's suffering. For he had asked her so plaintively to stay with him, and she had shaken him off and left him to die alone.

"The jewels, Miss Broad?"

Carolina batted the moisture away from her eyes and tried to look wounded. She *felt* wounded, but still there was this urgency to put on a face that could be clearly read as dolorous. "What jewels?"

Mr. James waved a stack of receipts at her. "Seems Longhorn purchased a lot of jewels over the last six months of his life." His eyes widened threateningly. "Those belong to the estate."

"Mr. Longhorn purchased a lot of jewels over his lifetime," Carolina snapped back. She was experiencing a tingle of dread, but still her voice was hard. "You can't hold me accountable for all of them, and anyway, the ones he bought with me in mind were gifts."

"They were on loan to you," Mr. James returned firmly. He waved the receipts. Across the room, blue afternoon light played against the finials and crests of antique furniture and washed out the gold threads in the upholstery. "We own them."

"I wonder how you'll get them, since he *gave* them to me." There was nothing Carolina could do about the insolent look on her face. The anger had come back, the way it always did when she knew something was going to be unjustly taken from her and that there was nothing she could do to stop it. It had not served her well as a child or as a lady's maid, and it was unlikely to serve her well now, but it was a reflex she could hardly control. "Or perhaps you're planning on dragging every woman Longhorn ever took a grandfatherly interest in into court."

"I highly doubt you want to go to court, my dear." Mr. James's lips were full and moist, and though her ire was strong as ever she found she had to look away from him. "And my people are over in your rooms now, packing your things. They'll put what you need in some of the bags nobody has any use for. The jewels we will be taking custody of—your maid told us where they would be."

The volume of her black skirt, with its tiered ruffles below

the knee, made her instinctual response to this undetectable:
She stamped her foot—twice, silently—against the polished
wood floor. All the guests were gone now, and across the room
men from Mr. James's office were moving to wrap up what finery remained and cart it off. Soon all the parties, the whole life
Mr. Longhorn lived there, would be scrubbed away. She saw
clearly what she had half-consciously feared during her train
journey: This game was over. She saw, too, why Mr. James had
been so conscientious in seeing her to the graveyard; so that he
could have his staff go through her things while she watched,
through a black net veil, Mr. Longhorn being lowered into
the ground.

"I don't think this is how he would have wanted it," she
said quietly. It was the truth, though she knew very well that
it mattered not at all to the gentleman lawyer.

"Well, if you like, you may come hear the will being read
next week. Maybe there will be some special compensation
for you. But if you ask me—and I am usually paid quite handsomely for advice of this kind—I'd say you've gotten away
with quite enough already."

Carolina left the New Netherland carrying far fewer possessions than she'd arrived with and badly in need of some

company. Neither Penelope nor Leland would do, and not only because both were still in Florida. The former was pledged to help her, but she was still not exactly the kind of friend you wanted to show your weaknesses to; and the latter could never know how dependent on Longhorn she had been—she wouldn't allow that. He knew of course that the old man had looked after her, but she had explained that this was because Longhorn and her father had been great friends, and that she lived off her own inherited income. As she left the hotel and watched her two beaten black trunks loaded into a hansom cab, she couldn't help but think of the one person in New York who knew perfectly well what she was.

She gave the driver a downtown address and refused to look out the window as they passed out of the charmed avenues and into the dingy old world. Outside it was all humdrum skyline, a gaggle of disappointing faces, a barrage of bold advertisements trying to convince everyday New Yorkers that their lives really would be different if they bought some cheap hair product or other that she now knew to be beneath her. There was no answer when she rang the bell on that faraway street, which she had visited only once before, and so she paid the driver a little extra out of her dwindling cash, and sat waiting in the seat with her black silk ladies' top hat tipped forward over her profile.

They had taken many of her gowns away and most of the

jewels, although there were a few items that fit her so perfectly that even sour Mr. James saw no point in stealing them. She still had her pride and her name, she told herself as she bent forward over the hard seat—however serendipitously come by, it was hers now. But even that small gift seemed to diminish as she waited and waited on the cobblestone street. The driver was growing impatient, she knew, and she wondered if maybe it wasn't time to move on, when the face appeared in the glass.

"Miss Carolina Broad!" he said, as though there were no one he would rather have happened upon. Her face turned hopelessly to sunshine. She couldn't wait, as she knew a real lady would, for the driver to come around and open the door for her. Already her gloved fingers were pressing down on the handle and she was spilling out onto the street.

"Tristan!" she cried as she threw her arms around his neck.

"And to what do I owe this honor?" he asked, as he pried her away just enough to get a look at her.

"Oh, Tristan, it's the most terrible . . ." she began. Now that she was with someone who'd always looked at her with such gilded intention and given so freely of his advice, she believed she might be able to let her guard down. Even though the air was still biting—Tristan's neck was protected by a thick, brown scarf—she began to feel a little warm. She wanted to show him all the sadness and anxiety and indignity of the day, and was grateful to him for even small things, like the fact that he knew her name.

"Will you come up for some tea?" he interrupted, after a good deal of babbling on her part.

Carolina let her sage-colored eyes roll ashamedly to the ground. "I have a few bags . . ." she said in a more tentative tone than before. The last time she'd been without a home, she had felt stupid and cloddy. She was only a little surprised that this time she was able to wear her distress like loveliness, and she imagined that she must be as delicate and fine as some rose petal veined with color that has just been picked off by the breeze.

Tristan's body was lean and strong, and he moved with assurance and purpose. She couldn't help but take a little pleasure in the fact that he was now instructing the driver to help him with her bags, and leading them up the narrow wood floors to the small flat he kept. It seemed neater and more welcoming this time, and when she felt the strong blast of the radiator she realized how cold she had been.

Tristan tipped the driver and gave Carolina a devilish smile as he took her coat from her. She had meant to mention, somewhere in all this, that she had met Leland Bouchard and was in love with him. But she hadn't done so by the time he put on the water and poured her a spot of brandy to warm

her up. Then it felt too late, and anyway, the natural thing to do when he turned and gave her well-fitting black silk dress an appreciative look was to lean forward, put her hand into his wayward blond hair, and press her lips against his.

Thirty

My Di—

I am thinking of you always,

and when we'll be together.

How soon that will be.

But in the meantime, keep your

wits about you, and act like

everything is normal.

Love,

H

THE WATER WAS FINE, THOUGH DIANA WASN'T, AND she swam out without looking back. The women in hats and stockings clinging to the rope that extended out to sea took no notice of her, and went on shrieking as though the ocean contained some perpetual surprise. For Diana, there were no surprises—the ocean went up and down, it carried you in and out. She felt soothed, a little, by the repetitious rocking, although she had an almost inexhaustible need for solace just then, which no act of nature could fulfill. Three days had passed since she had seen Henry on the balcony with his wife, and she had kept quiet since then, and thrown all of Henry's notes into the waves. It had been an awful thing to lose Henry the first time, to matrimony, but to discover what a false front he was capable of was another kind of blow, and it had left her almost speechless. Then there was the fury with herself—for she had known what Henry's love was, and still she had gone back to suffer a little more at his hands.

She floated on her back and paddled aimlessly, and the

shouting from shore grew indistinct. The beach cabanas and umbrellas were far away, and the hotel, with its place settings and carpets and lawn games and bicycles, farther still. Grayson was sitting in the sand, waiting beside her wicker chair, but he wasn't in much of a mood for high excitement, either. He followed her dutifully, but some of the recklessness had left him, and he seemed to have run out of things to say. Whenever she turned to him she was met only by great, sad, yearning eyes. Meanwhile, Henry seemed to believe everything was as it had been between them, and she was playing along with his game. Diana had directed whole scenes in her head, imagining what it would be like to confront Henry, and all the witty, devastating insults she would hurl at him. But another part of her wondered if she would have the chance. Perhaps he would go on sending her little notes forever, never noticing how hard her heart was to him, and the only difference would be that they would have returned to New York and she would have to put them in the fire.

Meanwhile, she'd grown trusting of the ocean, and in the midst of her contemplations a wave picked her up and then buried her under its arm. She had to swim hard to get back to the surface, and when she did she shook the water and the bright sun from her eyes. She kicked to keep her head up and pushed the hair back from her face. Then she blinked, trying to see in the light again, and realized that Henry was bobbing a few feet away from her. His eyes were attentive, and his sharp shoulders just emerged from the water.

"Are you all right?" he said, paddling toward her. But there was a smile secreted in his concern, and she knew he was proud of having found her like this. "Say, nice spot you found here."

"I'm fine." She gave him a steady, unkind look, and began to swim away.

"Diana, I think I've realized something about—what's wrong?"

"Are you asking what's wrong with me?"

"Yes. . . ." He paddled toward her. "You seem . . ."

For a moment, it was too vast and terrible to put into words, but she felt another wave come on, and this saved her from any silence or outburst. She ducked under it and held her breath, and when she came back up she looked for Henry. She was ready to get out of the water, and as soon as she told him where things stood, she could.

She spun around, and when her sun-spotted vision settled on the place where Henry surfaced, she said, "I saw you."

"You saw me swimming out to find you?" he asked. Then he looked over his shoulder, as though he feared some other witness.

Diana's legs and arms worked to keep her afloat, and she breathed in gulps. "I saw you and Penelope on the terrace of your suite, and so I know that all those stories you told me about there being no love between you, and all the lies about leaving her, were just as false as every sweet song you ever sang me."

A few seconds passed before Henry appeared to comprehend what she'd said, and then he cried out, "No!" He swam closer to her and tried to reach for her arms, but she floundered away. His fingertips grazed her skin, and she sensed a kind of desperation in them. "You don't understand what you saw. I mean that it's not what it seemed. I *am* going to leave her, I told her—"

"There's nothing between us anymore, Henry." This line had occurred to Diana in the hour after she realized his deception, and she had thought it to herself and even whispered it in the mirror hundreds of times since. She had no idea how she would wince when she finally had to say it to him, and she was relieved to feel the water swell under her with the current. "We're quite done," she added, as though that finalized things.

In the next moment another wave crashed over them, and it sent her wheeling head over heels back toward shore. She didn't fight this one. She let it drag her in. When she could feel the sand below her, she stuck her feet in, and then she began staggering out of the water. She was unsteady at first, but she kept on bravely and didn't look back.

Thirty

One

My spy at the Royal Poinciana, where many of our brightest New Yorkers have been enjoying the sun, has gone silent. The last note informed that Diana Holland has been paid much attention by her sister's former fiancé's new wife's brother, and that the young lady would seem to be blushingly returning his affections. . . .

—FROM THE "GAMESOME GALLANT" COLUMN IN THE *NEW YORK IMPERIAL*, WEDNESDAY, FEBRUARY 21, 1900

*I*T WAS THE HOUR WHEN THE WOMEN WENT UP TO their rooms to dress for dinner and the sky went from tedious blue to a kind of fireworks. All along the wide veranda of the hotel, fathers and husbands and brothers drank afternoon cocktails and reclined in the large rattan chairs in the fading orange and purple light. They folded newspapers across their knees and accepted telegrams on silver trays. They smoked cigars and talked about the golfing and the hunting and the driving they had done that day and, in lower tones, how the markets back in town were doing. Down on the far end, leaning against the white wood railing so that he would be least seen, Henry was trying to get drunk in a hurry all by himself.

There was little else for him to enjoy. Days had gone by in Florida, each one like the last. He was formal with his wife in public, and avoided being with her in private. He watched Diana laugh with Grayson Hayes and go off to the beach with him after breakfast. Now he knew she no longer hoped for him, and he felt the full idiotic weight of his many missteps. He had known that morning, after having been with Penelope, that he was a fool, but until a few hours ago he'd believed that Diana would never find out about it. Moreover, he'd seen that look on Penelope's face when he'd called her bluff—she could no longer ruin Diana as she'd once threatened. Her own reputation was too much at stake. But that was a precious insight that he couldn't use now. It was useless to him, just like every other pointless thing in the whole pointless world.

He had taken for granted his own smoothness and taste, his ability to discriminate and have his pick. It was an unhappy realization that when something mattered, when he actually cared, he was a hopeless boor tripping over himself and destroying everything in his path. That morning, before Diana had told him how much was changed in her, it hadn't been so bad to see her in Grayson's company. But he'd made the mistake of reading the society columns over one of the other gentlemen's shoulders, and it had confirmed his worst fears.

"Henry!"

Even the sound of his own name irritated him, although he did glance up dutifully in time to see Teddy approaching over the rim of his julep. Teddy was already wearing his dinner jacket, and, unlike Henry's, his tie was neatly in place. Henry was wearing a dress shirt of fine Italian linen, although he had forgotten his cuff links and left the top two buttons undone. He sipped from his glass and grimaced a little, even though there was no one else whose intrusion he could have tolerated at that moment.

"Henry," Teddy said again, when he had crossed the thick boards of the porch and reached his friend's chosen column. "Where have you been hiding?"

Henry shifted his black eyes away from the Coconut Grove, where a few women who had completed their post-tea transformation were strolling with men they thought were in love with them. There were a lot of flounces and parasols being twirled idly, and he couldn't stand any of it. "I wasn't hiding—I just haven't had the stomach for the party anymore."

"I know just what you mean," Teddy replied.

"I doubt that," Henry said darkly. He was being ridiculous, he knew, but Teddy had long suffered Henry's silly behavior, and that was too old a habit to change now. He didn't, anyway, seem to mind too much.

A waiter appeared, and Teddy gestured at Henry's drink. "Two more, please."

"You might as well order four—that man takes forever," Henry muttered, although the waiter was by then already gone. He waved his hands lethargically, as though the futility of every little thing was too great a problem to get very worked up about.

"I am tired of it, and I think my reasons are not so different from yours."

Henry looked at his friend slantwise, and noticed for the first time the furrows above his brow. "Oh?" was all he managed. He was sure that Teddy's reasons could not be half as devastating as his own.

"Yes." Teddy's tone was firm as he looked out toward the sea, and for a moment the orange light of sunset was reflected in his gray eyes. It made them look washed out and much older than he was. "I think I'm going to give it up for a while."

Henry, who had been experiencing his life as though it were a well that he was at the bottom of, was irritated by this turn of phrase. "Give it up?" he returned ironically. That would be easy enough for Teddy, he supposed, who had finished college and managed not to get himself married.

"You'll be all right without me," Teddy replied with a rueful smile.

"You're serious?"

"Oh, completely so." The waiter appeared with their drinks, and both men turned toward the porch railing and looked out contemplatively for a moment. The light was still blazing on the grounds, and it reflected on both heads of slicked hair. Henry's jaw worked as he anticipated his friend's response. "I'm going to war."

"To *war*?" Henry found that he was too stunned to sip.

"Yes, I'm joining the army." Perhaps because Henry went on staring at him with incredulous, bulging eyes, Teddy added: "I was in the cadets in prep school."

Henry had to look away. They had gone to the same prep school, but he couldn't remember his friend doing anything like that. "But where—?"

"I hope to become an officer and to see action in the Philippines. I've already written to my father's contacts at Fort Hamilton, and hope to enlist as soon as I return to New York. I can't wait for tomorrow—I'm going to be leaving tonight, after dinner."

This all sounded hopelessly far away to Henry, and he could not help but look appalled. Just thinking about it made his skin crawl under his shirt. He considered several more profound responses, something like "My God" or "Bravo." What he did finally say was: "But you could *die*."

Teddy put his elbows against the rail and leaned forward. "Of course I could die." He clutched his drink and smiled a little. "But I can't stay here forever, staring appreciatively at the new girls in the latest dresses and drinking from four in the afternoon till four in the morning. No, that would be a poor use of a life. I don't want to hide from danger—that's not what it means to be a man. I don't think so, anyway. To look in the face of hard things and keep moving forward—that's what one has to do."

It was not lost on Henry that what Teddy described as a poor use of a life was more or less *his* life. But he found that he was not insulted. He was rather affected by the phrasing, in fact, and so only half-listened to what Teddy said next.

"I've been speaking to that lovely creature you were engaged to once, Elizabeth Holland, and I find she makes me want to search out the profundity in things. She is so tiny and frail, and yet she came back from harrowing experiences, and seems no longer to tolerate frivolities. How could she, now, when she knows what it is to be alive as we do not?"

Teddy paused to put his hands over his face. Henry might have wondered if his friend wasn't stricken by impossible love, too, if he had not so quickly changed the subject.

"Anyway, it's a young country. And I want to be responsible to it, to its interests and its standing in the world. If not me, who, Henry? I am a good leader; I know how to explain men to themselves."

They both pressed their elbows against the wood rail and gazed out. The atmosphere was warm and full of virtually imperceptible disturbances that caused the palm fronds to rise and fall as though they were sighing. Henry was thinking of the younger Holland sister, of the way she could go from being an impetuous girl to a knowing woman in a few seconds and never lose the stars in her eyes, and of how his life had seemed to him when he'd believed he had her. Surely that was not a waste.

Then Teddy hung his head, and in a slightly different voice, went on: "Perhaps when I come back I will deserve the life I want."

The women in their ruffles were heading back toward the hotel, emerging from the palms like whitefish in a stream and heading up the stairs. Down the veranda, the sound of greetings and high heels on wood planks rang out; it was dinnertime, and no one could hide now. First Teddy and then Henry pushed away from the railing and finished their drinks. Henry clapped a hand on his friend's shoulder as they joined the crowd.

"I'll miss you," Henry said. "You had better not really get killed."

"The same goes for you," Teddy replied lightly. "On both counts."

Henry chuckled agreeably, and thought to himself that there was no need to worry. He had made the situation with Diana very bad indeed, but he was beginning to see the glimmer of a chance that he could fix it. Teddy was right. Life was a short window, and there was no sense in doing the wrong thing over and over even if it was so difficult to stop. When they got back to New York it would be all different for Teddy and different for him as well, and he would be very careful to

do the right thing and not get killed by his wife or himself or by anybody else. There was something to live for, after all, if only he could keep his sights fixed on it.

She was coming up the stairs on the arm of Grayson Hayes, wearing a dress of ecru tiered eyelet and a vast hat, and though she wouldn't meet his eyes, he still felt her loveliness in his knees. He didn't mind that she was on Grayson's arm anymore, and the thing he had done to her had to be faced. There was plenty of life left, and if he had to, he would use it all to get her back. The time had passed for making promises to her—all that was left for him was to act.

Thirty Two

Always stay sharp on railways and cruise ships, for transit has a way of making everything clear.

—MAEVE DE JONG, *LOVE AND OTHER FOLLIES OF THE GREAT FAMILIES OF OLD NEW YORK*

*T*HE GUESTS OF THE SCHOONMAKER PARTY—WHAT was left of them, anyway—took the same elegant private car back to New York, although they were far quieter and more subdued on the return trip. Penelope remained frozen in her seat, imperturbable and still despite the jerks and shakes of the train. The light came through the window in lively stripes, but her face remained unchanged, her eyes fixed on the carpet at her feet or at her husband, who sat opposite her. He wore a cream-colored shirt, which she had given to him, and his black trouser–covered legs were crossed. He was reading a volume of poems, a thing she had never known him to do, and he did not bring his eyes to meet hers even once. When he had to speak to her he looked at her knees. She was still suffering from that horrid, choked feeling that had been stifling her ever since her husband had rejected her in the hotel suite, and she was having difficulty finding a reason to do much of anything. Though he had been civil to her since their confrontation, and she was beginning to doubt his resolve to leave her, she could not bring herself to feel triumphant.

Even getting dressed that morning had brought her no pleasure, and now Penelope was paying for it in a mauve linen day dress that was perfectly in style but did not—she knew—show off her best features. Or not exactly suffering, because she felt so blank that even that didn't really matter. She slumped, in heaps of mauve, and managed to gaze a little farther down the aisle, where the Holland sisters sat cozily beside each other.

Diana drowsed on her sister's shoulder, her face as soft and pink as a little cherub. *A very young cherub*, thought Penelope. *A very irksome one.* Elizabeth, who was only partially visible to her, stared out the window, very much awake, as though she were contemplating the end of man. For the first time, Penelope wondered if Liz truly was carrying the dead stable boy's child. In the hotel, she had mostly suggested this possibility out of a desire to say something as nasty as she felt. But now Elizabeth was looking so stone-faced that Penelope wondered if it weren't the case.

The other sister, meanwhile, looked as though she hadn't a care in the world. Her face tilted upward toward the light in her sleep, her dark curls falling gently across her rosy skin. As far as Penelope could tell, Grayson had succeeded only in tiring her out. He had disappeared again, to the bar car, where

he was spending a lot of time. That had seemed normal enough until just that moment, when his little sister remembered a muttered comment of Grayson's about how much money he had lost in Florida—some of which Henry had loaned him—and how that was just the beginning of his debts.

Diana now persisted in looking neither wrecked nor ruined by his attentions. She was a tramp, of course, Penelope thought, although it was a shame that, as Henry had pointed out in their Florida hotel suite, she could no longer tell the world about it. Despite a devastating case of ennui, Penelope managed to cock a listless eyebrow, for it suddenly began to occur to her that she might be able to use that information, after all. The whole world didn't need to know the girl was a whore—there was only one man who needed to be made to see it. Then she rested her pale oval of a face on her own sharp shoulder, and let the rocking of the train soothe her into sleep.

Had New York ever been so cold?

Penelope wasn't sure if it was her brief period in the sun that made the bone-chilling end of February seem so intolerably dark and sad, or if it had always been that way. She had had too much of Henry's silent indifference on the train, and so on the evening of their return she pretended that her parents had missed her too much, and she went alone to their house to dine. Her mother had invited some "amusing" people, as usual, and she spent all of the meal rendering them completely unamusing with her barrage of inane questions. Penelope let her large, painted eyelids fall slowly, portentously, shut and allowed herself to feel the full tragedy of having worn such a becoming dress—it was black lace overlaying an ivory satin, and showed off her slim waist to fullest advantage—on a night when only imbeciles would see it. Candles flickered in the center of the long, squat Romanesque table. When her brother pushed back his chair and excused himself, she half-smiled her apologies and followed him into the adjacent smoking room.

"You've really failed me, you should know," she said as she swept over to the little heart-shape-backed settee next to the leather wingback chair where Grayson sat. His ankle was rested on his opposite knee, and he had just lit a cigarette. His gaze darted in Penelope's direction and then away. She noted the faint purple quality of the skin under his eyes, and realized that he was tired out, too. There was another quality to his posture, she decided, something like anxiety.

"How so, Penny?" he asked after a pause.

"With Diana Holland, of course." Penelope reached over and took a cigarette from the silver case that her brother had left sitting on the chair's arm. He kept a wary eye on her as he leaned forward to light it. "You were supposed to entertain us all with a game of cat and mouse."

"I'm sorry if you weren't entertained."

Penelope paused and inhaled daintily as Rathmill, the butler, entered the room and crossed the floor to stoke the fire. He refilled Grayson's cognac, and when he exited, the younger Hayes sibling went on cheerily: "Of course I was! Only I don't think you went far enough."

"That's a dangerous phrase coming out of your mouth," he muttered.

"I'm sure I don't know what you mean."

Sparks flew upward from the fire, illuminating the dark room, with its sculptured paneling and vaguely medieval air. It was a room without windows, at the center of the house, and for once Penelope was grateful to be so far from the public's attention. She exhaled and let her long, slender arm droop over the side of the settee, leaving a subtle burn mark on its magenta and gold upholstery.

"Anyway," she continued, when it became obvious that Grayson wasn't going to expand on his comment, "I want you to bat the mouse around a little more."

"Oh, Penny, haven't you had enough already?"

Penelope showed him her patient smile. She had become fixated by the idea that had occurred to her on the northbound train; it had given her something upon which to focus all her ambition and scheming—which had sagged briefly at the end of the disastrous Florida trip. This allowed her to feel more like her usual self, and anyway, he should have known that even in her weakest moments she was an insatiable person to whom the word *enough* didn't mean very much at all.

"You haven't even kissed her yet," she said eventually.

"I did *try*," he replied hotly as he relit a new cigarette with an old one.

"Maybe you've lost your touch with the fairer sex," she speculated with a wan smile.

Grayson's large blue eyes flashed in her direction as he threw his old cigarette into the fire. "I doubt that."

Penelope suppressed a giggle at his evident pride on that point by pressing her plush lips together firmly. "Then why stop now? Let's have some fun with her."

"I don't know." He shrugged uncomfortably. "She's lovely, but she's very young, and anyway, I'm busy with other things."

Penelope considered confessing all to him, but then decided that her other method of persuasion would be more effective. "That's not very brotherly, Grayson," she cooed sweetly. "If you assist me in this, I will see that it's worth your while."

Grayson waved his hand and went on looking into the fireplace.

Penelope stood, so that her next statement would have the maximum impact. "I'll pay your gambling debts if you keep the game up." A crescent emerged at the left corner of her mouth when she saw the reaction to this in her brother's face. He looked up at her very quickly, and his wide-eyed gaze remained on her as she moved toward the fireplace. She rested her right elbow against her left wrist, and brought her cigarette very elegantly to her lips.

"How did you know . . . ?" He trailed off. "Anyway, where would you get the money?"

"You forget that I am a married woman. You know how much my allowance from Father is, and Mr. Schoonmaker gives me twice that monthly. I order all my clothes on the elder Mrs. Schoonmaker's account, so you see, I have saved quite a bit."

Grayson's lips parted slightly as the possibilities began to sink in. He swallowed hard, and then he said: "What do you want me to do?"

Penelope smiled broadly now, and tossed the end of her cigarette into the fire. "Bat the mouse, Grayson, but harder this time, all right? Make her fall in love with you in a way that she'll end up regretting forever."

He put both of his feet against the floor, and rested his elbows against his knees.

"I know you've made lots of women feel that way

already." She could see that he was going to acquiesce, so she let her voice turn a touch patronizing now. "It won't take too much effort."

Penelope returned to her settee and took Grayson's crystal snifter from the little regency side table and sipped. He must have been desperate, for he ignored her insinuation and looked up at her with focused eyes. "How soon can you have the money?"

Penelope opened her own large blues magnanimously. "Oh . . . as soon as you agree to wipe that aura of innocence off our little Di." She let one eyelid fall in her signature smoldering wink. "And Grayson? Don't bother being too discreet. It would be so much more *fun* if everyone"—by which she meant Henry—"knew she'd been compromised."

Thirty Three

Miss Diana—

When I come by you are always

out. When I send messages to you,

it's as though you've disappeared.

When you grow bored of torturing

me, please call at the Hayes

mansion for a visit.

—G. S. H.

$\mathcal{D}$IANA LOOKED OUT HER WINDOW AT THE INEVI-
table snow that fell on the middle lot yards. She
pushed a stray curl away from her nose and wondered at all
that enormous feeling that remained within her, even after so
many blows. It was now clear that she had deceived herself
all those long months—and yet she still yearned for Henry.
When she thought of him she thought of the breakers in
Florida, which had swayed her back and forth during the day
and then later on in bed, too, even when they were only a
memory of sensation and the faintest sound in the distance.
Henry was like that too—he still swayed her, even so long
after the fact. She was tired of it. She closed her eyes.

Her small body slumped against the window frame
and she tried to imagine that all the pull she felt in Henry
Schoonmaker's direction could be formed into a tight ball of
newspaper and casually dropped into one of those fires that
tramps made on street corners in weather like this. It would
smolder to ash, and then the soft snowflakes would fall on

top, melting and disintegrating it to nothing. When Diana opened her eyes, she knew that her trick of the mind had failed. She made a little petulant noise—"Gah!"—and pushed herself away from the sill. Somewhere in the house, Elizabeth was moving from place to place like a ghost that had an axe to grind with the living, and their mother was clasping and unclasping her hands. Every being in No. 17 was distracted, and so it was easy enough for her to locate a wrap and slip out the front door unnoticed.

"Will you place the bet for us, Miss Diana?"

Hearing her name out loud, in a shadowy house of chance—over the constant noises of dice hitting hardwood and cards mid-shuffle and pealing laughter—caused an uncontrollable shiver up the younger Holland girl's spine. But then she reminded herself that all eyes were on the clubs and spades, or the black and red wheel, and that even if they had been curious about her, she wore a cat-eye mask dripping with black jet beads. Grayson had handed it to her when he met her at the door of the Hayes mansion, just before he whisked her into a waiting coach. He had kept a sheltering hand on her as she placed her foot on the little iron step, and his physical closeness had not abated since they arrived at the gambling hall somewhere on West Twenty-third. She had been unnerved by this at first, but she had come to see that—despite the red velvet seats and the chandelier that hung over them like some vast, illuminated jellyfish—this room was very different from all the rooms she had been in before. No one here was in the least shocked that she was positioned on Grayson Hayes's lap, or that his hand went back and forth across her knee.

"But I don't know how," she cooed, like some ingénue in one of those French novels that she kept under her bed. She had been watching the roulette wheel spin, and had by that time figured out how the game was played. But she enjoyed feeling his broad arms come around both sides of her as he whispered in her ear what to do. The low-lit room was reflected in the vast ormolu-encrusted mirrors, which faced each other so that the scene of black-suited men clustered at tables across the carpeted floor and, here and there, a woman like her whose hair was still covered by her evening wrap, repeated over and over again.

The place Grayson had taken her to was a short drive but a long way from Gramercy or Fifth. Diana liked the idea that this distance brought her far from Henry, too. Oh, he was still there, thumping in her head, but now there was also Grayson, who, while hardly the same man, was at least in the same *category* of man. They wore the same bespoke suits, for instance, and carried similar cigarette cases, and harbored like dishonest intentions, and anyway, every moment she spent with Grayson, he eclipsed the memory of Henry a little more, so that soon she was fully in the blooming moment of spinning wheels and whirring ceiling fans and cigar smoke thick and dusky in the air, and there was no past and no future and only the man whose barrel chest she leaned back into a little dizzily.

A waiter in a deep purple waistcoat paused to refill her champagne glass—she was unused to having her glass refilled so casually, or so often. Grayson whispered again in her ear, but she didn't hear what he said, and was not bothered by the fact. She placed their bet.

"Are you sure?" She could hear that he was a little frightened and a little thrilled by where she had placed their chips.

She only nodded and winked at the croupier, who called out for the rest of the men crowded around their table to place their bets. Then he let the roulette wheel spin and the little white ball fly in the opposite direction, above the blur. She closed her eyes and imagined that she was floating, that she was unattached to everything in the whole vast universe. That Gramercy was gone and money a game that children played at. She would have to go back to that sad house and her own sad room, but not just yet. She would go later. When she opened her eyes again, the ball had fallen into a pocket.

She blinked and it was only a moment later that she

realized that the pocket corresponded to the single number on which she had put every one of their remaining chips. All around them, gamblers gasped and clapped Grayson on the shoulder. She felt his hands tighten around her, one palm on her belly, and then he brushed his lips against her cheekbone.

"I can't believe it," he whispered. And then: "You must be my lucky charm."

It took another few moments before she could believe it, either, and then she was able to finally take a breath. Perhaps it was the sweet fizz of the champagne, or this very foreign realm she had too easily slipped into, but she did feel, in that moment, anyway, very lucky, or very lovely, or whatever it was he had said.

She threw back her head and laughed, raising her small white arms into the air, full of some feeling approximate to joy.

My readers know that I am exceedingly honest, and that I strive to give every question its full and most accurate answer. Yet, there are some things that never go said, and that still each mother knows in her private way to do, in order to protect her young and innocent daughters from the harsh glare and opinion of the world. Try to think on such things only in the winter, and pray you do not have to keep too many secrets.

—MRS. HAMILTON W. BREEDFELT, *COLLECTED COLUMNS ON RAISING YOUNG LADIES OF CHARACTER*, 1899

ELIZABETH PAUSED AT THE DOOR. SHE HAD BEEN hoping that if she lingered before knocking, her slight shoulders might cease to shake. But she had been there some minutes already now, and she was no steadier than when she'd arrived. On the other side of the door was the morning room, where so much of the work of the house was done by the Holland women's own hands these days. Her mother liked to crochet and worry there, crochet and worry, although when that lady went into the room after dinner she had still believed her greatest trouble was that her daughters had gone to Florida and back without securing marriage proposals. Elizabeth raised her fist to knock; she was going to have to tell her mother that there was something else to worry about, and better to do it before the physical evidence became overwhelming.

"Come in," was Mrs. Holland's sharp reply.

Elizabeth came around the cracked door. She had chosen an old dress of rich brown muslin, with a high waist and puffed sleeves, although inside she was all white fear. The gown was too large for her in some places and too small in others, and it blended with the dark stained wood of the room so that Elizabeth's soft, pale heart of a face must have seemed almost to float as she leaned back into the door to press it closed. This invisibility did very little to alter the heaviness she felt within, for she was weighed down by all the things she had done and could not take back. She had meant to live only for the good of her family, but now she carried in her a stark fact that would make them suffer all over again.

"What is it?" The quality of Mrs. Holland's black eyes changed when she saw her daughter; she brought her chin up and the skin of her throat tightened, for perhaps she already sensed some very large piece out of order. There was a fire going beside her, which flickered in her watchful eyes. She put down her hook and yarn and appraised her daughter, before gesturing gently that she should approach.

Elizabeth crossed the room and sank down beside her mother. The older woman's face was hard as always, with its tough lines around the thin mouth, but she gazed at her daughter with an imperturbableness that had warmth deep at its core. "Tell me," she urged.

And then Elizabeth did. Her confession came in tumbling breaths and was punctuated with little sobs. "Before Will . . . before he died, we were . . . as one, as man and wife. . . ." She paused to put her forehead against her mother's knee. There was some wetness on her lashes, and she did not want it seen. "And now I believe . . . I know." She gulped air. "I know I am. In a family way."

By the time Elizabeth raised her face up to confront her mother's reaction, the lady's expression had become implacable again. If she had been shocked or wounded by this final misstep of a once-prized daughter, she did not show it. There were many lifetimes of disillusionment behind her steady gaze, and she did not attempt to coddle her child.

"That is unfortunate," she replied formally. "Though not wholly unexpected. I blame Will as much as I blame you." She inhaled sharply, and moved her crocheting tools from her lap to the floor. "I told you that I would not force you into another unhappy engagement, Elizabeth, but I'm afraid this changes everything. You know this will be the end of us if anyone discovers it, don't you? Yes?"

Elizabeth nodded unhappily, her pillow of blond hair bobbing with her.

"You will have to marry now, or, if you can't manage that, we will have to take care of it. I know of a house where such things are done." Now it was Mrs. Holland's turn to be racked by a shudder, although it passed so quickly that if Elizabeth had blinked she might have missed it. She was glad she had not, for in that moment she knew how her mother really felt about this suggestion, even if she did find it so necessary.

"I will talk to my friends, the friends I have left, and see if there aren't some possible suitors for you. Perhaps it can all be done quickly and quietly. But I fear it will be the other path, and for that, my child, I am very sorry." She placed a small hand on her daughter's head and sighed. "Go now. Get your rest. In the morning we will do what needs doing."

Elizabeth nodded again, feeling strangely like a child even as one grew inside of her. She couldn't bring herself to look at her mother again, and instead rose solemnly and turned to the door. She thought of all the things she had wanted to say—how sorry she was, what a disappointment, how she had meant for things to be now and why they had gone awry—but she found that she had no energy or will to explain herself. She went out into the barely lit hall, and then carefully one step at a time down to the second floor and her own bedroom, where there was no fire, but at least a space where she could be alone with her secret.

There she lay back against the mahogany sleigh bed with its white matelassé bedspread and let her arm drape over her face. She waited for her breathing to calm down, but it did not. She remembered for a moment how she had felt with Will—how safe and sure that he would always know what was right. But that was a precious thing that had been taken from her. She was alone now, and if there was a right thing to do, she could not see it. A month ago, all the correct behaviors had seemed possible. Her family had needed her so terribly badly, and she had planned to do everything for them. She had allowed Diana to go follow Henry Schoonmaker, and it only seemed to have caused her more harm, and since then the elder sister had been so absent. She had scarcely spoken to her younger sister since their return; she had been too absorbed in her own fears to see how Diana was holding up. And her mother—it was almost too much to think how far she had strayed from her mother's expectations of her.

She drew her hand over her forehead and looked listlessly toward the window. The snow had stopped at some point during the night, and there was now a clear view of the half-moon in the sky. She wondered if Will could see her now, and she felt guilty all over again, not just for her family but for the days of ease and happiness she had experienced in Florida. The memory made her wince, and she wondered if she weren't being punished for it; if her current predicament weren't somehow retribution for having, for a moment, slipped back into the old subtle pleasures of the life she'd been born to, with all its soft texture, its politeness, its oblique glances.

Then her breathing did finally begin to relax and she blinked in the darkness that was now cut with white moonlight. She was thinking of Teddy again, and his presence in her mind made her wonder, however briefly, if maybe her situation weren't so fraught and impossible after all.

Thirty Five

In New York nowadays one is always hearing about new women whom one is supposed to keep an eye on. The latest of these is Mrs. Portia Tilt, whose husband's fortune is in coal or some such, and she seems to be throwing a lot of parties. Reader, dear, you know I have ever been the skeptic, and with my skeptical eyes, I will be watching.

—FROM THE "GAMESOME GALLANT" COLUMN IN THE *NEW YORK IMPERIAL*, WEDNESDAY, FEBRUARY 28, 1900

CAROLINA KNEW IT WAS HER DESTINY TO SEE LELAND again, although she would have been hard-pressed to explain how that would ever come about. Luckily, thoughts of the man she had imagined close to a proposal in Florida were all in her head, and so there was no need to make any of it logical to anybody else. She tried not to dwell too carefully on her current circumstances, either, which were a million miles from just a week before. She was wearing a plain black dress again, though this one at least had a high, stern neck and some attempt at ornamentation around the chest. She had lived for a few days in one of those rickety places downtown, and now she had her own room—close to the servants' quarters, in another woman's grand home. There was nothing about this new situation that made Carolina feel even a little bit grand.

"Miss Broad."

"Yes?" Carolina's eyes fluttered innocently, and she knew that her face assumed that serviceable, cowlike expression that it had worn so often in her years as a lady's maid. Her voice became suddenly girlish too, like that of a woman who has not yet learned to ask for what she deserves. "What is it, Mrs. Tilt?"

"Miss Broad, you need not look so frightened!" Portia Tilt was already a little drunk, and it did not do kind things for her garishly done-up face. She was smiling charitably at Carolina, but only because she now felt more powerful than her. It was quite evident that the western transplant, upon whom Carolina had not wasted even a minute of thought when they'd crossed paths at Sherry's, liked having someone whose name had been in all the columns to boss around. "I was only going to tell you that you are welcome to play bridge with the guests if you like. You will have to borrow against your wages if you want to bet, but maybe you're a good player and will come out ahead."

Carolina blinked her wide-set, sage-colored eyes. She nodded a little dumbly, and then let her gaze drift so that she could see through the satinwood doorframe. Arranged at little French antique card tables were people who once had been her peers. They had all dressed in their finest to see this new Tilt woman, just as they had once done to meet the Broad heiress. She recognized, for instance, Mrs. Carr's high trilling laugh, although she would have been aware of that lady's presence at the Tilt town house anyway, for Carolina had handwritten her invitation. Mrs. Carr never turned down an evening, which was one of the reasons that Carolina—in her capacity as Mrs. Tilt's new social secretary—had recommended her as a guest. A woman beginning her career must take friends were she can, Carolina had advised tactfully, although she would do well not to exclusively associate with divorcées as her reputation grew. It had pained Carolina to give away such wisdom, but then she no longer had very much to barter.

"No, thank you," she said quietly. "I'd rather not tonight."

Mrs. Tilt shrugged her shoulders, her indifference to Carolina's suffering exaggerated by the vast heaps of red satin ribbons that crowned her lace sleeves. Yellow curls sat above her undistinguished face, catching the light of the chandelier. Mrs. Tilt's social secretary had held that title only three days by then, and already she resented everything about it. She loathed it, in fact, and feared that others would get wind of this indignity, which was the true reason—although the idea of borrowing against her wages certainly was humiliating—that she preferred not to play bridge that night. Longhorn had taught her, and she was in truth a canny player, but the idea of being pitied by Lucy Carr was too much for Carolina, and so she hung back against the doorframe as Mrs. Tilt swept forward into the room and took her place beside Tristan.

He looked up briefly at Carolina, causing her to draw backward into the hall, where she was invisible and could only see a sliver of the goings-on in the Tilts' second-floor card room. It had been Tristan's suggestion that Carolina take the social secretary position, and also he who had planted the idea in Mrs. Tilt's mind. That lady swerved past the salesman now, planting a red kiss on his cheek as she made her way to the adjacent high-backed chair, which was covered in new grass-colored jacquard. It was a gesture that was meant to mark her territory, Carolina knew, but she didn't mind particularly, even though she had allowed Tristan to kiss her twice. She saw now that he was like an illusionist who captivated women with a little sleight of hand, and once she had seen the mechanism, it had lost all power for her. The kisses had only been accepted in loneliness, she told herself, and there was no reason Leland would ever have to know.

Now the chandeliers—far smaller than the ones in Leland's home—bathed society guests in twinkling light, and the smell of cigarettes was sickly sweet in the air. Carolina closed her eyes, and remembered how she had been a prized part of similar circles in rooms that smelled like this one. That she should be hiding in the hall, in a house like this—too far west and too far uptown to have any real importance—made the skin under her collar burn. The house of a woman, more-over, who didn't think twice of baldly touching her lowborn lover in the house that her husband's millions had afforded her. It was the kind of behavior one would have thought more rightly at home on a Nevada ranch.

A waiter was passing her, into the card room, a carafe of white wine in his hand, and she reached out and tapped his arm.

"Webster Youngham prefers red." She had seen this same man unwittingly pouring the great architect white earlier, and knew that he would not accept another invitation if things were not done more correctly. He was a very entitled gentleman, and rightly so, or at least that was what Mrs. Carr always used to say. The waiter nodded and retreated. A moment later, he reappeared with a bottle of red.

"Pour from the right," Carolina added, before the man crossed into the card room. It had been a kind of instinct, and she felt immediately angry with herself and Tristan and Portia Tilt for having put her in a situation where she might again act so slavishly over someone else's desires. She let out a breath of embittered air and turned in a hurry from the irritating scene. Mrs. Tilt wouldn't be needing her anymore, and it was just as well to wallow in her room as right there. The self-pity that Carolina felt in that moment was of an irascible and overwhelming nature; if some little bird had suggested that her life was far more comfortable here than at the Hollands', or than it would have been on the street, she would have shot it down.

She strode forward on the oak floors, not bothering to step lightly in her high-heeled slippers. She was too good to make herself quiet for anyone, to hide, or to look after stray waiters who had not been given proper instructions. She was very nearly mouthing these facts to herself when she heard her name, spoken with what she would have formerly believed was the correct stress and reverence.

"Miss Broad," said Leland Bouchard.

"Oh." Carolina came to a stop, and her face fell. She was horribly conscious of the simple arrangement of her hair, which was parted down the middle and drawn up in a bun behind her head, and of the dress which her new mistress had considered more appropriate for her than any of those that Longhorn had paid to have made just for her. She managed a little curtsy and tried to say hello.

She must have seemed strange—she knew very well that she appeared dumbstruck and terribly off—but you would not have known it from the way Leland was looking at her. He was beaming; if she hadn't been so unhappy about his finding her in reduced circumstances, it might have occurred to her that he was pleased to see her.

"We haven't met at all since Florida. Have you been hiding from me?"

"You mean you haven't read the columns?" Carolina whispered numbly.

Leland laughed. "I never read the columns."

"Oh." Carolina nodded. Of course he didn't, she reflected,

as she found herself improbably liking him even more. "It's only that I haven't been feeling so social," she lied.

"No, I should say not. You look pale, and a little tired. Are you feeling ill? You ought to get your rest. A body needs rest, you know. You ladies work yourselves too hard." The broad, masculine lines of his face softened suddenly in concern. "It was a long trip," he added kindly. There was a quality in his voice that she wished could be produced over and over, and held in a great vat, so that she could dive into it.

"Yes," she seconded, although for her it had not been long enough. "Why are you here?" she went on, knowing that the question sounded neither sophisticated nor polite. But it had just occurred to her that she had made up the guest list, and his was a name she would never have added for Portia Tilt.

"Youngham and I have some business, and he told me to come here to meet him." Leland shrugged, and brushed back his wheat-colored hair. She noted his handsomeness with a certain searing pain. "I wouldn't, ordinarily. You know I have no interest in cards. But I am leaving on a long trip soon, and am short on time."

Carolina looked up at Leland with sad, childlike eyes. "Where are you going?"

"To London first, and then Paris. At the Exposition Universelle in April there are to be many automobile demonstrations and races, and you know of course that I would never miss a thing like that." He grinned widely, and then, when Carolina's lids fluttered shut, he added: "Say, are you quite sure you aren't ill?"

"Yes, I only—"

"Miss Broad!"

The couple who had gotten on so well in Florida looked up from their private moment to see Mrs. Tilt emerge from the more flattering light of the card room. The step she'd taken in their direction had been wobbly, but her tone had been perfectly precise. Carolina had known what it meant—it was the way a high and mighty person spoke to her minions—and she was sure Leland had heard it too.

"Mrs. Tilt," Carolina replied, drawing herself up. She pressed her lips together so that the fine lines of her cheekbones emerged in shadows. Without trying very hard, she soon had a look of haughty carelessness, and then she heard herself go on in the old way. "Thank you so much for a lovely evening, but I fear I am not feeling so well and have lost my appetite for cards. Mr. Bouchard has been so kind as to offer to escort me down and to hail a cab."

Mrs. Tilt's mouth opened up like a capital *O*, but she was apparently struck dumb, for she said nothing more as Carolina curtsied, took Leland's arm, and descended the stairs at the end of the hall. They paused in the lobby, where Carolina gestured for Mrs. Carr's otter coat, and then she was again out in the cold.

As they waited in silence for a cab to come clomping down the street, Carolina tried desperately to think of something to say or do that would ensure her seeing Leland again. But she had no permanent address, save the one that she had just exited, and no planned social engagements where she might hope to meet him again soon. There was the same strained silence as a cab finally came to a halt and Leland helped her up to the seat.

"I leave Friday, and am afraid I'll have no time to see you before I go. But you'll let me know you're feeling better?"

Carolina moved her head up and down mechanically.

"Send me a telegram at least," he said. He grabbed for her hand and held it, tightly, in his own.

"I will," she promised as she reluctantly released her grip. "Goodbye, Mr. Bouchard."

Then there was the sound of a whip and the horse moved forward into the night. Carolina closed her eyes, and tried to imagine that she was still with Leland and not wrapped up in a stolen coat riding in a cab to which she could give no directions home.

Mr. William Schoonmaker, whose political
ambitions are well known, has been in Albany
all week, meeting with the governor and shor-
ing up allies, now that he has joined the Family
Progress Party. By all accounts, the would-be
candidate will return to Manhattan today....

—FROM THE *NEW YORK TIMES*, THURSDAY, MARCH 1, 1900

"WOULD YOU LIKE A DRINK, SIR?"

"No."

Henry kept his chin down and his gaze steady as he walked past the waiter and into the second-floor drawing room where his stepmother did much of her entertaining. Louis XIV furniture, which had been oiled that morning between breakfast and luncheon, was arranged with affected carelessness across the deep purple Hamadan carpet. A few of the men and women who fit the elder Mrs. Schoonmaker's idea of "right people" were now talking in imperious tones over very little. They perched on the corners of divans and reclined in bergère chairs, sipping only occasionally from paper-thin china cups. The late-afternoon light streamed through the lace undercurtains, and one could be sure that on the other side of the glass the parade of carriages down the avenue was moving briskly along.

The skin of Henry's jaw was freshly shaved and tender. He did feel a twinge of regret that he had turned down the drink, for that particular waiter had been attentive to his empty glasses for many years, perhaps over the objections of Henry's father, and he felt a little disloyal about the rejection. But he was trying to keep himself fit and clear. He had been trying all week, as he awaited the return of the elder Schoonmaker from Albany. He had gone over all the arguments in his head, and he felt ready to present his wish to leave Penelope in a rational and straightforward manner and then let the old man do his worst. And anyway, there would be other drinks and other glasses—with Diana, he hoped, in some wonderfully unrecognizable future.

His gaze darted across the room, but he didn't see his father anywhere, and eventually he focused on the blue-eyed brunette with the long neck who was sitting on an oval-backed, black velvet settee in a day dress of emerald green satin. Beside her was his stepmother, her blond hair done up and her cheeks pink with all the compliments she liked to receive when there were guests. Both women looked toward Henry, and then Isabelle laughed and turned away.

Penelope, however, went on watching Henry as he moved through the little tables and marble statuary that filled the room. He passed Adelaide Wetmore and Lydia Vreewold, ensconced in conversation, and the painter Lispenard Bradley, who appeared to be waiting for a vacancy beside Mrs. Schoonmaker. Once Henry had drawn close, Penelope turned a bright, counterfeit smile back on him.

"Have you missed me terribly?" she said loud enough for several known gossips to hear.

The bodice of Penelope's dress was braided and layered, and the effect was something like armor. Despite the abundant fabric, there was an angular quality to it. There seemed to be nothing capable of movement underneath the fitted satin, and Henry wondered not for the first time if her blood ran red or black. The answer didn't matter to him anymore.

"No," he said finally.

Penelope's long black lashes batted back just an eighth of an inch. She pressed her oversize lips together and let the perfect oval of her face assume an implacable expression. If she felt embarrassment, she was trying awfully hard to make sure no one else noticed it.

"I was looking for my father. Is he here, Isabelle?"

Isabelle, who had been engaged in a silent exchange with Bradley, showed Henry an innocent face that betrayed just how carefully she had been monitoring the words between her stepson and daughter-in-law. "No," she said eventually. "He went to the club, but we expect him for dinner at the Hayeses' tonight. You can talk to him there, later. But do stay now, Henry—you are never any help when we have good people over."

The glow coming through the windows was fading slowly to evening light, and the colors that women wore during the day began to appear garish. Already Isabelle was thinking of the next gown she would wear, he knew, although, as usual, she would not want to part with those who had kept her company during the day. She collected furniture, but somewhat indifferently—her real passion was for collecting people.

"I don't feel so much like socializing now," Henry replied curtly. "There's something that I need to discuss with the old man—it's important, and I won't be much fun until we've had our talk."

He nodded his goodbye, and moved to leave the drawing room. He'd nearly reached the door when he realized that his wife had matched his every step. All the heads in the room twisted so as to better observe her, and when Henry fully comprehended that the attention of the assembled was on them, he paused and tried to appear a little normal.

"What is it you want to talk to your father about?" she asked in a low voice.

Henry's eyes went everywhere—to alabaster torchères and angels carved out of wood, to the postures of people who were trying not to seem to spy, to anything but her. "I'd really rather not—"

"If it's about me, I hope you'd have the courage to say it to my face."

Henry's hands moved awkwardly across his black jacket and he sighed.

Penelope's eyes brightened with a prideful gleam. "Here it is," she replied, extending her neck so that her head came closer to his. Though her tone was sweet, there was a challenge in it, too.

The Schoonmaker guests had gone back to their little talks and were at least keeping up the illusion that they had no interest in the newlyweds by the mahogany doorframe. He had told her once before: He didn't know why he was finding it so difficult to muster the words now. Maybe she seemed a more pitiable figure to him after everything.

"Is this about that nonsense you were babbling about in Florida?" She laughed, as at a very urbane joke. There must have been something in his countenance that affirmed this, because she went on: "What would people *say*, Henry. It would be so awfully irregular." She brought a gloved hand up to cover her mouth and laughed again, this time in a more quiet, simmering way. "Would you like to know what I think? I think you don't have the guts to tell your father."

Henry took a hoarse breath. There was a taunting quality in her voice, and it made him pity her somewhat less. He held her gaze, and pronounced his next statement with great care. "I'm going to tell him tonight."

Only now did Penelope's smile begin to falter, although she held it enough that her sharp cheekbones emerged against her skin to catch the last of the outside light.

"You wouldn't." Her voice had fallen to a hiss, and she stepped forward as though she might find a way to physically prevent him from altering her plans.

"Yes." Now that he'd said this much aloud, he felt as though the conversation with his father was a foregone conclusion. Henry thought maybe a parade down Fifth Avenue should be planned to honor his bravery, and he was already almost experiencing the thrill of falling confetti. "I would."

There were many more things he might have gone on to say—about how she deserved it, or that she was cold and venal, or how flimsy his interest in her had ever been—but he knew somehow that the right thing to do at that moment was to keep quiet. There was no need to prolong the war when his exit strategy was so perfectly clear.

He nodded a polite goodbye, turned on his heel, and left the room, his blood charging through his veins and his thoughts soaring to a triumphal tune.

Thirty Seven

It is a truth universally acknowledged that there will always be a gentleman to dance with, except at just the moment when you require one most.

—MAEVE DE JONG, *LOVE AND OTHER FOLLIES OF THE GREAT FAMILIES OF OLD NEW YORK*

*I*T WAS THE DAY FOLLOWING ELIZABETH'S CONFES-
sion to her mother, and by afternoon she was
struggling for her old composure. The guilt and fear were still
tremblingly there, not to mention the nausea and fatigue, but
she tried hard for some steadiness in her fingers as she did the
row of tiny buttons that ran along her sleeve from her wrist to
the inside of her elbow. She arranged her hair high above her
forehead, the blond strands at the nape rising upward from her
tall black collar. Already you could see where her small body
was growing larger—but not dressed, not with the thick wine-
colored skirt hugging her waist and falling down past her toes.
There was some time yet, although the idea of how little made
her feel sick all over again. Will had died two months ago
now—her predicament would be visible quite soon.

"Claire," she said as she descended the main stair into
the foyer. The red-haired maid looked up at her tiredly
from her work. She paused in the dark wood–paneled space,
but did not release the broom from her hand as Elizabeth

placed her foot on the final step. "I am going to call on an old friend."

If Claire noted something unusual about this—for it had been months since Elizabeth had done anything of the kind— she did not show it on her face. She rested the broom against the wall, wiped her hands against each other, and went to the cloak- room, which was built under the stairs. As she waited, Elizabeth gazed out through the glass in the doorframe. She could see the slight movement of the trees in the park, but no passersby, and realized that it must be very cold outside. Over the past months, with the Holland household staff so reduced, Elizabeth had taken to fetching and putting on her own coats, but she resisted that impulse when Claire reemerged with the brown tartan cape. She waited to be helped into both arms and have the large cloth buttons done up in the chest. Then she met the maid's eyes, but only for a moment, and only with the most cursory of smiles.

She had recently become conscious of the possibility that Claire was behind the revelation of Diana's indiscretion with Henry Schoonmaker, and though she had always trusted the girl implicitly she found herself acting guarded around her now and pinning every stray piece of gossip one heard about the Hollands on her. She certainly didn't want her to get wind of any brewing scandals.

"Tell Aunt Edith that I will be back for dinner, unless I am invited elsewhere," she said as she came down the final

step. She wasn't sure quite what she meant by that statement, but she blinked as though it were perfectly obvious and moved forward toward the door. She wavered for a moment in front of the glass, wanting to give Claire a reassuring look, or perhaps to receive one. But then she remembered how dire her situation was—every time it occurred to her it was like a bath in ice—and she fortified herself. She had once had a deft hand for perfectly manipulating any social situation; she might yet have it again. But she could not vacillate or pause for niceties or succumb to the nervous energy within.

The city was very still at that hour, and if she had not known better she would have thought there was nothing doing. But she did know better. She knew that the end of tea was coming soon, and the ladies of New York were employing all their daintiest gestures while thinking of what sort of antics they would get up to at dinner. They were thinking of slights and how to make them and engagements and how to enter into them. She was on a mission herself, one for which she would be well advised to keep a cool head and her wits in regimental order—and yet, she was surprised to find a warm and pleasant anticipation fanning through her chest as they rode up Madison Avenue into the thirties.

She told the hansom not to wait and presented her card at the door.

"Is Mr. Cutting in?" she asked, and though she had planned to smile, the one that came was so natural, glistening on her face like a sunset on waves, that she was embarrassed by it. "Mr. *Teddy* Cutting."

She could not see the Cuttings' butler's expression through his beard, but his initial silence made her wonder if she hadn't been too forward or if her delight in saying the name aloud had not been too obvious. She knew that, for herself and according to her own standards, it had been inappropriate. "I will see, mademoiselle," he said eventually, and then he led her to the drawing room.

A fire was going under the restrained marble mantel there, and the ferns overgrew their pedestals. The walls were covered in striped purple wallpaper and all the surfaces were populated by cut crystal, and on the ivory Turkish love seats sat Mrs. Cutting and two of her daughters, Alice and Julia. They were looking unusually dour—that was the first thing Elizabeth noticed. The second was that there were fewer people than she might have anticipated in a drawing room of this stature and at that hour.

"Miss Elizabeth Holland," the butler said, and when the three women looked up she realized that they had all been crying. Elizabeth's small mouth began to work, but she could not get hold of any appropriate words. The butler withdrew and she stepped forward into the warmth of the room.

"Oh, Elizabeth," Alice wailed. She hurried across the room and threw her arms around her brother's old friend's neck. Like her mother and sister, she wore black, with a little American flag ribbon pinned to the chest. "If you only knew! If you only knew . . ."

"Whatever's happened?" Elizabeth felt the tight clump of hope within her begin to dissolve. Something much darker was coming. For a moment she wondered if she wasn't some kind of curse, and if a violence hadn't been visited on Teddy just like the one that had taken Will. "Why so sad today?"

Alice drew her into the sitting area, and Julia poured her a cup of tea. She passed it to Elizabeth, who managed only to hold it politely. As she waited for the bad news, which she could already feel nipping at her toes, she sensed that even tepid liquid might scald her.

"It's Teddy, of course." Alice sat down beside their guest and rested her hands on the other girl's knees. Her gray eyes were just the same shade as her brother's, and she had the same broad and slightly horselike features. "He's gone."

Elizabeth's eyelids squeezed shut, but only for just a second. "Gone where?" she asked, when they opened again. Her teacup had begun to clatter in her saucer, and she brought her other hand up to stop the shaking.

"Gone to war." Julia, who was sitting beside their mother on the opposite love seat, looked at Elizabeth as though it might somehow be her fault. For all she knew, it was. "He said that he met some soldiers on the train who showed him what it meant to be a real American, and that even Elizabeth Holland had endured more hardship and fought back more bravely in her life than he ever had from anything. . . ."

Elizabeth put down the tea and her hand moved involuntarily to her waist. She looked backward to the memory of her time with Teddy in Florida as though at a best friend standing onboard a ship moving inexorably out to sea. What had she said to him that made him want to go so far away? She couldn't place it, and only wished that she'd let him know how very heroic he might have been to her, right there in New York. She would have traded a great deal just to have stayed a little longer on the dance floor with him the night he had tried to propose.

"So soon?" she said eventually, as though it were only the timing of this news that shocked her, and not the revelation of absence itself.

"Yes." Mrs. Cutting's voice broke over the word, and she brought a handkerchief to her face. Her fair hair was going gray and her whole soft body shook a little with the sorrow of it all. She had ever been a lady whose singular joy in life was the presence and success of her children; her only miseries,

their pain. "He enlisted and already they've shipped him out to San Francisco! From there he goes to the Philippines."

Elizabeth wondered at what point in that journey her old friend was at now, for after all, it was one she herself had made. But then, that did not make him any more reachable.

"You must be terribly proud of him," she said sincerely.

The three Cutting ladies nodded wretchedly, and then went on to discuss all their greatest fears and nightmares, all their prayers for his safety, and what drastic measures they would take upon their own lives if anything should happen to him. Elizabeth knit her brow in sympathy and crooned in agreement, but her spirit had already left that parlor. That morning she had had a plan, and that afternoon she had felt a rising optimism, but by the end of tea she saw these things anew, for all their foolishness and futility.

Thirty-Eight

The happy, rich Henry Schoonmakers are back from Florida and apparently cannot spend a moment apart. They will be attending a small, intimate dinner at the home of the bride's family, the Hayeses, this evening, along with a few select guests. One can only conclude that for their happiness they depend very little on those outside their circle.

—FROM THE SOCIETY PAGE OF THE *NEW-YORK NEWS OF THE WORLD GAZETTE*, THURSDAY, MARCH 1, 1900

W HEN, UPON HER RETURN FROM THE SOUTHERN sojourn, Penelope had insisted that her mother throw a dinner for her family-in-law, she could not possibly have imagined that so little would have been accomplished in the intervening days, or that she would have been so incapable of improving upon her situation even to the slightest degree. While it was true that there had been very little in her favor on the return trip, still she would not have believed that so much time and so much of her own effort and beauty would not have turned things around.

Even now, sitting in front of the large, beveled mirrors in the ladies' lounge, where on the evenings of grand balls scores of women crowded around, trying to look even half as beautiful as the hosts' young daughter, she found it incomprehensible. For those were her slim shoulders and her unblemished forehead and her almost phosphorescent complexion. That was her exquisitely fitting pale pink chiffon dress, which was layered and tucked so that her décolletage might reflect the candlelight and her waist could just barely exist.

"Henry will stop being such a cad and pay more attention to you soon," said Isabelle, who was sitting next to her in a dress of ivory overlaid with beige lace, as though she had been reading Penelope's thoughts. Though her words seemed intended to reassure, her tone did nothing to enforce that sentiment.

"I'm not worried," Penelope replied, sitting back against the little stool. She looked at herself in the mirror and willed her white neck to lengthen. She was a girl long adept at saying precisely the opposite of what she meant, and yet there was a little strain in the lie tonight. She wouldn't have believed that Henry had the nerve to tell his father he wanted to leave his wife, but there had been some awful determination in the way he carried himself that afternoon in Isabelle's drawing room. She was full of trepidation, wondering what he might do tonight, and she felt woefully devoid of any idea how she might fight back.

Grayson appeared just then in the doorframe and Isabelle stood up hopefully—a gesture that the younger matron could not help but regard with a little internal scoffing, for truly, Isabelle should have been over him by now. Though he had once paid her sweet attention, Mr. Hayes didn't appear to so much as register her presence. It was clear that it was his sister he had come for.

Out in the hall, Penelope noticed Buck, his huge chest covered in a blinding white dress shirt. Penelope couldn't be quite sure why, but she had lately found his presence insufferable. Perhaps it had something to do with how little he had been able to do for her during this, her time of need, or maybe it was because he knew how very much she wanted in this world and what a slight percentage of it she truly had. For too long a moment Isabelle waited for Grayson to turn around for her, and when he did not she allowed Buck to take her arm instead so that he might accompany her in to dinner.

Grayson put on a serious expression and offered his arm to his younger sister. "You look very lovely this evening," he said as they stepped onto the black-and-white checked marble flooring of the halls. Buck and Isabelle were far enough that they wouldn't be able to hear the Hayes siblings' conversation, and the sound of all their custom-made heels rang out through the intervening yards. Penelope noted the seriousness of his tone, and wondered for a gleeful moment if perhaps he had already found a way to punish Diana. Then she'd have that to dangle in front of Henry, and perhaps all would not be lost.

"Thank you."

Penelope walked at a relaxed gait, leaning against her brother's arm. Isabelle was probably now longing to turn her head, which was heaped with blond curls, but propriety and pride made even a small gesture of that kind impossible.

"I will need to give you the money back."

The tight grin that Penelope's lips wore began to slacken. "The money?"

"Yes."

"Don't you need it anymore?"

"Yes."

There was something new in his voice, almost like earnestness, which Penelope found both mysterious and painfully annoying. But she would have disliked what he said regardless of tone. "Well then, *why*, dear brother?"

They had reached the entryway to the parlor that adjoined the dining room, with its burgundy club chairs and gold vases filled with pampas grass. Inside that oak-paneled space were her family, and Henry's, and the painter Lispenard Bradley and a few others, loitering on the camel-hair rug and fingering their drinks. The gentlemen were moving slowly to take up the ladies' arms to escort them into the dining room. They appeared very stupid and useless to Penelope at that moment, and then she noticed something else.

"What is she doing here?"

Diana Holland could not possibly have heard her, but still she looked up from her place by the fire and her old aunt Edith, who was apparently the best she could do for a chaperone, and looked directly at Penelope. There was no smile on her face, and in her eyes a certain veiled challenge. She was wearing a pale green dress, the color of melon, which Penelope distinctly remembered her wearing on more than one occasion during the fall season.

"I invited her," Grayson said.

"My God, why?"

"Because you asked me to—" He broke off and his eyes glazed dreamily. "And because I'm beginning to think I might be in love with her."

When Penelope saw the expression on his face, and the puppy-dog look in his eyes, she felt the full crushing weight of his idiocy. What was it about that short creature with her wild hair and spurious air of purity, and why would anyone, much less two men, love her, and to such disastrous ends?

They could linger on the threshold no more, and she felt herself pulled by his arm, which was—even after this latest betrayal—still linked to hers at the crook of their elbows. If her mother hadn't been there searching out compliments about their enormous house, or her father muttering into his drink, or the elder Schoonmaker looking judgmentally at all the objects in the room, she would have pointed out to Grayson that his was a desperate situation, or insisted that they had made a deal he could not back out of. But there was the low hum of people greeting each other in the evening, and Penelope reluctantly assumed the smile of a gracious daughter and new wife as she went forward into the room.

She had never hated the word *love* quite so much as at that moment.

Now old Schoonmaker, who had just arrived, was saying something kind to Diana, and Henry, who had paused at the arm of Mrs. Hayes, had turned to stare. He was only there, Penelope knew in a glance, because of the intentions he'd declared that afternoon, and he was only waiting for the moment when he had his father to himself. His neck was twisted for a better view, and lamplight played against his clean-shaven throat. For once, there was nothing inscrutable about his black eyes. The way he was looking at her made Penelope want to shriek and throw something. She would have liked to charge across the room and pull the humble ribbons from Diana's hair. She could have proclaimed to the whole room that these Hollands, with their superior poverty and their old-fashioned airs, were in fact two perverse girls—one of whom had given away all to another woman's husband, while the other had quite possibly conceived a bastard. But just as the tide of fury was rising within, a perfect solution crested in her consciousness.

Grayson was moving like a man possessed through the exclusive gaggle of people, but Penelope was quick enough on her feet that she made her presence at his side appear very natural. She followed close behind him to the place where seemingly all eyes were focused. She followed him all the way to Diana.

"Miss Diana, I am so pleased you were able to attend," he said.

"I am very glad to have been invited," she returned. Penelope noted the tone, and deduced that there was a private joke between them, and then Diana turned her pointed chin and gave the older girl a jaunty smile that in private might have been an invitation to a slap. But Penelope's idea was a good one. She felt no need for violence anymore, and instead smiled back at the little twit and waited until Rathmill, the butler, appeared from the dining room and announced that dinner was served.

"May I escort you?" Grayson asked Diana. She smiled and they moved together, Grayson in his black tails and Diana in her tiered dress, leaving behind the lady that he had entered the room with.

Penelope looked around affecting an expression of helplessness, knowing full well that everyone had already paired up. Then she met old Schoonmaker's eyes. He was a large man, his face a bloated version of Henry's, although the dark eyes and hard jaw were still intact. He offered his arm, and they took a step in pursuit of Grayson and Diana. Behind them came Henry and Isabelle, and then all the rest.

"Don't they look handsome together?" Penelope whispered airily, gesturing with her chin at her traitorous brother and the petite tramp.

"I suppose," William Schoonmaker, ever the discriminator, answered.

"Oh, you must agree, on a night like tonight, you could almost imagine such a couple on the altar."

Schoonmaker made a vague grunting noise, of neither agreement nor disagreement.

"But don't worry, Father," she went on, her voice growing more delicate and feminine even as she added volume. She had never called him "Father" before, but it seemed to her like a nice touch. "I am not one of those women who, once wed, can think of nothing to do but make matches. It's not that I don't enjoy the pastime! Perhaps just a little less than other ladies. But the real reason is, I fear I will be not much in society this summer and fall, and after that I believe there will be a new addition to our family."

Penelope phrased this with quiet care, and at the precise moment she knew those within earshot would understand her meaning, Old Schoonmaker's face lit up as though she had just told him she'd found a cache of Standard Oil stock in his safe, and his response was so voluble that she knew there would be toasts. She would have loved to see Henry's face then, but the thing to do was to keep controlled and go on facing her husband's father with that aura of angelic magnificence.

The full genius of her coup was only just occurring to her—soon everyone would know how tightly bound she

and Henry were—and she could not resist the satisfaction of glancing away once or twice, to observe how the younger Holland sister's shoulders had jumped and locked together, and also the stricken expression she now wore. She had the look of a starving rabbit run out of her hole by a fox. That one hurt, Penelope knew, much more than anything Grayson could have engineered for her.

Thirty Nine

It is difficult for the once poor to ever play truly rich. But this is a city full of those who will try.

—MRS. L. A. M. BRECKINRIDGE, *THE LAWS OF BEING IN WELL-MANNERED CIRCLES*

$\mathcal{D}$ARKNESS FELL QUICKLY ALL OVER MANHATTAN, and those who could huddled near a fire. There were waifs in doorways who would not make it through the night, though Carolina was not like those unfortunates, and for plenty of reasons. She was wearing a coat of brindled otter fur, which she had borrowed temporarily from the divorcée Lucy Carr, and even as she stumbled through the anonymous and gloomy streets, she knew that she had been chosen for a destiny that had far better lighting.

This had not, however, been the opinion of Mrs. Portia Tilt. The western lady had imagined a more modest future for Carolina, one that involved remaining in the shadows whenever handsome or rich people, or those with fine names, were about. She had imparted this opinion to her former social secretary with particular vehemence and an articulateness that she had not heretofore exhibited, late on the previous evening when Carolina had returned from an hours-long cab ride without a destination. It was lucky that the Tilt staff was an unhappy one, and the head housekeeper had seen to it that the fired employee had a bed for the night. But in the morning there was nothing more they could do for her, and so Carolina had taken up her little suitcase and gone out into the city.

The sun had still been high then, and the memory of Leland, and the kindness in his pale blue eyes, still fresh. All of Carolina's self-regard had been renewed, and so while she might have gone back to Tristan's she did not seriously consider it. The kisses they had shared seemed tawdry now, and the ways that he had helped her inexcusable. It had been a moment of weakness, she told herself, something she had done to survive, and then she thought of it no more. Meanwhile, she carried with her all the true ingredients of her career—her height, her carriage, and her taste, which was not innate but had been one of Longhorn's many gifts to her. All she needed was an inconspicuous job, only for a little while, and then she would find a way to be herself again. She had managed thus far—why should this crater be any different from any of the other holes she had clawed her way out of?

There had been several places she had considered going in and asking for employment, although in each of them the idea of Carolina Broad and where she had come from stood in her way. First there had been the ladies' tearoom, where she had imagined for herself an office in the back overseeing

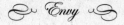

the décor of the place and scolding the waitresses for their slovenly appearance. But then she had seen, through the wide windows, the girls in their uniforms, like a little herd running scared, and the prospect that the owner might make her wear one of those black-and-white getups had caused her heart to sink. Later, passing a newly opened hotel, she'd wondered if perhaps she could dust the rooms of wealthy visitors when they were empty. But she knew there would be more than dusting, and that if she were lucky enough to acquire a job like that, it would come with the title of maid. Bile rose in her throat at the thought of that terrible word.

It was only now that the color had gone out of the sky and she seemed to be the only female left on the streets that she began to wonder if a tearoom or a hotel wouldn't have been a good place for her after all. Just for a day and a night. Maybe they would have had a cot where she could have slept or a place for her to put down her small suitcase. Maybe Leland would appear there by chance, in the morning, his chin freshly shaved against his stiff, new collar, and upon seeing his love in such duress, would spring into action. Maybe he would even carry her out, like a princess in a bedtime story. Carolina pressed her teeth into her bee-stung bottom lip at the thought of it, but then she opened her eyes and saw the cobblestones and pools of water ominous in the night, and all her nice fantasies flagged and the desperate ones began to loom.

She couldn't help but think sorrowfully of Longhorn, who had protected her so gallantly and who had made so many of her evenings comfortable and light. The world outside was a very harsh place, and her chin trembled a little to think how furious he would be to see her thrown into it. But here she was now, with nothing to do but trudge on. She did so, stepping forward along the pavement, but she came down on something soft. Squealing followed, first from the rat underfoot, and then from her own throat when she jumped back and felt the little creature crawl across her other foot and skitter off into the gutter. "Oh," she said, feeling the shudder up to her shoulders. After that, coat or no coat, she was chilled to the bone. She hurried now, and the next time she saw light spilling from windows onto the sidewalk, she went and pressed her nose into the plate glass.

Inside, young women with clean faces were bent over tables piled with lustrous materials. They ran their fingers over seams and brought dresses and skirts and little jackets under the arms of churning sewing machines. They were all bathed in a modern electric light, and for a moment, out in the cold, Carolina thought it actually might be nice in there. Moving between the tables was a full-bodied woman with reddish hair fading to gray, arranged in a fan above her head. She bent to see what the younger women were doing, occasionally pausing to undo their stitches. Carolina craned her neck to look up at the sign above the door, which read, MADAME FITZGERALD, DRESSMAKER, and then took a deep breath and opened the door.

It was warmer inside than she had imagined, and the air was thick with floating fibers. The machines whirred and there was also the sound of fabric swooshing, although the girls themselves were very quiet. When the door swung shut behind Carolina, the older woman turned to stare. She had a face as broad and unyielding as a man's, and though it seemed for a moment that she might say something welcoming, it soon became clear that she had no intention of speaking first.

"May I talk to Madame Fitzgerald?"

Now several of the girls did glance up to see what was happening, although their hands kept moving over their projects, and their feet never let up on the pedals.

"You're looking at her," replied the woman.

"Oh, I—" Carolina found herself blushing furiously. "Hello."

The older woman sighed in exasperation and put a fist on her hip.

"I was just passing by and your shop seemed so nice and I thought—I wondered if—I hoped that—"

"You hoped what?" the woman prodded. Her voice came down hard through her sinuses.

"That you might have a job for me."

The woman's painted red brows soared at that. "Oh-ho? And why would I give you that?"

The muscles of Carolina's face loosened in surprise. She had imagined that the difficult part would be bringing herself to ask for the job—that actually acquiring it should demand more from her was quite a shock. "This is a business, isn't it?" Carolina asked lamely.

"Yes, it is," Madame Fitzgerald snapped back. She let her eyes go all the way up and down Carolina's fine fur coat. "Not a shelter for high-and-mighty types who've bit off more than they can chew. What would you do anyway? Sit in the window?"

"No, I . . . I . . . can sew." She took a faltering step forward. She clutched at her coat, but suddenly wanted to show her old self, too. "This coat was a gift from a friend of mine, but it doesn't mean anything. I was for many years a lady's maid for the"—here Carolina's throat dried up, but she forced herself to say the name— "Holland family."

"Were you, now?" Madame Fitzgerald's earlier irritation subsided as she savored this amusing revelation.

"Yes." Carolina marched on through her humiliation. "Until this last fall."

"Well"—the woman shrugged, coming around a table and toward the door—"show me how you work, then."

"All right." Carolina tried to put on an eager smile, and

placed her suitcase on the floor. She stepped forward, but was stopped by the expression on Madame Fitzgerald's face.

"Take that coat off."

Carolina involuntarily brought her hands up to her chest. She thought first of turning on her heel, and second of the rat that had run across her foot. Slowly, reluctantly, still protesting in her heart, Carolina removed the coat and hung it on the stand by the door. Then she brushed her hands across her lap and tried to steel herself for what was coming next. Madame Fitzgerald gestured through the rows of girls at worktables. There was both envy and animosity in the way they observed the former maid with the coat that would have cost any one of them a year's wages. Now that she was on the other side of the window, Carolina saw the shade under their eyes and the roughness of their fingertips, but still she wanted to be one of them. Just for a night.

She sat where Madame Fitzgerald pointed, and took a breath of hot, dry air. The proprietress brought a skirt made out of ivory material and dropped it in Carolina's lap. There was something terrible about the fabric, far worse than anything she would have imagined herself wearing, or even touching, again—it seemed to be sloughing off in rough bits all over her.

"Hem that."

"What?" Carolina's thoughts had been diverted for a

moment to a very different dress of pale gold with a scalloped and embroidered hem that Longhorn had had made especially for her. She'd worn it that night at Sherry's, when being the inferior of a Portia Tilt had been so impossible to her. . . .

"Hem it." Madame Fitzgerald leaned back and somehow managed to smile by turning down the corners of her mouth. "It's a test, sugarplum."

Carolina nodded. She removed her gloves, pushed back her sleeves, cleared her throat, and reached for the skirt. She brought it close up and ran her fingers across the rough, unfinished bottom. The skirt had been let out, just like her sister Claire's hand-me-downs used to be let out for her. She was too tall and grew out of things too quickly, always needing more length, more fabric, more everything. Carolina looked up briefly at the proprietress, as though to make sure that she was supposed to do what she thought she was supposed to do, and that using one of the machines would not be good enough, and then she took up a needle from the pincushion on the table and threaded it.

After a few careful stitches, Madame Fitzgerald moved away. She peered over the shoulders of the other girls, but kept an eye on Carolina, too, who was trying to keep her head down as she tentatively pressed the needle through the fabric. This kind of work made her chest feel tight, and her shoulders grew tense with the idea of doing so much for so little.

She thought for some reason of Will—poor Will, who had suffered so, and who never even got to go to Sherry's, or the opera, or to wear clothing that had been made especially to fit his body. She thought about him and all the injustices of his life and of her own, all the foolish events that had brought her here, and she went on making stitches, although with less care each time.

A little bell rang and Carolina glanced up from her work to see the door open again. A man had come inside, the high lapels of his coat obscuring his face but not his light brown hair, which he had grown overlong. She felt her lungs swell with air and her hands flutter with the thought that it might be Leland. That it *was* him. He had come back for her—he had found her against improbable odds. She smiled and her freckled skin stretched taut over the cheekbones. Then Madame Fitzgerald made a happy, guttural sound and went over to take his coat. She removed it, and then the young man turned his face to survey the room. Though he was tall and handsome and wore his hair in the same way, he was not Leland.

The proprietress kissed the man on the cheek, and it was clear that they were from the same stock—he had her face, the way a son or nephew might. Before Carolina's disappointment occurred to her, she began to feel the pain.

"Oh!" she said out loud.

Several of the girls turned to look at her, and then

Madame Fitzgerald did, as well. Carolina looked down, and saw how she had jammed the needle into her thumb, just under the nail. For a minute there was only the stunned hurt, but now the blood had begun to flow, across the skin and onto the unfinished skirt.

"You stupid girl!" Madame Fitzgerald crossed to where she was and jerked the garment away from Carolina, who could only go on staring at her wounded finger. The older woman grabbed her hand and roughly pulled the needle from the skin where it was lodged. "Now look what you've done," she said, in an only slightly less angry tone.

Indeed, the skirt was now marked with her blood, and though Carolina would have liked to point out that the skirt wasn't really worth wearing anyway, she knew that that logic would be lost on present company. She stood up with what pride remained and pulled on her gloves, first one and then the other. The second began to soak up the blood. Then she crossed through the rows of rabid-eyed and underfed girls, slipped her coat over her shoulders, and gave a final look at the proprietress and the young man at her side. Their faces were full of contempt. When Carolina could look at them no more, she went out into the night.

She imagined how it might appear in print—CAROLINA BROAD WALKS THE DARKENED STREETS—although she no longer felt worthy of that name. It seemed to her that everything had

gone numb, and that the sensations of her body were terribly remote. She'd lost feeling in her fingers, and soon she forgot about her toes. Then, later, when she sank into a doorframe, and huddled in her coat, and laid her ear against her shoulder, it was as though she were some other girl this was all happening to—perhaps Lina Broud—and that Carolina, whoever that was, could only watch from afar.

Forty

Mothers write all the time to thank me, many of whom benefited from my wisdom before they were matrons. It is one of the great joys of my life. Still, some girls never learn, and I hear the stories of their mistakes with even greater chagrin as I grow older. . . .

—MRS. HAMILTON W. BREEDFELT, *COLLECTED COLUMNS ON RAISING YOUNG LADIES OF CHARACTER*, 1899

$\mathcal{F}$AR NORTH ON FIFTH AVENUE, ALMOST TO THE park, the rain had begun to fall. It came softly at first, blown at an angle by the wind, but it was soon a true downpour; Diana listened to it beat a tattoo against the walk. Inside the Hayes mansion another bottle of champagne had been opened, although nearly everyone within was already thoroughly sauced. Henry Schoonmaker was—he drooped on a couch while his new wife smiled at his side—and so was his father, who had initiated the bacchanal. He had been dancing with Edith Holland, who had had not a few drinks herself, and was reminding those with long memories of the girl she used to be, and of an episode from the seventies when certain members of society believed for the first time that there might be a Holland-Schoonmaker alliance in the works. Meanwhile, his second wife, Isabelle, spoke quietly to Abelard Gore, whose wife had attended some other engagement that night, and Prudie Schoonmaker went on chatting—it seemed that she had talked more that one evening than she had over her entire life—with the painter Lispenard Bradley, who kept glancing in Isabelle's direction. Edith's niece Diana was sitting on a divan in the corner, carelessly holding a champagne glass, and when the waiter came by with the bottle, she extended her arm to have it filled up.

Everyone in the room was drunk, but no matter what she did, Diana could not seem to join them. She wanted to feel anything but the seething hurt that Henry had dealt her, but champagne was of no use. It was as though she'd been taken captive by some mad scientist who was conducting an epic experiment to document the furthest, Antarctic reaches of pain. He had given Henry a knife, and told him to twist it deeper, and somewhere, behind one of these mirrors, he watched to see how the sensation played out on Diana's fragile face. Occasionally he would add mitigating factors, only to override them with more vicious experiments. Surely this— realizing what a colossal lie it had been that Henry didn't sleep with his wife, that in fact they would soon be a happy family of three—was the most pain he could cause her. Although, Diana reflected as she put the champagne flute to her mouth, she had thought exactly that several times before, and here she was again in uncharted waters of anguish.

"There are good paintings in the galleries, is that right?" she said to the man sitting beside her, Grayson Hayes, who she knew full well had been instructed by his sister to show her how charming he could be and whom she had tried to use to make Henry jealous and then to forget Henry, neither time with very effective results. Poor Grayson—the pawn in two losing games. She did not ask about the galleries in a flirtatious way or a suggestive way or a cagey way. She asked without guile, except in the sense that it was not so much a question as a request to be taken far from the smoking room, which was now so purple with joy.

"Yes," he replied, hearing her request clearly and rising to offer his hand.

She rested her palm just lightly on his, and allowed him to lead as they exited. The party had now reached such a pitch that no one noticed the absence of these two, and they strode through the halls of a house that could have fit ten of the Hollands' home inside of it. If Diana had thought that leaving the room where Henry and his wife were celebrating their happiness would soothe her, she was finding herself very wrong now. Her small frame was still trembling with the knowledge of what the Schoonmakers' life together was—what it must have always been, even while she'd imagined all the different ways that Henry might truly, secretly belong to her. He had taken advantage of her, or at least he had intended to. She tried to feel lucky that she had discovered the truth so soon, but her ability to see silver linings had been thoroughly damaged by this last shock.

"The paintings in this gallery are particularly nice."

They had entered a dimly lit room, and Grayson raised a candle, which he had acquired somewhere on their walk, although Diana found herself less than interested in examining the canvases.

"Miss Diana, I am glad we are alone. I've been wanting to tell you how often over the last week I have found myself thinking about you."

She turned to Grayson, and found that his face looked not only handsome, which of course it always did, but open and earnest. That was a surprise. "Is your interest in me sincere, or is it some scheme of your sister's?" she asked in a plain, quiet voice.

"My interest—and that word doesn't do it justice—is beyond sincere. Now. Please don't make me tell you how it began, but believe me when I say that doesn't matter anymore." Grayson reached forward to tuck a curl behind her ear, and his eyes stared into hers with an adoration that she could not possibly match. She saw that his aim was true, or that he was at least intent on making her believe that. But could she ever trust herself to know the difference?

"Tell me why." After Henry's treatment of her, she wasn't sure that men could honestly love women, but she wanted to believe it. She wanted to be told pretty things, and for the frightening clip of her heart to slow to something more reasonable.

"Well"—Grayson laughed softly—"because you are beautiful and curious and because you like to go places and feel life. Because I feel free with you, and unbound from all the stupid constraints of my dull self."

"Oh." Diana moved backward against the wall. She wondered if Henry had ever felt that way—maybe at the beginning, before he'd realized how easily she could be manipulated? But there was Henry again, invading her thoughts, twisting the knife, and she groaned a little without meaning to.

Grayson put a hand on her waist gently.

"Do you think you'll go on feeling those things?" she asked after a pause.

He took a breath. "I can't imagine stopping."

She opened her eyes, but did not meet his before blowing out the candle. Then she reached for him, placing her hands on his shirt and shoulders and pulling him nearer. The brass holder clattered to the ground. She could feel his breathing against her neck, and decided that she liked it. She had never imagined being touched by someone other than Henry, but she found in the event that close proximity to another's body made the knife wounds somewhat less excruciating. She opened her mouth and brought it up to Grayson's.

"I've never felt so much for a woman before," Grayson said, when, after a minute, he pulled back from her. "I find that I want to be with you always and—"

Diana was nodding along with him, but she didn't want to hear more. She wanted to be kissed again until the kissing subsumed all her other feelings. She put the crown of her head against the wallpaper, inviting him to kiss the skin of her throat. There was a hesitance at first, but then he did bend to put his lips there, before moving again to her mouth, where he kissed her lightly over and over. She wrapped her arms around his neck, spreading her fingers just below his hairline. She had nearly forgotten the hour, or the people they had left behind in the other room, when Grayson protested again.

"Do you think they will miss us?" He was panting a little.

Diana tried to catch her breath. "Not yet," she answered. Grayson blinked at her—perhaps he was trying to determine how well she knew her own desires. In the dark, he looked just like Henry, or close enough.

"Miss Di," he went on sweetly, "I don't want to seduce you into . . ."

He trailed off as Diana stared at him. She had been thinking of the way Henry used to be able to gaze at her from across the room and make her feel that he was at her side drawing his fingertips across her skin. Still the memory made her weak. At that moment, with the shouts of the Schoonmaker party still faintly audible off in the next wing, with the rain falling against the elaborate eaves and sleep still too far away, it seemed that only one thing might possibly make her stop thinking of what

Henry had done to her. She raised her finger and pressed it across his lips, urging quiet.

"Please," she whispered.

Then he hoisted her up, so that she was rested against the top of the oak wainscoting. Her pale green skirt and white crinoline were all around them, like a wave breaking against a jetty, and she felt her whole self butterflying open. He bent to press his mouth to her shoulders, and she discovered that that felt nice. His arms were under her, holding her aloft, and she found she liked that, too. Then she pressed back against him, knowing full well that she would give him all, willing him to take her down into some abyss of forgetting.

She had lost all sense of herself, and turned away from Grayson so that he might more easily bury his lips against her neck, when she saw a figure in the umber halo of the door-frame. Was it Henry, or did she only imagine him everywhere? Then the figure was gone, and she knew she would never have anything quite so sweet and new and pure as what she'd had with Henry again.

Forty One

Men's reaction to the news that they are to be first-time fathers is often inadequate, if only out of nervousness; if they are wise, they will look to their own fathers, who have had plenty of time to get used to the idea, for cues.

—MAEVE DE JONG, *LOVE AND OTHER FOLLIES OF THE GREAT FAMILIES OF OLD NEW YORK*

"WHAT A JOY AN EXPANDING FAMILY IS," THE elder Mr. Schoonmaker declared as his heavy body sank back into his chair. He had, for the moment, grown tired of raising his glass in celebration of his son and daughter-in-law and their family manqué. It was a lucky thing for Penelope, who must be weary—Henry could only assume—of trying so arduously to blush whenever his father referenced her condition. It was a lucky thing for him, too, as there was no expression he even knew to attempt. At the head of the table, Penelope's father stared, stultified, into his dessert wine. On the other end, her mother was beside herself with giggles, and winked at anyone who so much as glanced in her direction. The other guests went along, gamely enough, with the calls for more champagne and every time a greater need for congratulation and excitement.

"That was lovely," Richmond Hayes offered halfheartedly as the waiters descended on the oak-paneled dining room to remove the final course. The guests paused in their chatter and looked over at the man of the house, for even they knew there would be more. Henry wondered if they were as exhausted by it all as he was. But everyone likes a party, especially when it is already well under way, and their eyes were very bright.

"Mr. Hayes," said Mrs. Hayes, "shouldn't we invite our guests into the smoking room for digestifs?"

The men and women arranged along the long table murmured their approval, and then Richmond Hayes agreed, not altogether convincingly, that it was a good idea. Henry could not bring himself to glance at Diana, who sat across from him only partially obscured by the arrangements of pink begonias. Everyone was pushing back their chairs and standing. The gentlemen were reaching for the arms of the ladies they had escorted in, somewhat less tipsily, several hours ago.

"Henry, sit by your wife," old Schoonmaker commanded once they had all, somewhat stumblingly, relocated.

Penelope turned to him, from her place on a settee, her eyes as large and trusting as a doe's. It was dizzying, he thought, all the different emotions she could feign. In her pale pink, expertly tailored dress she looked just the part of the young mother who cares for nothing so much as her children, although he could never believe again that she was even partially such a person. Not after the way she had used them long before they were so much as born. He walked around to her and sat at her side, but could not bring himself to meet her gaze.

Hours passed like this. At first, Henry rejected the champagne that was poured for him. He'd been sober all week, and he still felt that he should keep himself strong and ready and brave. But then he began to wonder about the slight possibility that Penelope might be telling the truth, and the very notion caused him to demand a drink and down it in a hurry. Then he ordered another and another. When the sounds of the others' voices had grown giddy and loud enough to drown out what Henry had to say, he addressed his wife.

"You can't really be." His voice was hushed and a little slurred, but he managed to focus his black eyes carefully on her and remain hopeful.

"What do you mean, Mr. Schoonmaker?" she returned innocently.

Henry glanced across the room, where women were rearranging their skirts in order to appear to the best advantage of the chandelier light and the waiters were circling with full decanters that he would have liked to have gotten both of his hands on and absconded with to some dark corner. There was a huge, gilt-framed mirror over the fireplace, tipped slightly forward to give a view of the room as though from above. In the far corner of the scene Henry saw his own reflection, in his black slacks and tails, and beside him his wife, in her subtle and artistic dress. For a moment, he saw what they all saw: two perfectly matched, tall, dark, lithe people, too in love to join in the shrieking of all the others. He hated himself for having glimpsed that picture.

"It was only once, a week ago, two—I can't remember." Henry sighed and shifted his jaw. "I don't believe it."

"All right, then." Penelope let her white shoulders rise and fall in careless acknowledgment.

"You're not." For the first time that evening, Henry's dread ebbed.

She rolled back her eyes and let her mouth open slightly. "Well, I'm not completely positively *sure* that I am." Then she brought her gaze to his. "It's possible, of course."

Henry let out a sigh from the bottom of his chest and shook his head in relief. There was no baby, there was no family. He could leave her after all. It would only take a little longer, and the conversation with his father would be somewhat more awkward. But he could still do as he had planned.

"Oh, Henry, don't be cruel."

Her face had gotten all crumpled, and though he didn't know what she was about, he felt the fears creeping back from the base of his skull.

"I told you how it is," he said carefully.

"But now it's all different!"

"Penny, don't be stupid, you said yourself—"

Penelope looked down at her gloved hands, with their circles of rubies at the wrists, and began to squeeze them together. "I'd be careful whom you call stupid," she said quietly. "For instance, you haven't even considered how it will look when you leave your pregnant wife. It *is* awfully different now, don't you see?"

"I don't think that lie is leaving this room, my dear." Henry closed his eyes briefly and rubbed his forehead. "After all, what are you going to do in nine months, when there is no baby?"

Penelope moved closer to him, and her eyes drooped down sadly as though what she was about to say had already come to pass. "Wouldn't that be so much worse?" she went on in a whisper. "If you left your wife because she couldn't carry your first son to full term?"

Henry swallowed hard. He glanced around him, as though the walls and the furniture and even the guests were made of iron. They might as well have been. In a few seconds he realized that they all constituted a kind of prison. They looked back at him now, smiling, not knowing what their belief had changed them into. They beamed and watched the Henry Schoonmakers, thinking they were trading lovers' secrets. Penelope must have gleaned this too, because she moved forward and into the illusion, bringing her body less than an inch from his, pressing away from the soft cushions.

"Anyway, I don't think you have much to leave me for," she whispered in his ear. "What do you think your little Di has been up to all this time?"

When she fell back against the armrest she giggled show-ily in a way that reminded him of the rest of the room, with its jovial din and witless pitch. The air around him had grown smoky and almost too thick to breathe. Everyone was talking at a level that made it impossible to hear any one conversa-tion over another. Henry turned about in his seat, searching for Diana, but saw her nowhere. There was her chaperone—visibly drunk and dancing with his father. He saw the divan where Diana had last been, but it was empty now.

Up above the empty seat was a painting of a man, drawn to scale, in vaguely military dress, riding a horse that had reared up on its hind legs. The horse's hooves clawed the air and his eyes were full of fear and fire; meanwhile, his rider looked proudly, calmly, at some battle down below. Henry would have liked to believe that he was like the rider, but he knew he was now playing the other role. His gaze fell to Penelope, who winked knowingly.

"Don't you wonder where she's run off to?" She smirked, and placed her hands demurely in her lap. "Or *they*, rather. So do I, especially since my brother told me some very interest-ing information just before we came into dinner. He told me he *loves* her."

"Stop it!" Henry wanted to shout—to his wife, to everyone in the room. But he did not. He recalled all the things Grayson had said in the casino about Diana, and what

a wild, desperate sort of man he was. Maybe he believed he loved her, and Diana was probably in such a state right now that she might actually believe he did too.

"Excuse me," Henry said.

His body felt dull, and it moved too slowly through the halls of his family-in-law's home. He used to know his way around there, for reasons he no longer liked to acknowledge. His heart beat and his feet carried him forward without any conscious control. All he knew was that he had to find Diana, which he did, eventually, but then he saw that it was too late.

He put his hand against the doorframe of that darkened room and witnessed for several horrific seconds the way Diana's body was entangled with Grayson's. He might have cried out, but he had no breath. It was he who had brought both of them here, to a point from which there was no returning, and it would only be foolish noise if he yelled at anyone but himself. There was nothing for him to do but stumble away with the full knowledge that all his planning and heroics were no more than half-formed thoughts dying in the mind.

Forty Two

There is in this city, behind a brownstone façade like any other, a mistress of abominations who deals in powders for immoral girls, and who gives operations when those powders fail. . . .

—REVEREND NEEDLEHOUSE, *SERMONS FOR OUR TIMES*

ELIZABETH WENT LATE AT NIGHT, AS HER MOTHER had told her to do. She had memorized the address—respectable, off Washington Square, a town house like its neighbors, although the light over the high stoop burned somewhat brighter than at the buildings on either side. The rain had died down and she wore a dark, hooded cloak that covered her face, and she was careful not to be noticed on the street. It was for that reason that she paused so long in the shadows and, when she was sure there was no one peeking from a window or loitering on the corner, went quickly up the stairs. She carried with her the last of the money that Snowden had given her family, from their father's gold rush interest, and her mother's final words before she left the house.

"I always thought better of you," Mrs. Holland had said, before announcing that she was going to bed. Edith had already left to chaperone Diana, and so there was no one to see Elizabeth into the bracing night. She had been told to take a hansom cab, but she could not bear for even one person to be complicit in what she was going to do.

She was sick of the nervous fatigue, but still it took her too long to pound the knocker against the door. She closed her eyes and hesitated and then finally raised her slim wrist. After that it all happened very quickly. She was ushered into a second-floor parlor, lit with antique lamps and furnished with soft fabrics and animal skins. The richly dressed woman who had let her in disappeared behind a Japanese screen that obscured an entryway. It was just like any other parlor, except finer than many, went Elizabeth's thoughts as she waited.

There was the sound of feminine voices, very faint, from adjoining rooms. Elizabeth clutched her hands together, loosened them, and then tightened her grip. It was so strange that she should have ended up here—she who had been so admired for her dress and manner, and then later on, during nights she would have given anything to live again, so well loved. She didn't know what to make of it, of all the turns of fate, or the room she was sitting in, with its offensive finery and false air of normalcy. It would have been difficult for her to say with certainty who she was anymore.

Once upon a time, she had been a girl who lived for her family, and its own particular idea of what was correct and beautiful. She had failed at that but found a better ideal to pursue. And now that something better had been taken from her in a blast of gunpowder. Without Will, every footstep was tentative. Even the borders of her body felt somehow hazy and indistinct, and perhaps that was a blessing, because whatever was going to happen to her next was not something she wanted to feel. She sensed a gale of sorrow coming upon her, and she shut her eyes and willed it to pass. The skin of her forehead folded at the center and she prayed that Will was in heaven, looking down on her, and that he would help her not to cry.

What would he think of this room, with its neatly framed pictures of women wearing unsmiling faces and their staid best? How many girls, she wondered, had sat in that room before her, feeling somewhat calmed by the similarity of the environs to their own homes, wanting it all to be over so they could go to balls again and be proposed to and have everyone see them as they always had—as good, pure girls who were born to marry well, in ceremonies that depicted them as blank slates. They were all hypocrites, every last one of them, she realized. The girls in their white dresses and the men who put them on pedestals but still brushed up against them when they danced. And not least her own mother, who had told Elizabeth she had "always thought better of her," but would have been pleased to do something as venal as marry off her child for money.

The only person Elizabeth had ever known who was not

a hypocrite was Will. She felt the hard stone in her throat and brought her hand up to her belly. It was stunning that she should have to suffer this way for love, and that the punishment should be so bodily, so humiliating, so absolute.

"My dear," said a woman as she came around the screen.

The light was low, but the suddenness with which Elizabeth's eyes opened caused her to see spots. A little moisture had collected along her bottom lids. The woman was dressed in black velvet and was full in the chest and in the face, and she smiled at Elizabeth the way a person does before they demand payment. Perhaps, Elizabeth wondered for the first time, she was not being forced to suffer. Perhaps this wasn't another tragic twist of fate.

Suddenly it began to occur to her that what grew inside was the last thing Will had given her, and she could not possibly be ashamed of that. He had been her husband, she reminded herself.

"I have to be going," she said as she stood. She was fatigued but not in the least ready to sleep, and she felt blearily capable of anything, just as one does after staying up all night.

"But my dear, your condition—"

Elizabeth backed toward the door. "I'm sorry," she said. Her voice had grown loud and clear. "But that was all a mistake."

Envy

The house was dark when she crossed the threshold, but no sooner had she removed her cloak then she heard the rattle and creak of the parlor pocket door and saw her mother come out of the darkness.

"I would have thought they'd keep you all night," she said, and though her words were harsh there was something strained in her voice.

"No." Elizabeth tried to catch her breath and let her eyes adjust to the lack of light. It was good to be inside; although the real chill had gone out of the weather and she had sensed a moisture in the air and the return of rain as she climbed the steps. "I couldn't stay there."

"What do you mean you couldn't stay there?"

Mrs. Holland stepped into the foyer, bringing with her that smell of ash that follows all clothes that have lingered by a hearth. Elizabeth could see her face now, and she recognized in the older woman's expression the same nervous indecision that she had been experiencing not an hour before. But for Elizabeth, the nervousness was gone, and she felt in its place a strange fortitude.

"I am going to have a child," she answered calmly. "Will's child."

Her mother made a noise as though she had been hit in

the stomach and all the breath had gone out of her. "You will ruin us," she said. But she did not say it harshly, and somehow when the phrase was in the air, it sounded like not such a bad fate after all.

Elizabeth discovered that she was smiling. She kissed the little lady on either cheek and said, "Good night." Then she turned and walked up the stairs to her bedroom. She hadn't the faintest idea what she would do in the morning, but she knew that for the first time in many days she would sleep through the night.

Forty Three

The last will and testament of Carey Lewis Longhorn will be read today at the New Netherland Hotel, where the late Mr. Longhorn resided for the last years of his life. Though he was a bachelor, many a society lady will mourn the loss—some of them, of course, hope that today his largesse will live on.

—FROM THE SOCIETY PAGE OF THE *NEW-YORK NEWS OF THE WORLD GAZETTE*, FRIDAY, MARCH 2, 1900

"MISS BROAD, WHAT HAS BECOME OF YOU?"

Carolina, or Lina, or whoever she was now that all of her dignity had been scrubbed off her, stepped into the lobby of the New Netherland where she had once been so grand. Her coat dripped a little onto the shiny mosaic floor, and though she had planned to appear slightly less wrecked at this moment, the first familiar whiff of the perfume and coffee, and the sight of Mr. Cullen, the diminutive clerk who had so often handed her the key to her room, brought tears to her eyes, and before she could even begin to explain, she was wailing like a baby.

"There, there, Miss Broad," said Mr. Cullen, as he removed the rain-soaked coat from her shoulders. "Did you get caught in the rain?" he went on dubiously as he examined the coat, which had in truth spent all night inches from the downpour, and now smelled unmistakably of the street. He gestured to a bellboy, and when the offending garment was out of sight he placed a hand on Carolina's shoulder and said,

"We will send that to the cleaners and see what can be done. But my dear, you are freezing. We must get you warm and into some dry clothes."

Carolina put her face into her hands and nodded vigorously, although she had not yet found a way to stop crying.

"Do try to contain yourself, my dear," Cullen went on as he drew her into the office. "You are here for the reading of Mr. Longhorn's will, aren't you? Surely the old gentleman must have left you something. . . ."

Carolina pushed her hand against the underside of her nose, wiping away the snot, and tried to believe this. In truth, she didn't hope for much anymore, and had only come to the hotel because she had woken up in a doorway and had no place else to go. She could see, too, in Cullen's face that he was only trying to make her feel better, and this was such a rare kindness that it took all her will not to begin crying again. He called one of the housekeepers, and had her find Carolina a dress, and only when she was properly put together again did he himself escort the young lady to the suite where she and Longhorn had spent so many evenings, talking over what his youth had been and what hers then seemed to promise.

Mr. James, the lawyer, was sitting at a wide table and he looked up at Carolina in a way that made plain how unwelcome she was. Luckily, Cullen was still there with her, and he walked her to one of the chairs that had been set out, and only once he was sure that she was solidly placed in her seat did he leave her side. There were a few other women, occupying chairs and crying theatrically into their hankies. Lucy Carr was among them, but she would not meet Carolina's eyes.

"Welcome, ladies, gentlemen . . ." Mr. James began, before coughing rather disgustingly into his hand. A preamble followed that Longhorn's former favorite could hardly listen to. This was a document that the old bachelor had ordered drawn up when he was contemplating his own end, and she had failed him so miserably there. She was still enduring the consequences of that selfish decision, and she suspected she would endure them for a long time to come. Most of the beautiful objects in the room had been wrapped up, she observed, and the life had gone out of it.

"To my second cousin, Mrs. William Barre," Mr. James was saying. That lady gasped a little and sat up like a rod. "I leave all my large silver platters and one thousand dollars."

Mrs. William Barre then loudly praised Longhorn's generosity, even while looking slightly disappointed.

A series of small bequests followed, to which the people in the chairs made tepid responses. Carolina couldn't expect anything from the old man—she had known him only a few months, and had failed him when it most mattered—but still she couldn't help but think how much more five thousand dollars would mean to her than to the Society for Young Girls

Orphaned by Fire, which had been her former benefactor's favorite charity. She too was an orphan, she thought as she dabbed her eyes.

Then she heard the words that let her know it was the end, and she stood to leave.

"And the remainder of my estate," Mr. James was now saying, somewhat reluctantly, "including all of my holdings in real estate, stock, business, and cash, I do leave to my dear friend, who gave me such joy in the final chapter of my life, Miss Carolina Broad."

Everyone in the room gasped and turned to look at the girl who already appeared headed for the door. For a moment, Carolina thought that she had been called out for bad behavior or some other infraction against good taste, and her eyes roved back and forth from the women assembled there to the lawyer. Then she saw Lucy Carr smile at her, and she knew that her fortunes had turned around again. She was still cold, and it would take several hours before she began to really understand how utterly her life had been transformed. But already a sense of safety was returning to her limbs, and the women who had come with hopes of their own crowded around her to wish her all the best. Longhorn had seen promise in her youth after all, and oh, with what infinite kindness, what eternal magnanimity had he gone about ensuring that that promise would be fulfilled.

Some hours later, and outfitted from the wardrobe that had been rightfully restored to her, Carolina arrived at a west side address of no particular distinction and instructed the hansom to wait in the street. The rain had finally stopped and you could feel the coming of a kinder season in the air. Still, she pulled her coat—the old broadtail one, which Longhorn had purchased for her in the springtime of their friendship—close around her shoulders as she crossed and approached the stoop.

The housekeeper, when she opened the door, did not at first have anything to say.

"Don't worry," Carolina said with a smile that showed off every one of her teeth. "I am not here for my back pay. Nor will I ever be."

The older woman's eyes darted down the hall, and she was evidently nervous, because she had to pause to wipe the sweat on her palms against her dress. "I don't think Mrs. Tilt will be happy to know that you came here."

"Oh, I don't give a fig about that!" Carolina laughed. "And anyway, I didn't come for her. Is Mr. Wrigley here?"

"Yes, but—"

"Good." Carolina brushed past the woman and into the hall, where she turned just enough so that her long, lavender skirt could twist up sculpturally behind her and catch all of the electric light from the ceiling. "Where are they?"

The housekeeper glanced at her hands. "First-floor parlor."

"Ah, yes."

Carolina entered the room with her furs still on and her face incandescent with victory. She knew perfectly how well winning looked on her, and posed in the doorway so that Mrs. Tilt and her friend Tristan could take in the full glory of the effect. At that moment, all of her suspicions about her own greatness seemed to have been confirmed, and so she had no trouble at all using one of the tricks of fine ladies everywhere, the proper employment of which had eluded her until that evening. Her timing was all right.

"I told you never to return here," Mrs. Tilt said eventually, and though she was trying very hard for cold, the strain melted some of the ice out of her tone. Tristan, sitting next to her in a red and white upholstered wing chair, appeared uncomfortable for perhaps the first time in their friendship. She was gratified to see that he was already dressed up, however, in a black jacket and waistcoat, and with his light-colored hair more neatly arranged than usual.

"Did you? Since I have no desire ever to return to this place, I believe I shall be able to do as you ask." Carolina leaned insouciantly against the doorframe. "Tristan," she went on, lowering her voice and taking her gaze permanently off Mrs. Portia Tilt, "come with me."

Tristan's chair scraped against the floor as he adjusted awkwardly, but he did not yet stand. "Mrs. Tilt and I were planning on dinner at the Waldorf. We were just having a cocktail to begin the evening and then—"

"Nonsense. You are having dinner with me, at Sherry's. You see"—and here she paused to smile Carolina's smile—"I have just inherited a great fortune, an amount higher than I think your Mrs. Tilt even knows how to count to, and I want to toast myself."

Tristan did not hesitate after that. He came to Carolina's side without so much as acknowledging the western lady, and they left the room without bidding her goodbye. Carolina did decide to glance back at her one last time, and the look of wounded pride and indignation that her former employer wore at just that moment was something the Longhorn heiress would have paid quite dearly to see. As it turned out, though, this was a sight Carolina was able to enjoy for free.

"It will be in all the papers tomorrow!" she called over her shoulder.

Tristan helped her into the hansom, and as they sat beside one another being jostled by crosstown traffic, she found that all of a sudden she had run out of things to say. The story was too large to begin to tell, and she only wanted someone to

celebrate with for a night. Her old friend the Lord & Taylor salesman would do very well for that—not for much else, she had come to realize over the last few months, though he had been very useful in putting Mrs. Tilt in her place. She would have preferred Leland a thousand times over, of course, but she had read in the paper that afternoon that he was already on a ship many miles out into the Atlantic, and so she had resigned herself to waiting a few more months before their romance resumed. For now, the rain had cleaned the air, and she was dressed regally, and her escort—whoever he was— looked very handsome indeed. The night was young, and so was everything else.

Forty Four

More than one new society bride is with child,
although I am not yet at liberty to say which
ones....

—FROM *CITÉ CHATTER*, FRIDAY, MARCH 2, 1900

THE FIRE SNAPPED, AND ELIZABETH'S BROWN EYES twitched upward to meet her mother's. Neither woman flinched, and they went on staring at each other for a long minute. The rain was again falling outside after clearing for a time that afternoon, and Diana was still asleep upstairs despite the fact that the evening was nearly upon them. Edith had the look of death about her, and could form no words about the party at the Hayeses' the previous night. So they had run out of things to talk about, and now the elder of the Miss Hollands could do nothing but try to keep warm by the fire and suffer her mother's accusatory glances. She felt a little nervous and unsure of the future, but now she had some-thing greater than herself to protect, and it made her feel less frightened.

"Mrs. Holland," Claire said, adjusting the pocket door as she came through it. The shadows of a gray day played across her milky face.

Edith made a grunting noise and covered her eyes. "For

God's sake, be mindful of my headache and keep a little quiet," she said, even though Claire had most certainly spoken in a quiet tone to begin with.

"I'm sorry," Claire whispered. Since Mrs. Holland steadfastly refused to look up from the hearth, the maid glanced at Elizabeth, who nodded for her to go on. "There's a guest here."

"Who is it? We're in no state to receive anyone," Mrs. Holland went on sharply. Edith groaned, but did not mention her headache again.

"It's Mr. Cairns."

"Ah!" Mrs. Holland's expression changed. "Show him in."

Elizabeth straightened as he entered the room. She had been so absorbed in her own troubles that she had not noticed the outdoorsman's absence since her return from Florida, and indeed his thick features, and the extreme paleness of his blond hair, were almost unfamiliar to her. She felt a little bad about this, because he had done so much for her family, and she tried to smile more broadly at him to make up for it.

"Mrs. Holland, Miss Holland, Miss Elizabeth," he said and bobbed his head.

"How lovely that you've returned to the city," said Mrs. Holland as she rose from her chair. She looked less worried somehow, and Elizabeth felt grateful to him for it. Her father's old associate had such a knack for showing up when the family was in the greatest need, she observed, and that made him seem not so strange to her. "I wasn't sure you'd be back."

"Yes, and I plan to stay awhile. I know how compulsively hospitable your family is, and I didn't want to disturb you until I had settled in. I have taken an apartment at the Dover on the park—it is not as charming as all this, of course, but it will do for a man like me." His gaze was steady on Elizabeth, who turned to her mother, who looked at Snowden. "I received your cable," he added, addressing her mother, Elizabeth assumed, although he went on watching her.

"Welcome back to New York, Mr. Cairns," Elizabeth said sweetly as she stood, touching her belly unconsciously as she did. She hoped that that was all that was required of her in the moment, but she was not to be so lucky. His gaze covered her whole body, and then he crossed toward her and sank on one knee.

Elizabeth's eyes darted to her mother, but that lady was facing elsewhere now.

"Elizabeth, I hope you don't think it is overly forward of me to say that I know of your situation and that I feel I can be of service to you. I know how you loved Will—after all, it was I who married you. Of course you must have his child. But you will do that child, and the late Mr. Keller, a disservice if you bring it into the world outside of the traditional covenant of marriage. I know you do not love me, at least not as a wife loves a husband, and I do not expect you to try." He paused, to adjust his knee's position on the floor, and looked up at her cautiously, as though his words might unintentionally do her harm. "I want to settle here in the city, and have a home. I think that if we wed, we could form a family of a kind—I could offer you protection from the world's censure, and you would make this city a happy place for me. . . ."

He trailed off, and Elizabeth closed her eyes. For a moment, the room was quiet and there was only the sound of the flames snapping and, outside, the rain against the pavement. Then he spoke again. "Will you marry me?"

Her mother had raised her to be such a marriageable girl, and so she had seen not a few men on their knees before. It was a bizarre twist that this man—perfectly acceptable, but hardly the social ally a debutante should seek out—was to be her husband in the end. Elizabeth knew Mrs. Holland would have preferred Teddy Cutting, though not as much as Elizabeth herself would have. But Teddy was nowhere in sight.

The full meaning of Snowden's offer swept over her slowly, and when she realized everything it would mean to her, and what a sacrifice it was for him—for he would give up any chance of finding true love himself, to protect her and Will's unborn child—she reached out for his hand.

"Oh, yes," she whispered. "Thank you."

When she opened her eyes again, he stood and, still holding on to one hand, kissed her lightly on the cheek. "I will give you a good home, Elizabeth."

She could not quite bring herself to smile, but she did nod. Then her mother came over to them and put her hands over their hands.

"Mr. Cairns," she said. Her dark eyes flicked rapidly as she stared at him. "You must take good care of my child. She is everything I live for."

Then she embraced him. Edith had come across the room, and though her headache was still obvious in her face, she tried to smile a little. She put her arms around the young couple-to-be and whispered her congratulations.

"I remind you that I knew Mr. Holland not a little," Mr. Cairns said to none of them in particular. "And I know how he would want me to treat you right."

Elizabeth nodded again. The world was such a marvel— it gave you trials, but if you were still and concentrated, if you tried to do the right thing, it always provided you with salvation. She had imagined that a solution lay in one direction, but that didn't matter now, for the road to there hadn't yet been built. It was not to be. This was to be, and it was just as well. She was going to be a mother—the thought suffused her with joy.

"I think you will agree with me that it must be done

quickly, to avoid suspicion, and that in fact we should move as soon as possible. . . ." Snowden was saying to Mrs. Holland, or maybe Aunt Edith—Elizabeth wasn't paying attention anymore; she was thinking of Will, of his honorable nature and his willingness to work hard and everything he had done for her, and how perhaps she would finally be able to do right by him.

Forty
Five

Many of my usual sources have been silent at this quiet time of year, although some of my new friends have pointed out to us the striking presence of the younger Holland sister, Miss Diana, at the Hayeses' last night, where she was said to be the special guest of the family scion, Grayson. Whatever could it all mean?

—FROM THE SOCIETY PAGE OF THE *NEW-YORK NEWS OF THE WORLD GAZETTE*, SATURDAY, MARCH 3, 1900

$\mathcal{W}$HEN THEY RETURNED FROM THE CHURCH, Diana wanted nothing more than to go up to her room. The ceremony had been short and dour and there had been no guests outside of their little family and a few members of Snowden's retinue. Reverend Needlehouse had officiated, glancing occasionally over at the bride's sister as if she had a bad smell about her. Afterward the bride and groom had gone to their new apartment house, and the Holland family had returned to their home on Gramercy Park, and Diana was once again the lone sister in a sad home. She put her foot on the stair, but before she could return to her own private anguish, her mother blocked her path.

"Di, your sister is very lucky."

Diana looked back at her mother, still dressed in black as she had been for over a year now. The youngest Holland's clothing—a navy wool dress in a modest cut—was not much less somber, and she would have been at pains to declare which of them was the gloomier.

"I know," she said after a moment.

When her sister had revealed to her the secret she had been bearing in silence all these weeks, a stone had flipped over inside Diana and all the vague disquietude she had been experiencing over the thing she had done with Grayson, in one of his family's galleries, showed its full, mossy form in the light. For she had committed an act that could have terrible and unexpected consequences, and the knowledge dragged her further down.

"If it is true what I read in the papers—that Grayson Hayes has taken a special interest in you—then that would be very good," her mother concluded, and then Diana knew that her mother was disappointed by the marriage that had just taken place. For while it would smooth appearances and allow Elizabeth to have her child, it was not the glorious match that Mrs. Holland had so clearly hoped for. "I have not always approved of the Hayes family, as you know, and there might be other suitors whom I would prefer for you. But their fortune is large, and though it pains me to say so, they are the future."

There was no way for Diana to respond to this without telling her everything; and of course that she could never do. So, wincing, she nodded her understanding, and then she went up the dark, paneled staircase, which heaved a little under her weight. The whole house was showing its age. Or its youngest member, at least, was feeling a hundred years older than she had on her return from Florida, and it was with weariness commensurate with this feeling that she drooped into her own bed. What else would she have to go through, she wondered, to fill up the pages of the story of her life? That volume was already very crammed.

The physical act that had joined her and Grayson was not so different from what she and Henry had shared, all those months ago, and yet she felt so different this time. After Henry there had been a wonderful, peach-colored halo all around her body; now she felt sodden with regret. Every time she closed her eyes she was forced to relive those heated moments with Grayson, and the memory scorched her. There was that ghost of Henry in the door in all her recollections, and it hardly mattered whether it had been a real or imaginary witness to her transgression. What she had done had not been for love, and that was all the difference.

No matter what her mother said, she knew she would never marry Grayson. He had told her that he loved her, and for all she knew it might be true. But she could not return the sentiment—she had never felt so little doubt about any-thing—and that meant she was very tawdry indeed. She had just watched her sister promise herself to a man whom she did not love, and while the expression on her face had been muted, Diana had seen clearly how much it pained her to marry again,

so soon, when her love for Will had been so pure and was still so recent and alive inside her.

Diana brought her knees up to her chest and made herself into a ball on her bed. It was there in that room, with the salmon damask walls, the white bearskin rug, the old gold-upholstered wing chair, that Henry had come to her that first time. They had lain together on that rug, over by the small tin-covered fireplace. She would have given anything to return to that moment in time, before she discovered that Henry was not what he had seemed to be, and what gross errors she was capable of. She was exhausted by all she had done, but she could not cry. There was no changing any of it—it was an inescapable part of her now.

She had gotten what she wanted, although not in the way she had imagined. She had wanted to feel different, and indeed she did now—she felt worse. She was older, and she had lost a good deal of innocence, but if she had believed that Grayson could make her stop thinking about Henry, she had been outrageously mistaken. Henry had taken up permanent residence in her mind, and for the first time what he had done to her no longer seemed so terrible, for she had done exactly the same right back to him, and now knew how thin the rewards were.

Forty Six

By this evening Elizabeth Holland will have wed her father's former business associate, Mr. Snowden Trapp Cairns, in a private ceremony at the Grace Church. One can only assume that after all she endured last fall, she wants a quieter life, and a less showy man than Henry Schoonmaker to share it with. . . .

—FROM THE "GAMESOME GALLANT" COLUMN IN THE *NEW YORK IMPERIAL*, SATURDAY, MARCH 3, 1900

T HE DOVER WAS A CREAM-COLORED BUILDING OFF
the park in the mid-seventies, and its apartments
contained parlors and libraries and maid's quarters. There were
elevators and laundry chutes on every floor, and the whole
place gleamed with its brand-new modernity. The Cairnses'
unit took up the whole fourth floor, and to its new mistress
it looked very strange. The furniture had never been used, by
her or by anybody, and it appeared to have been arranged with
more practicality than art. Everything looked expensive, and
yet there seemed to be not nearly enough objects.

"What a beautiful place," Elizabeth said as she came
through the door.

Snowden smiled at her, and held out his hand for her
cape. One of his men had made a fire in the fireplace, and
her husband gestured for her to sit near it. The rain had
continued on, and now that everyone knew under whose protection her child would be born, their attention had shifted to
Elizabeth keeping healthy and not moving about too much.

They had gone together as a family to the church, and then, in case there were any watchful eyes looking to see if there wasn't more to this match than the papers were reporting, Elizabeth and Snowden had returned home alone just like any married couple. "No one ever thought a Holland would live that far north," her mother had said obliquely when they parted.

Elizabeth had never been so tired. It was that exhaustion that comes only after a prolonged and terrible worry has been put to bed. But she was far too weary to parse her mother's choice of words, and after a moment she followed Snowden's gesture and went to the white muslin–upholstered Eastlake sofa and sat down. It was soft but a little boxy, and she wasn't sure quite how to sit on it. Tomorrow she would make this place look more like home, and on every following day, until her child was born. But there was no need to worry about all that just yet.

Snowden was still standing in the entryway in his dark brown suit, which he had bought earlier that same day at Lord & Taylor, the department store. Elizabeth's simple ivory dress had been purchased there as well. It had a mandarin collar and sleeves that were full almost to the wrist, and it had been ready-to-wear and not crafted especially for her. There had been something discomfiting about all this, and she realized during the exchanging of vows that this was because it was all so similar to her and Will's wedding day, and that in fact the suit that Will had worn was strangely like the one that Snowden had chosen.

"What are you thinking, my dear?" her husband asked from the shadows.

"Oh," Elizabeth sighed. She took a quick breath and attempted a smile. Then she moved forward on the seat and shrugged. "It's only . . ." Perhaps it was the fatigue, but Elizabeth suddenly feared she might cry. That seemed awfully ungrateful after everything that Snowden had done for her, and she frowned, trying to will away tears.

"Go on," Snowden said gently. "You can tell me. There's nothing you can say that would bother me."

She closed her eyes. "I was just thinking that until this evening I was Mrs. Keller," she whispered.

Snowden came over and sat down beside her on the sofa. She looked at him a little reluctantly, and then when she saw that his expression was a kind one she sighed, and fluttered her hands, as though to say it was all just ridiculous sentimentality, even though that couldn't be further from her true feelings.

"Of course." Snowden smiled at her. "I know you will always be Mrs. Keller in your heart."

"You were only being kind," Elizabeth replied remorsefully.

A maid was hovering in the doorway, and Snowden gestured for her to enter. She came over to the little geometric oak table in front of the pair and poured them each a glass of red wine. Snowden waited until the woman in the black-and-white uniform had disappeared, and then he raised his glass. Elizabeth blinked and picked hers up too. Their glasses met, and then she tried to take a polite sip, although in truth she had no taste for alcohol just then.

"To our family," Snowden said before he drank.

Elizabeth smiled and placed her wineglass back on the table by the stem. Then something else occurred to her.

"I suppose I am legally married twice now." She said it almost as she thought it, and without concern for how it would sound to Snowden. Then she looked at her new husband, and saw something strange behind his eyes. "I am—aren't I?"

A terrible silence followed, and at the end of it, Elizabeth knew that the next sentence she heard was going to be a lie.

"Yes." Snowden faltered a bit on the first word, but by the second he was speaking smoothly and assuredly again: "Of course you are, but since the paperwork for the first marriage was filed in Boston, and since there are sure to be more than a few Elizabeth Hollands and Will Kellers in this world, I am sure that there is nothing to worry about."

Then he smiled and cupped his hands over hers, where she had placed them primly on her lap. She wanted to tell him that she wasn't nearly so worried about being found out as she was about honoring the memory of Will. The peculiarity of that moment stayed with her, though, and try as she might, she could not stop herself from feeling unnerved. But then she closed her eyes and told herself that she was married to someone else now, and perhaps Will's memory was something she would have to nurture in secret, and there would always be strange moments between people that never need be explained.

"Are you tired, my dear?" Snowden asked.

"Yes, very," she replied.

"Come, I will show you to bed." Snowden stood but held on to her hand, so that it lifted up off her lap and into the air.

Elizabeth's wide-set brown eyes opened in bewilderment. For a moment, she feared that their domestic arrangement had been terribly misunderstood, and she brought her other hand up over her heart protectively.

"I thought we might—"

"To *your* bed, my dear. My bed will be down the hall."

"Oh." Elizabeth showed him a relieved smile as she rose to stand beside him. She felt a little silly for making trouble where there was none, and so she reached for his hands again and said, in her warmest tone, "Thank you, Mr. Cairns."

"Do not think of it."

Then he led her down the hall, with its new parquet floors and high picture moldings, and at the door to the room where she would now end all her days, he paused to kiss her lightly on the forehead. She could almost feel her head against the pillow and sleep coming over her. Then she would dream of Will and their child, and for a few hours they would all three be together.

"Good night," she said as she placed her hand on the knob.

"Good night," Snowden said, turning to leave her. "Good night, Mrs. Cairns."

Forty
Seven

We applaud Mr. Edward Cutting's heroic move to join the army and serve his country abroad. Will other blue bloods follow? We can only hope this is the case. It would be a small step to right the inequalities of our great nation.

——FROM THE EDITORIAL PAGE OF THE *NEW YORK TIMES*, SUNDAY, MARCH 4, 1900

*T*HE SCHOONMAKER MANSION FELT VERY MUCH LIKE home to Penelope that morning, and she moved through its halls with a certain swishing, imperious air that might have intimidated several of the crowned heads of Europe. She was holding a dainty china coffee cup aloft and pulling her vermilion skirt up from the floor. There was much to do that day. She would have to pick an appropriate wedding gift for her husband's former fiancée, to begin with—and what did one get a girl in a situation like that? Penelope's summer wardrobe had not yet been completely settled upon, and there were so many events in the coming weeks, several of which overlapped, that she would have to consider. Behind every door there was a difficult choice, but she was feeling very light and a little naughty, and she trusted herself utterly to make the right decisions. She very nearly buzzed with energy.

"Henry," she called as she came into their suite. The bed had been made while she was having her hair arranged and picking at a croissant, and now the room appeared in its full, smoothed over, white and gold glory. She smiled, because everything was in its place. Of course Henry was not there. She had gone to bed without him again; no doubt he had stayed up late drinking, as he had the previous days, and was still now asleep on the couch in the adjoining room. By the time she had left the party three nights before, she was the lone guest still possessed of a clear head, and so she'd been the only one to notice and interpret Henry's return from an odd ramble, and later Grayson, and then Diana, both of them with their attire somewhat wrinkled and askew. She could only imagine what Henry had seen, and she did try to do that. After all, it was only a matter of time before he sobered up to his situation and realized it was actually a quite pleasurable one.

She sipped her coffee contentedly as she considered the spoils of her planning and scheming. It had all come off just right in the end, she thought with a smile. Of course, the pampering she was now receiving from the Schoonmaker staff was based on an inconvenient misunderstanding that would have to be cleared up sooner or later. Now that Henry knew Diana had been tainted forever, he would come back around, and her predicament could be easily remedied, although Penelope knew that she didn't want to start making grandchildren for old Schoonmaker. Not right away. It was her first season as a married society lady, after all, and there were new clothes to be shown off and so many gatherings to attend, and she didn't want to grow fat and immobile just yet. It was a hand she had not yet figured out how to play. But all the cards were right, and she knew she would. The old her was back.

She smiled a little at the thought that soon Elizabeth would be unable to do anything fun, for surely her quick wedding confirmed what Penelope had suspected in Florida—that Elizabeth was going to have a child, and sooner than anybody had any right to expect.

"Henry?" she called again. She put her china cup down on the little carved table at the end of her bed and brushed past the various trunks that had arrived that morning via steamer—for she was not *totally* unprepared for the coming season—and stepped up into the adjoining room.

She was dismayed by the darkness within, and realized in a few seconds that the curtains had not been opened.

"Henry?" she said again as she went over to draw them back. Light flooded the room, illuminating the couch with its kilim pillows and soft leather cushions and the silly idyllic mural overhead. That was the place where Henry was supposed to be, and her head ticked to the side to see things out of order. She went over and brushed her hands across the cushions, as though that might give some indication of where he was at an hour of the day that was much too late for him to be carousing, but still early, for him, to be out in the world.

"Yes, Penelope?"

She turned around and put her hands behind her back as though she had something to hide. Her husband had come up through the bedroom, and he was now standing on the threshold staring at her.

"I was just . . ." But Penelope couldn't finish the sentence. She was too distracted by Henry's outfit, which was unlike anything he'd ever worn before. "Where did you get that?"

"This?" He looked down at the fitted navy coat with the brass buttons and the light blue trousers that were brought even closer to his legs by leather gaiters. The sight of Henry in uniform made her heart speed up a little, and she found herself staring into his eyes and moving toward him. He was holding a hat with two peaks in his hands, and he looked good enough to eat, though his gaze was as steady and uninviting as ever. "From the United States Army, to which I now belong."

For a moment this notion seemed to Penelope terribly romantic, and her mind wandered to all the things a man shipping off might ask for. She smiled hazily and clamped a hand on her hip. Then she looked at Henry's posture and knew he was not dressed up for her personal amusement. Her hand and face fell, and she moved toward him more quickly this time.

"I am shipping out today."

A fearful urgency surged within her. "Shipping where?"

"I don't know." He cleared his throat. "Teddy has departed for the Philippines. I am not sure where they'll have me stationed."

It was just beginning to sink in that she had done something to prevent his ever leaving, and that he had countered by finding another route out of town. "You aren't *actually* leaving New York?"

"I am going to serve my country, Penelope." He sighed and looked away from her. There had been fight in his eyes for a minute, but it was gone now. "It will be in the paper tomorrow, but I thought I should tell you myself. I've caused everyone enough harm, Lord knows, and I wouldn't want to cause any more."

Her whole body was ticking with energy, and her mind had already traveled from what the columns would make of it, to what Henry's father would think of her now, to the desolate feeling that was sure to settle in at the pit of her stomach when he was really, truly gone. He stepped back down into the main room. She couldn't stand the idea of this departure, and hurled herself forward so that she fell at the feet of her husband. She would rather have him there to spar and bicker with, she would rather have him in the city doing unkind things than to lose him this way, to some foreign location. Her knees were on the floor—she could feel the unyielding wood, even through her skirt—and she reached for Henry's legs. Her arms, which were encased in a crepe de chine of a slightly deeper shade of red, not to mention a collection of gold bangles, clung to him then. He was still stepping backward, and as he did so he dragged her some inches.

She looked up at him and found that wetness had quite naturally flooded her eyes. "What about the baby?" she cried. She knew she was being ridiculous, but it was all she could think to say.

Henry bent and put his hands firmly under her armpits and pulled her up to her feet. "There is no baby," he said when they were again at each other's eye level.

"But—"

"I wish all the best for you, my dear," Henry said in a way that made Penelope feel she'd been boxed and stored in some back closet of his life. She could feel the seconds slipping away, and knew that she had precious few to figure out a way to prevent his leaving.

"But *Henry*."

He let his dark eyes linger on her one second longer, and then he put the hat on his head. He was only a few feet from the door, and Penelope rushed toward the bed, pulling back her skirts from her feet but not caring particularly if she ripped them. She hit the blankets wailing.

"Henry, Henry, Henry, don't leave!" The tears had become a hot torrent now, and her whole torso shook with the terrible fate of being abandoned in Henry's house alone. "I'm nothing without you!"

It was true, she realized just after she'd said it. She balled up her fists and pounded them against the gold-embroidered bedspread, but minutes passed to no avail. When she did look up, Henry was gone. He had been gone a long time.

She sniffled and blew her nose into her sleeve, not caring if she ruined it. Tomorrow she would order another one made. She pushed herself up on her elbow, and tried to dry her cheekbones with the heel of her palm. Eventually her chest stopped heaving, and she began to slowly regain normal breath.

"Oh, Henry," she said quietly to herself.

Outside, the rain, which had been interminable for two days, was beginning to weaken, and she knew that if she got up, and put her face back together, that she would be able to see her situation anew. She couldn't stop him now; for now, he was gone. But there was tomorrow, and the day following, and forever after that. She stood and called for her maid. She was no one's fool, and she had plenty of time to figure out how to get him back.

Forty Eight

Please read all of it.

—H. S.

THE LETTER ARRIVED IN THE AFTERNOON WHEN the rain was still strong, and the messenger had gotten drenched. Diana had looked at the thing fearfully as it sat on the ceramic platter by the door, for she had become certain that Henry had seen what she had done, and that he'd written down his invective toward her. It was only after dinner, when everyone else was asleep—somehow, superstitiously, that made Diana feel that her thoughts were less likely to be read—that she went to fetch it. She wasn't yet sure if she would be able to consume his message in its entirety.

Edith, who had still not fully recovered from the debauchery at the Hayeses', had glanced at the letter before dinner, but she apparently lacked the energy to pry. "Oh, to be young as you," was all she'd said, before going to bed early.

Still, some hours passed, and the sky began to turn purple, before Diana found the courage to break the seal.

That act gave her little tremors, and so she put the letter down for another while. She gave herself a speech, and decided that she was nothing if she didn't face the consequences of her actions. So she picked up the letter for good and went over to the white bearskin rug and folded her legs, and her skirts, up under her. She took a breath and then began the heartbreak. By the time she set it down she felt quite different again.

My dearest Di,

I've really mucked things up.

It would probably look comical from the outside peering in, and I might indeed laugh if it weren't me, and especially if it weren't you. But it is you, and nothing could be more tragic to me.

It is probably difficult, given the

outrageousness of my missteps, for
you to believe that I was always only
trying to protect you. But that was
my intention, however poorly borne
out. That was my intention when
I married Penelope, and even during
all the blunders that followed. It was
my hope that I could keep you safe
from censure. Now I've seen how
stupid and futile all that was. My
actions have caused you great suffering,
and I have put myself in the
permanent agony of seeing you courted
by others. It is no doubt a great

failing on my part, but that is what
I find I cannot stand.

In fact, I feel I would sooner
die than see you as the beloved of
another—some part of me died
already when I saw you with
Grayson at the Hayes mansion. It is
for this reason, as well as for a need to
atone for all the things I have done
wrong, that I am leaving the city and
enlisting in the army. I am going
to fight for our great nation in the
Pacific. I know that I might die, but
that seems a happier end than being

without you, and anyway it seems to
me that looking in the face of hard
things and still being able to move
forward, even when the end includes
grave danger and the possibility of
death, is the mark of a man. After
all I have done, I could certainly do
worse than to try to prove I am still a
man.

I have gone on too long, and you
are probably tired of me by now. But
I wanted to tell you before I left how
completely, abjectly sorry I am for all
the pain I have caused you, and that

if I die, you were the one true Love of my life. By the time you read this I will be gone, but please know, I am still always at your side. . . .

Yours forever,

Henry William Schoonmaker

Diana read the letter three times and pressed the back of her hand into her face and tried not to cry. She blinked furiously, but it was no use. She cried in front of the fire and then she moved to the bed to cry some more. She cried over her willful actions, and all the stupid misunderstandings that had passed between her and the only man she had ever loved, and most of all for the distance that now separated them. It had yawned to a great expanse and was now too wide to bridge. The worst of it was that so many betrayals seemed to have grown from lack of faith on both their parts, and not because of any bad intentions.

She went to her window and looked out at all the twinkling windows and above them all the faint stars. How many false impressions lived out there? she wondered. How many hearts broken through carelessness and failures of nerve? How many decades-old mistakes festered behind fine window dressings? Then she cried a little more, until her small body felt dry and spent. There was no use, she knew, crying anymore.

She went over to her vanity—it was an elaborate piece of dark wood furniture, ornamented with carved flowers and angels, and it had offered up her reflection on so many nights when she had still been full of girlish wonder. She looked older now, she knew. The skin under her eyes appeared trampled on, and her features stood out more starkly from her face. Still, she suspected that she was young enough that a few real kisses and a good night's sleep would be enough to make her look fresh again.

She rested her elbows on the table and cupped her forehead with her palms. She pushed her fingers up into her hair and clutched it in fists. "Oh me, oh me," she whispered to herself as she began to agitatedly draw the pins out of her hair.

When she had finally pulled them all out, and her rich brown curls stood out around her head like wildfire in the brush, she knew that the sleep could wait, but she had to get those real kisses. Her hands fumbled across the table until they took hold of a pair of scissors. For a moment she clutched their gold-plated handles and wondered if she hadn't gone a little mad. But there was a pure, reflective quality to her eyes that had been missing over the past week, and she knew that what she was about to do was the only thing that made any sense at all.

She began to cut. As she made slow and exacting movements, the hair began to fall away. It collected in tufted hills at her feet, but she kept steady and focused on the mirror in front of her, until her head was crowned by nothing more than a boy's short wisps. She had such a soft and feminine face, it was difficult to imagine that she could pass for anything but a girl, but her conviction had grown all the while, and now a niggling thing like that couldn't stop her. She was going to follow Henry, even if it meant joining the army, even if it meant living as a man. Anyway, there was that new, aged quality to her features—maybe that was all she needed to complete the illusion.

It was very late when she turned her chin a final time, and examined the newly bare nape of her neck in the old vanity. She felt a hundred pounds lighter, and when she stood up, she knew she was carrying only the most crucial things. She packed a small case and tucked Henry's letter inside it. Then she put out the lights and slipped down the stairs.

Diana wore a men's bowler with the initials *H. W. S.* sewn into the lining and an old French army coat. She looked at No. 17 for a long moment, before she at last began walking toward the river. The rain had stopped, and the air was clean and just chilly enough to make one feel alive, the way all promising beginnings do.

Acknowledgments

I am tremendously grateful to everyone who has worked so hard on this series. Many big thank-yous to Sara Shandler, Farrin Jacobs, Josh Bank, Les Morgenstein, Andrea C. Uva, Nora Pelizzari, Lanie Davis, Kristin Marang, Allison Heiny, Cristina Gilbert, Melissa Dittmar, Kari Sutherland, Barb Fitzsimmons, Alison Donalty, Ray Shappell, Elise Howard, Susan Katz, and Kate Jackson.

TURN THE PAGE FOR A PEEK AT

Splendor

THE EXCITING CONCLUSION
TO THE LUXE SERIES.

Prologue

FIFTY YEARS AGO, EVERY AMERICAN GIRL WANTED to be a European princess. One could detect it in her gowns and gestures, for they all tried to dress as European ladies did and to imitate the manners of Parisian salons. But now they come from the old world to see how we behave and decorate ourselves here in the United States. They stand on the decks of steamers, gloved hands gripping the guardrail as they catch their first glimpse of Manhattan, that island of towering buildings and smothering secrets, brimming with its millions of lives celebrated or forgotten in almost equal measure. What a narrow strip of land, those sea voyagers inevitably remark in surprise as they begin to take in the new world, for so *very* much to happen upon.

Of course, roughly as many ships go out of the harbor as come into it. Even those whose names are regularly cast in the smudgy glory of gossip columns, and followed in every detail by an eager public, must sometimes leave. How many top-drawer souls were entrusted to the hands of the Cunard

Company, whose twelve o'clock steamer was already drawing resolutely away from land, en route from New York to Paris? The crowd on the worn wood planks of the dock was growing smaller, as was the city that cropped up behind them. A gentleman or lady leaning against the rail could not even make out the handkerchiefs waving at them anymore, although they knew that fine examples of embroidery were still being held aloft in the thick summer air. Did they look at their own city with love or nostalgia or resentment? Were they glad to see it slip by, block by block, or did they already miss its drawing rooms and shady clubs, the verdant park at its center, and the blocks of mansions that lined it?

There, those fine New Yorkers looking back at their city might think, *if I followed that street I would arrive at Mamie Fish's house. Or I could take that one to where the William Schoonmakers live, or to the Buck mansion, or to any number of Astor holdings.* They might reflect, thinking of those landmarks, that it has always been a world that holds its children tight to its breast, or else sends them away to wander like exiles. What slights and embarrassments, what suffocating marriages and unforgivable deeds, what grand social missteps might the voyagers under that cloudless July sky be trying to escape?

For any bright sets of eyes gazing a last time at the city of their birth, there will be a certain glow of longing for what was left behind. But the anguish of leaving will dim with

every passing second as the excitement of what they are yet
to see grows. Especially for a girl who, say, has only recently
come to understand what hearts are capable of, or where love
and a healthy sense of curiosity can take her; or a fellow who
has just experienced the thrill of truly cutting ties for the first
time, and of stepping out as his own man. After all, it takes
only a few seasons to learn how everything changes, and how
quickly; to realize that the glorious and grotesque lives lived at
the currently fashionable addresses will soon seem quaint and
outdated. New York will always be there, but it grows stranger
every day, and staying put will not make it stay the same.

And in the end it doesn't matter, because these eyes had
to go, and the distance from shore has rapidly become too
great to swim. There is no going back now.

One

With the younger Miss Holland, Diana, away
in Paris for a finishing season, it is a most
lonely social era, and we have all had to content
ourselves with lesser beauties. There are those
of us who remember those chocolate eyes and
glossy curls and sulk in the corners at gatherings awaiting her return.

—FROM THE "GAMESOME GALLANT" COLUMN IN THE
NEW YORK IMPERIAL, FRIDAY, JULY 6, 1900

*I*N THE MORNINGS, SHE LIKED TO WALK ALONG THE sea wall. She went by herself and usually only passed one or two gentlemen, canes ticking against the stone, for the locals preferred to stroll later in the day, after siesta. Lately the weather had grown extreme, and there were occasions when the ocean would sweep over her path; at first this frightened her, but by a humid Friday in early July, she had come to view it as a kind of baptism. The force of the sea—as she had written in her notebook the night before, just before falling asleep—stirred her, and soothed her, and made her feel reborn.

Once she had crossed the Paseo del Prado, she turned and headed into the old town, with its shadowy arcades and glimpses of tiled and verdant patios just beyond the crooked streets. There were more people there, lingering in arched doorways or around tables in the squares. She wore a wide, drooping straw hat, and her short brown curls were pinned up at the nape to disguise the peculiar length. Not that it mattered—she was a foreigner, and all of her peculiarities were obscured by that one vast difference. No one recognized her here; it did not matter to any of the Habaneros passing in the street that she was Diana Holland.

That was in fact her name, and in other parts of the world it carried certain implications. For instance, that she had been taught from a young age never to show the naked skin of her hands outside of her family home, nor to walk on the streets of her own city unchaperoned. And although she had routinely flaunted these restrictions, she had never known what it was to be so thoroughly free of the rules of her hometown until she had arrived in Cuba. In her light-colored, loose-fitting dress, on the streets of a very foreign capital, she was both quite noticeable and, in a manner, invisible. She was anonymous, and, like the sea, this gave rise to powerful feelings.

The ocean was behind her now, as well as the slate gray clouds that were massing over the bay and beginning to crowd out the blue sky. The green of the palm trees appeared extreme in contrast. The air was thick and moody with the possibility of rain, and the weather looked bad, but for her there was something satisfying in such a landscape. The shades of dark, the looming quality of it, all seemed to her a kind of expression of what was in her soul. Sooner or later the downpour would begin, first in big drops, then in heavy sheets that would soak the striped awnings and flood the gutters. It was not long ago—a matter of weeks, although sometimes it felt

like forever—that she had arrived in Havana, but she was a quick study of atmospheric disturbances. This one had the color of suffering, and she would know.

She was alone and thousands of miles from home, but of course it wasn't *all* suffering. If Diana had been pressed, she would have had to admit that there was only one thing she really wanted for. Even the loss of her curly mane of hair had not been *truly* bitter. She had cut it because of Henry Schoonmaker—she'd foolishly tried to enlist in the army to follow him, even though he was her sister Elizabeth's former fiancé, and currently married to a rather terrifying girl, who as a maiden had gone by the name Penelope Hayes. A thing Diana wouldn't do in pursuit of Henry had yet to present itself. She had gotten used to the short hair, which had been a self-inflicted wound in the first place, and anyway there was nothing chopped tresses could do to contradict the rosy femininity of Diana's petite body. In the previous months she had found herself capable in ways she could not possibly have imagined back in the cozy rooms of the townhouses of old New York. She had never, during her adventures, gone without food or slept out of doors. But, oh, the lack of Henry—how that wrung her delicate heart.

Diana had been all manner of places since her boy-short hair had failed to convince the United States Army that she was ready for basic training back in March, but none of them had looked remotely like this. As she walked, she couldn't shake the sensation of being in a very old city—New York wasn't so much younger, she knew, but somehow it effaced its history more effectively. She liked the idea that the cathedrals she passed, the façades with their wrought iron detailing and the red roofs above them, might still shelter aging conquistadors. Before this she had been a barmaid on a luxury liner, and before that she had hustled her way to Chicago on trains. That was when she still believed that Henry was in a regiment headed for the Pacific by way of San Francisco.

Officially she was in Paris. That was what the papers were reporting, with a little help from her friend Davis Barnard, who wrote the "Gamesome Gallant" column in the *New York Imperial*. He was also the reason that she knew Henry wasn't where he was supposed to be, either—apparently, old William Schoonmaker held such sway that he had not only secured a safer post for his son in Cuba, but had managed to bully all the New York newspapermen into keeping mum about the transfer. Diana liked the idea that neither of them was where they were supposed to be. They each had a decoy self, out there in the world, and meanwhile their real selves were moving stealthily, ever closer to one another.

Presently she passed through a square where dogs lay languidly in the shadows and men lingered over their coffees in outdoor cafés. She had never been to Europe and so she

couldn't say for sure, but it seemed to her there was some-thing Continental about the city, with its long memory and crumbling buildings, the ghosts in its alleys and the warbling of its Catholic bells, its slow and pleasant traditions. There was that smell in the air that always comes just before it rains, when the dry dirtiness of a city rises up a final time before it is washed away, and Diana began to hurry a little in anticipa-tion of an onslaught. She wanted to arrive home, to her little rented rooms, and hopefully avoid being drenched.

She had reached the edge of the square, and was moving quickly enough that she found it prudent to put her hand up to better secure her hat. Ahead of her were two American sol-diers wearing fitted dark blue jackets and stone-colored slacks, and Diana's eye was inexorably drawn to the easy gait of the taller one with the jauntily cocked hat. It was magnetic, his stride, and familiar, and for a moment she swore the sun must have broken through the clouds to cast the skin at the back of his neck a golden shade she knew well.

"Henry!" she gasped out loud. It was characteristic of Diana that she spoke before she thought.

The tall soldier turned first, slowly. For a moment her lungs had ceased to function; her feet felt like unwieldy hooves and wouldn't move forward, no matter what urging she gave them. She forced oxygen in through her nostrils, but by then the man's face was disappointingly visible, and she saw that the features were too soft and boyish, the chin too covered by reddish beard, to belong to Henry. His face was confused, devoid of recognition, but he went on staring at her. His mouth hung open a few seconds before breaking into a grin.

"My name ain't Henry," he drawled. "But you, little lady, you can call me by whatever name you like."

His eyes went on gazing at her until they seemed a little fevered, and she couldn't help but return his smile faintly. She liked being appreciated, but she did not want to be stalled. She had made the mistake of straying from Henry when he had not seemed to be hers before, and the recollection still horrified her. There were American troops all over the city, and one of these days she would run into the right one. She was as sure of it as of something fated.

In the meantime, she gave the tall soldier a wink—though not a very special one—and then hurried on, toward the Calle Obrapia, where she would ready herself for evening. The day was young, and everything in the city was bright, and Henry was out there somewhere, and she wanted to prepare for the day when the stars arranged themselves auspiciously, and long-lost lovers came face-to-face.

Chris Mottalini

ANNA GODBERSEN

was born in Berkeley, California, and educated at Barnard College. She currently lives in Brooklyn, New York.

For LUXE secrets and gossip, go to www.harperteen.com/luxebooks and to visit Anna online go to www.theluxebooks.com.

For exclusive information
on your favorite authors and artists,
visit www.authortracker.com.

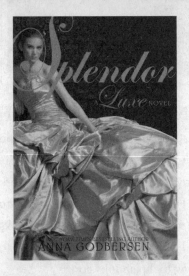

Don't miss a single scandal!

EVERYONE IN ULTRA-EXCLUSIVE ROSEWOOD, PENNSYLVANIA, HAS SOMETHING TO HIDE....

FIND OUT WHAT THE PRETTY LITTLE LIARS
ARE HIDING AT **WWW.PRETTYLITTLELIARS.COM.**

CHECK OUT **WWW.PRETTYLITTLELIARSBOOKS.COM**
FOR SERIES GOSSIP, GAMES, AND GIVEAWAYS.